THE LODGE

Other books by Stephen Williford

When You REALLY Embarrass Yourself,
Nobody EVER Forgets

Along the Way;
Taking Care of Each Other on Our Way to Heaven

365 Devotionals for Children

Stephen Williford

THE LODGE

This is a work of fiction. All names, characters, places, and incidents are either from the author's imagination or are used ficticiously. While a few establishments are mentioned, this book is not about any actual person, persons, or institutions.

Printed and Produced in the United States of America

For media and other inquiries contact:
Larry J. Tolbert, Publisher
larry.tolbert@radianpartners.net
6055 Primacy Parkway, Suite 160
Memphis, TN 38119
Office 901.202.3909
Fax 901.202.3975

Original cover art by Jeff Atnip

Interior and exterior design by Louise Koonce, LuraeDesigns

Author contact information: steve.will@radianpub.net

THE LODGE

Chapter One

The Lodge.

I had been calling it that for years. The only trouble was . . . well, there wasn't one. I had accumulated things to furnish it, like some beds and tables and chairs, some art and even a bird feeder. All I needed was the Lodge.

I wanted a place away from everything and everybody. A place to sit on the porch and listen to the birds. A place to build a fire in a big fireplace and watch the snow fall.

But on a teacher's salary, progress was slow. Combine that with the fact that I wasn't a carpenter, or plumber, or electrician, or roofer, and that might further explain why there was no Lodge.

I managed to secure some land from a dear sweet lady, Elsie Ross, who wanted me to have it. It was on a mountain with a spectacular view. Mrs. Ross really cut me a deal. Even so, it took five years to pay her in monthly installments. During this time, I met with an architect who used to be one of my students. He never gave me a bill. He said it was his way of saying thank you. Which might have been code for, "You couldn't afford it." Maybe he also secretly thought I could still change his grade or alter his permanent record. Whatever the case, I am very grateful.

A few months after paying off Elsie, I was able to take my first step to build the house. Another grateful student's father built the foundation at cost. He said that I saved his son from an extra year in school. He was right.

I was now at the framing stage. Well, several of my friends were at the framing stage. I was more *back* stage. They came on Saturdays. Some came out of friendship. Some probably out of pity. Some to keep from going to estate sales with their wives. Some because they liked being outside and building anything.

The Lodge would eventually consist of an open living area that included the kitchen, Great Room, dining area, and a bathroom. Upstairs would be two bedrooms and a bathroom.

I loved it, but it was not large. This made the word *Lodge* humorous to my fellow construction workers.

The site is about 50 miles out of Spruceville, a small town in East Tennessee, where I live and teach. Fortunately, the school year just ended, and I could spend much more time at the building site. It was early June, and I had the summer to work on my mountain home.

I was cleaning up on Monday from the weekend's work. I had collected most of the loose nails, stacked the unused lumber, and was sweeping the wood scraps and sawdust off the slab. Just another day in paradise.

I heard gravel crunch from far below. It wasn't necessarily a visitor for me. There were two houses above mine on the mountain. But they were seldom used. I kept sweeping.

In a couple of minutes, I heard a vehicle turn off the road and onto my long drive. As it turned the last corner, a white Range Rover appeared.

The car parked in front of the house. After about a minute the door opened. A woman with shoulder length blonde hair stepped onto the gravel. She was wearing bright blue pants, electric blue high heels, a white t-shirt, and a short red vest. She was stunning, radiant, and beautiful.

She stood beside the car for several seconds, taking in the framework. She saw me, smiled, walked over, gave me a hug, and kissed me on the cheek. "Hello Mr. Jensen."

"Hello Jillian," I said.

Jillian Renfro was a former student from several years ago. The years had been her friend.

She didn't seem to be impressed that I remembered her name. She should have. It had been over a decade since I last saw her. I taught over a thousand students since that time. Maybe she was used to people remembering her name. She looked around some more. "This was not an easy place to find."

"I guess you do have to know where you're going," I said. Also part of the plan. As I mentioned, the Lodge was designed to get away from people.

She looked at the framing. "You're building a house?"

I nodded. "I hope so."

"That is so cool! Can you show me around?"

That was a funny question. There was very little to show. The framing had just started. I showed her where the front door was going to be, where the fireplace would be, where the bathroom would be, and described the upstairs. I was still wondering what she was doing here.

She looked through the framing. "Look at that view!"

"Yeah, it's a big reason I bought this property. That and being so far away from town."

"Oh," she stopped looking at the scenery and directed her gaze at me. "I have intruded on your privacy. I apologize."

"It's okay, Jillian. I'm through for the day. It's always great to see an old student." I knew that came out wrong as I was saying it.

"I'm not *that* old, Mr. Jensen."

No, she wasn't.

"I didn't mean it like that," I laughed. "I mean you're from my earlier years as a teacher."

"Not much better."

"You're more of a vintage student."

"Ouch."

"What I mean is that you were always one of my favorites. And I'm very confident your visit will be the highlight of my day. Maybe my week."

"Perfect," she smiled a very bright smile. "And I'm not sure you could say I was your student. I never took Speech. But you were a Senior class sponsor, and since I was class vice-president, we got to figure out major events, like homecoming and prom, in your classroom. What is that?"

She was looking at the camper.

"That, Miss Renfro, is where I sleep and store my earthly belongings for the summer." It was a camper that came off the back of a pickup truck. I bought it at a salvage yard shortly after I bought the property. I paid them to deliver it.

"Really? That's where you sleep?"

"That's it."

"Does it have electricity?"

"No."

"A bathroom?"

"Nope."

"That means no shower?"

"Correct."

"No running water?"

"No."

"Was I really?" she asked.

"Pardon me?"

"Was I really one of your favorites?" Her gaze left the camper and was back on me. She was smiling.

"Yes. I guess I can say that now. I can't tell students while they are my students."

She laughed. "I'm still not sure you could call me your student. Whatever. It's been awhile, Mr. J."

"How long has it been?"

"Fourteen years."

"Wow, that long?"

"Hard to believe."

"I still remember you," I said.

"Really?" she said, smiling again. "What do you remember?"

"I remember you wore long dresses to school sometimes."

"You remember that?" she laughed. "I'm not sure why I did that. I guess I thought I was a trend setter. Or maybe it was easy and comfortable."

"Yes, and you and your friends brought your lunch to school."

"How can you remember that?"

"Because sometimes you'd ask if you could eat in my classroom."

"I remember! You were the only teacher who would let us do that. We thought you were so cool."

"Well, students and faculty only got thirty minutes for lunch. That's never changed. So, I have always eaten at my desk. I guess I sympathized."

"We thought you did it because you thought we were cute," she said, eyes still fixed on me.

"You were cute. Cute high school students."

"Too young?" she smiled as she sat on the makeshift steps to the foundation. "We were just fooling ourselves?"

"Way too young," I said.

"True." She was quiet for a moment, maybe listening to the Mockingbird's melody.

The breeze blew a few leaves in front of her. And a little sawdust I missed while sweeping the porch. I silently speculated that Jillian would be transporting some of that sawdust back to her Range Rover.

"I heard you and Mrs. Jensen got a divorce," she said.

I paused. "Yes, we did."

"I'm sorry. I didn't know her. I'm sure it had to be difficult."

I nodded.

She was looking at her vehicle, I think. Or maybe not looking at anything.

"So, tell me about you," I said.

She looked at me and smiled. "I became an attorney."

I paused to think about that. "Outstanding! Good for you!"

"Yes! I litigate. For the most part, I sue large corporations with lots of money. Maybe I should have taken your Speech class."

I thought about that for a second and laughed. She did, too.

"Well, congratulations, counselor," I said.

"Thanks," she said.

She stood up and walked in a small circle in front of the

framing. “I am here to ask you a question,” she said. “And I am very nervous. I did not realize I’d be nervous.”

I smiled.

She took a deep breath. Her eyes got bigger. “Okay, here goes. I have a deposition in a few days. It’s in Gatlinburg.”

“Okay.”

“The deposition is at a school. I have to depose a teacher.”

“I’m guessing Smoky Mountain High.”

She nodded and remained silent.

I did, too. When it was clear she was waiting, I said, “So . . . you are here to . . . practice on me? Pretend I’m the teacher?”

“No, but thanks for the offer if that’s what it was. Here’s the question. Will you come with me?”

I didn’t say anything because I didn’t see that coming.

“It would just be for a few hours.”

Finally, I opened my mouth and asked, “Jillian, why in the world do you want me to go with you?”

She looked at me. Maybe she was trying to decide if she wanted to tell me. “Well, the truth is that I need you to go with me. This is a male gym teacher. He doesn’t like women. I need a back-up.” She looked at me again and waited.

“I’m thinking,” I said.

“Yeah,” she said. “I was afraid of that.”

“I’m still trying to absorb this. I haven’t seen you for a long time. “

“Fourteen years,” she said.

“And you find out where the Lodge is and –“

"Lodge?"

"My term for cabin. Humor." I stopped. "How did you find out about my place?

She smiled. "I go to the same gym that Bill Linder does. I heard him talk to some other guys at the gym about helping you build a cabin – lodge -. I asked him about it and asked him where it was."

I nodded. I'd have to ask Bill about this conversation. "Bill has done more than help. He's been my guiding light. So, he tells you where the Lodge is. And then you go to the trouble to find me, and you come all this way to ask me to go to a deposition for a teacher at another school?"

She nodded. "Exactly. I'll be deposing a student first, in front of him, and then I will depose the teacher who is also a coach."

"And that – this – "I said, gesturing with one hand toward her car and one hand to her, "doesn't seem weird to you?"

She smiled again. "It does seem a little weird, doesn't it?"

I nodded. "Pretty weird. Okay, explain it to me some more."

She paused. She looked at me again and took another breath. "I shouldn't be, but I am intimidated by what I've heard about this coach. I know, I'm a trial attorney. I've done hundreds of depositions in all kinds of situations. But there's something about this one that makes me kind of unsettled.

"Call it intuition. There's something about this that makes me think I shouldn't go to the deposition by myself. I need someone on my team. Maybe it's not needed. But maybe I do need someone to watch my back."

"Why would -"

She held out her hand like a cop telling me to halt. She wasn't looking at me now. She was into her case. "I would have normally taken Zachary. You don't know him. He is an attorney and is also -

was my boyfriend. We broke up. So, I can't ask him. I don't have an assistant or another attorney to go with me on a Saturday."

Saturday?

I took a chance and spoke. "So, on Saturday, you want me to go with you because Zachary can't go?"

"Yes."

"Not to keep harping on this, but why me? There is a whole world of people out there. Much younger than me. People you hang with. People who might know something about the law. You have met many of these people in the last decade. Why pluck me from way back in your high school days?"

She walked to about two feet in front of me and held her arms toward me. "This is why I was nervous. It doesn't make too much sense when it's verbalized. It's not because I have some bizarre romantic interest in you. You are much older than me. No offense. How old are you?"

I hesitated. "I'm 47."

Then she hesitated, too. Maybe trying to absorb that fact. "You're 47 and I'm 32. You are a teacher and I'm a lawyer. I like being in New York and Chicago and San Francisco and you like . . . this." She pointed to the framing. This is not about hooking up, Mr. Jensen. This is because you are . . . " She held both arms toward me again . . . "safe."

"Safe?"

"Yeah. Guys my own age might misinterpret my invitation. And," she paused, searching for the correct words, "some might be intimidated." She gave a dismissive gesture with her hand. "I don't know. It happens. I can be myself with you. You're not going to be intimidated and I don't have to worry about you thinking I'm attracted to someone like . . . you."

"Perish the thought."

She smiled. “You know what I’m saying. I need a male to go with me to keep this guy in his place. An older male is even better. He’s not going to be as aggressive toward me if you’re sitting beside me.”

“So, after a decade –“

“Fourteen years.”

“After a decade and a half, you break up with your boyfriend, have a deposition coming up, flip through your directory of potential male . . . helpers and just happen to think of old Mr. J to protect you from another teacher?”

She smiled and let that sit there for a few seconds. “Yes. If it makes you feel any better, I did think you were cute when I was in high school.”

“Good to know that I used to be considered cute by a teenager.”

“You have aged gracefully.”

“Thank you. The people at the Home will be so pleased to hear that.”

She laughed. “You look good for someone your age. I think you’re still cute.”

I thought about that. “Maybe you can introduce me to your grandmother.”

“Ick. I will be happy to compensate you for your time,” Jillian said. “We can call you a consultant. And we will be back by 6:00 at the latest, I promise because I have - that’s when I need to be back.”

That wiped out the whole day. On the other hand, I was looking at a very attractive woman, who had come a long way to see me. That didn’t happen, well, ever. She was asking me to spend the whole day with her. And I was thinking about two-by-fours. Or why she didn’t pick someone else. *I was getting old.*

“What kind of consultant?”

"What?"

"You said I'd be a consultant. What kind?"

"I don't know. What kind do you want to be?"

"I need a title. What exactly will I be doing?"

"Just sitting beside me. "

"The Equalizer."

"Yeah, I guess so."

"Want me to be the muscle?"

"Show me muscle."

I picked up a length of two by four and held it over my head.

"Okay, you'll be an attorney."

"Same wages you're getting?"

"No."

Chapter Two

I stayed at my house in Spruceville on Saturday morning. Jillian picked me up a little before six. It was still dark. I walked out to the Range Rover and got in. It smelled new. It also smelled like coffee. And perfume.

I didn't know what to wear, so I chose a brown sports jacket, white shirt, my favorite tie and tan slacks. I think it's a crime in several states to wear a coat and tie on a Saturday, especially during the summer. She was wearing a black and gray striped business suit.

She smiled and pointed to a Starbucks cup. "I had no idea what you drank, so I guessed."

What I drank was not from Starbucks. Until recently, it was from the school coffee pot. Which should also be a crime in several states. I picked it up and tested it. It did not taste like school coffee. Always a good sign.

"It's the Medium Roast Coffee," she explained as she headed back down the drive. "I decided to go conservative."

"Good choice."

Less than two hours later, we landed in Gatlinburg. We were in a Range Rover, but Jillian thought she was piloting a Lear 45. The Smoky Mountain High School looked like a functional but not a necessarily pretty school. What it *did* have was a stunning view of the Smoky Mountains. It was just outside of Gatlinburg with several athletic fields around it. I was familiar with the school because of its successful football team through the years.

We walked in the front doors at 7:45. Our meeting was at 8:00. We were met by a man who looked to be in his fifties. He shook hands with us and introduced himself. "Hi, you must be Ms. Renfro. I'm Carl Winn. My firm represents the Sevier County School District."

"I'm Jillian Renfro. This is Stuart Jensen."

"We're set up in the conference room. Are you co-counsel, Mr. Jensen?"

"We're not sure yet exactly what role Stu will play, Carl. He is here today. Then we'll see."

Stu?

"Gotcha. Well, there's coffee in the room and the bathrooms are down the hall."

"Can we smoke in them?" I asked.

Carl paused and then grinned. "I'll leave that to your better judgment, Stu."

Stu. I was still questioning my better judgment for being at a school during the summer, before 8:00 on a Saturday morning, evidently now parading as an attorney, and in the company of a surprise female friend who said she needed me.

Boys' bathrooms in high schools are all the same. They smell like a bucket of disinfectant, have a bunch of stalls with doors that don't lock, a lot of tile, and echo. I was admiring my tie in the mirror. It was a tie some of my students had given me a few years back. It was from a service project, *Camp Good Grief*, for children who had lost a loved one during the year.

The bathroom door opened and a Recreational Vehicle rolled in. Well, it could have been. It was actually a man who was about 6' 5" and weighed enough to play on any defensive line in the SEC.

He probably had.

He had a large head. And a crew cut. As he squeezed through the door, he saw me. He looked to be about 30. He was wearing a very large sweat suit that had *SMHS* on the shirt and pants.

He fixed a gaze on me. "You must be one of the kid's attorneys," he said. I did not pick up any admiration in his voice. He looked at me like he might get into a three-point stance .

"Just came along for the ride," I said and smiled.

"You must have a boring life," he said.

"It's probably more similar to yours than you realize."

He paused to digest that. When that didn't work, he said, "Just so you know, I'm not happy about this at all. As a matter of fact, I'm really unhappy."

It occurred to me that I had no idea what *this* was about.

"I'm sorry to hear that," I said.

"No you're not. You're here to make money. I have a good mind to show you just how unhappy I am. He edged a little closer.

I pulled out my cell phone and began recording.

He stopped. "What are you doing?"

"I'm taking your picture. Video, actually."

He looked at me some more. I held the camera steady. He grunted and walked past me.

I waited for the breeze to die down and rejoined the party. Perhaps I should ask what the purpose of this deposition was. And check out the coffee bar. Not necessarily in that order.

Chapter Three

I found the meeting area, which was a modest conference room. Taking up most of the space was a table about ten feet long. Jillian was sitting on one side, beside a boy about fifteen or sixteen. A woman I presumed to be his mother was seated beside him in a row of chairs against the wall. The boy was handsome. I could see why. His mom was a beauty. She looked barely old enough to be his mom.

I found the coffee on a small table in the corner. I was delighted to see that it was in a thermos with *Donut Friar* on the side. That was a local Gatlinburg bakery. We dodged the lethal silver bullet of school coffee. Plus, there were *Donut Friar* donuts.

I sat down next to Jillian. Seated in the corner was a young woman with a strange looking keyboard and a computer screen. She appeared set up and ready to go.

On the other side of the table sat Carl. At the head of the table was a vacant chair. At the other end of the table was a tripod and video camera.

RV rumbled into the room and Carl motioned for him to parallel it next to him.

I noticed no one else was eating a donut. I didn't particularly care. I ate donuts when we had teacher conference meetings. This was about the same thing. Except there was a camera. And a stenographer. And lawyers who were getting paid that morning about what I made in a week. As I considered the scene, I munched on my donut. Jillian looked at me. I think it might have been a look of disapproval. I smiled and took another bite.

"Well, okay," Carl said in his friendly professional tone. "We're all here so let's get started. He motioned to the woman behind the keyboard who pushed a remote control. A red light came on the camera. "We are here in the matter of a complaint that Mr. Eason," Carl nodded toward the boy, "has lodged against Mr. Bodine."

Between bites, I noticed a legal pad and pen in front of me. I also noticed that Jillian was writing on her *Jordan and Wiser* legal pad. This presented a quandary: write something or finish the donut? With a sense of sadness, I placed the donut on my napkin and picked up the pen. Write what, I had no clue.

"Mr. Eason, we will begin with you. You will need to sit in the chair at the head of the table so we can record your deposition."

Jillian turned towards the boy and smiled. She motioned for him to move to the chair with the microphone in front of it.

Carl resumed, "Now, Mr. Eason –"

"You can call me Richard."

"Okay, Richard. Thank you. This morning, I represent the Sevier County School System and the Smoky Mountain High School. I am going to ask you some questions. I'm sure Miss Renfro has explained what would occur this morning."

"She has."

"So, Richard, please tell us why you have lodged this complaint against Mr. Bodine."

"Just to be clear, this is more than a complaint," Jillian said. "We are bringing suit against Mr. Bodine, the Smoky Mountain High School and the Sevier County Board of Education." Her tone showed no fear. No intimidation. Very professional. With an edge.

Carl exuded another professional smile. "Thank you, Miss Renfro. So Richard, please tell us why you asked Miss Renfro to file suit against Mr. Bodine, Smoky Mountain High School and the Sevier County Board of Education."

"I'm sorry that I had to do that," Richard said. "I certainly didn't want to."

Richard was very calm and composed. He wore a pressed oxford blue shirt, pressed khaki pants, and loafers. His hair was neat. He looked a lot better than Big Bodine over there. I wrote *Jillian and Stu* at the top of the pad.

"It's unfortunate for all of us to have to be here," Jillian said. "But sometimes lawsuits are necessary. Just tell them what you've told me, Richard."

"Okay, well I just finished the tenth grade. I was required to take a Phys Ed class for half the year. That was from January to the end of May. During this time, we played a lot of games. We played football, basketball, softball, dodgeball, and kickball.

"I did not grow up playing sports like most of the guys in the class. Maybe it was because I didn't have a father at home. Maybe it was because I didn't have an interest in them. For whatever reason, I did not play on the elementary sports teams. I did not have a basketball goal in my backyard. I did not play football in the front yard. I did not know the rules of the games.

"I have other interests. I am a Boy Scout. I have been in some form of scouts since I was in elementary school. Cub Scouts first. Now, Boy Scouts. I am currently a Life Scout. That's the rank just below Eagle. I will work on my Eagle Scout Project this summer as well as my remaining merit badges.

"I am not a lazy person. I love the outdoors. I hike. I backpack, carrying a thirty-pound pack on ten-mile hikes on the A.T. in the Smokies .

"A.T.?" Carl asked.

"Appalachian Trail," Richard explained. "I exercise. I run three times a week and have run in a half-marathon. I am a certified Red

Cross Lifeguard. I eat a healthy diet. I just did not grow up playing traditional sports."

I noticed that Big Head was trying to stare down Richard. Maybe he thought he could stare a hole in him. Maybe he thought Richard would be intimidated and run out of the room. Whatever he was doing, it wasn't working. Jillian was still taking notes. I picked up my pencil and wrote *Gimlet Eye ineffective.*

"Early in the past semester, we dressed out in our Phys Ed uniforms and assembled on the football field. It was cold and we were wearing shorts. Mr. Bodine walked out in a sweat suit, like he's wearing today, with a cup of coffee. We were all shivering. The temperature that day was 27 with winds gusting to 15 miles an hour."

"That's very impressive that you remember that," Carl said.

"I keep a record of the weather. I'm very interested in meteorology. That historical information is also available on any weather board."

I saw Jillian's mouth go into a smile. Big Head couldn't see it because he was trying out a different stare.

"Coach Bodine told us to grab a football and start passing it around. There was a ball for about every five or six guys. Most of the guys knew how to pass the football. So they were throwing the ball up to twenty yards. Since we were on the football field, it was easy to measure. They were commenting on how hard the football was. Someone threw the ball to me. I caught it. The footballs had been outside all day and were pretty much frozen.

"Since I didn't know how to pass the ball, I handed it to someone close by to pass. After a few minutes, Coach Bodine walked up and asked in a very loud voice, *What are you doing? Why aren't you passing the ball?*

"I explained that I didn't know how. He asked for someone to give him a ball. He handed it to me and said, *I want to see you pass the ball.* So, I tried. It went about five feet.

"He laughed and said that my parents must be proud of me and walked away."

"You're sure that's what he said," Carl said.

"Yes sir. Several of the other guys heard it, too. Miss Renfro has their names and statements."

Carl paused after Richard's response. He had served up a very soft pitch. I thought lawyers were supposed to know the answer to a question before they asked it. What was Carl up to?

"Okay, Richard, please continue. Obviously, this was an embarrassing moment for you. Correct?"

"I was not just embarrassed, Mr. Winn. I was disappointed. I wanted to *learn* how to pass the football. But no teaching took place. From then on, Coach Bodine would loudly ask me to perform a competency for each new sport we tried.

"In softball, he asked me to throw the ball from third to first base. In basketball, he asked me to take a jump shot from the foul line. In dodgeball, he asked me to throw the ball to hit someone at least twenty feet away. Each time I did not perform, he would shake his head and laugh. He would ask everyone to watch before he asked me to do something."

"So, he hurt your feelings," Carl said.

"Well, yes," Richard said, "but he did more than that. The entire semester was comprised of –"

"*Comprised?*" Big Head mimicked.

"That's one," Jillian said, looking at Bodine. "When you get to three, we are out of here. You can let your attorney explain why that's not a good idea."

Jillian still didn't seem to be intimidated. I wrote a *ONE* on my legal pad, under my *Gimlet Eye* entry.

Carl put a hand on Bodine's arm. I watched to see if Bodine might gnaw it off.

Carl said, "Please continue Richard."

"Our curriculum consisted of playing these games," Richard said. "As I mentioned, there was no teaching. For example, I expected Coach to demonstrate how to pass the football and make sure we all passed it correctly. He did not demonstrate a single skill for the required competency. He just watched us play. Since he did not teach us any skill development, it would be difficult to quantify improvement."

Quantify? RV mouthed. If Jillian saw it, she didn't say anything.

I decided to throw the flag anyway and wrote *TWO.*

"So, from what you've said so far, it's pretty clear you didn't like Coach Bodine," Carl said.

"No, I don't care for him. I think he's a poor teacher who doesn't like his students. He shouldn't be in a position in which his laziness and bluster causes harm to adolescents. But that's not why I pursued this. The unfair piece is that he gave me an F for the class.

"And you disagree with his assessment?" Carl asked.

"Mr. Winn, I have never made less than an A on my report card. Ever. I work hard on my classes. I took the ACT Test this year as a sophomore and scored a 33. I am also physically fit. There was no teaching and there was no assessment. If I had had been taught a skill, I would have worked on it until I mastered it."

I wrote: *ACT Score – 33.*
PE Grade - F
Coach –bona fide idiot
Jillian - fearless
And still cute

"It was unfair to give someone a grade when no teaching took place, and no tests were given. I'm confident that I could have learned how to throw a football or a baseball, but Coach Bodine did not show us a single time how to do that. All he did was to tell us to play ball while he drank coffee and talked on his cell phone. How is it fair to receive an *F* given that criteria?

"I asked him several times how he would determine our grade. I regularly asked what I needed to do. Each time, he stared at me and laughed. He also refused to answer my mother's phone calls and requests for a conference. The principal chose not intervene or set up a conference of any kind."

By this time, Jillian had filled up several pages of notes. I had less than half a page. To compensate, I began to draw a picture of Mr. Bodine's head. That would take up some space.

Carl was finished. Asking Richard questions was not in Mr. Bodine's best interest. He knew that beforehand. And yet he did it anyway.

"Miss Renfro, do you have any questions?"

She looked over at my pad and hesitated. It was bad timing. I wasn't through with the head. Then she looked up at Richard.

"Just a few. Richard, have you ever had a dilemma like this before?"

"No ma'am."

"Ever had a problem of any kind with a teacher?"

"No ma'am."

"As I look in the student handbook, it says on page 25 that *all students shall receive a class syllabus on the first day of class. The syllabus will explain course content, a schedule of activities and the types of tests that will be given to determine a final grade.* Did you receive a syllabus for the class?"

"No ma'am."

"Any handouts regarding how the course would be graded?"

"No ma'am."

"Have you ever received a *U* for conduct before?"

"No ma'am."

"Do you know who Coach Bodine was talking to on his cell phone?"

"No ma'am."

"And you say he used it daily."

"Yes ma'am."

She held up a sheet of paper. "And this is a list of fellow students who also observed Mr. Bodine using his phone each day?"

"Yes ma'am."

Jillian reached for a booklet and turned to a]bookmarked page. "That's unfortunate because this year's *Smoky Mountain High School Faculty Handbook* states that *no teacher is to use a cell phone during class except in case of an emergency.* The section goes on to say that *teachers who consistently violate this policy can be sanctioned, suspended, or terminated, while forfeiting employee compensation.*

"Richard, do you feel that Coach Bodine subjected you to public ridicule often?"

"Yes ma'am."

She turned to me and whispered in my ear. "I think Carl may want to settle before this goes further. Please don't let Mr. Bodine see your cartoon without police protection."

She looked at Carl. He nodded.

"Let's take a break. Miss Renfro, can I see you outside for a moment?"

Carl and Jillian got up and disappeared. Richard got up and sat down by his mom. Coach Bodine cleared his throat and leaned forward. I reached for my cell phone and pushed record. So, he stared at Richard for several seconds. Then he walked out. Maybe it had been a good idea for Jillian to have co-counsel.

I turned around and looked at Richard. He looked at me and let out a very large sigh. His mother gave him a hug.

"You okay?" I asked.

"Yeah, I'm okay," he said.

"You did a very good job," I said.

"Thanks, Mr. Jensen. It's a load off my shoulders just to be able to tell somebody what's been going on. I got nowhere with the school administration."

"I think you got somewhere today," I said. I looked over at Mrs. Eason. "Richard did what he needed to do today," I said.

"I know," she said. "I'm just frustrated and very angry that it has gone this far. Do you know how much damage that big . . . piece of . . . wasted flesh has caused? The principal didn't do what needed to be done. The school board didn't do what should have been done. Why did this even have to happen?"

"It didn't," I said. "But there will always be guys like that. And there will always be spineless, lazy bureaucrats. And they'll keep ignoring guys like the coach that are doing bad stuff until someone stands up and says that's not right. Richard did that today. It was awkward but it was the right thing to do. I know you're very proud of him."

We waited a few minutes until Jillian and Carl came in. Carl walked around and shook Richard's hand. "Richard, you did a remarkable job today in expressing an unfair situation. On behalf of Smoky Mountain High School and the Board of Education, I want to apologize for this unfortunate experience."

He shook hands with Richard's mother and said, "I know this has been a very trying time for you. I cannot change that. But what I *can* do is to try to make it better. Miss Renfro and I have come up with what she feels is a fair and equitable solution to this situation. First, your grade will be changed from an F to an A. Your conduct grade will also be changed from Unsatisfactory to Satisfactory.

"I understand that you are not seeking any financial remuneration. So, we, that is the school and the board, would like to make a donation to your Scout troop for whatever you and your Scoutmaster want to use it for."

Richard's face lit up. "I like that idea!"

"It's a significant donation," Jillian said.

"We are always looking for funds to support our Eagle Scout Projects," Richard said.

"What's yours?" I asked.

"I want to build a training facility for Guide Dogs for the Blind."

We all paused to let that one sink in.

"That's very impressive," Carl said. "I know the school would be honored to help with such a worthy cause."

"Coincidentally," Jillian said, "the school's gift will more than pay for the materials and other expenses needed for this project."

Richard was smiling from ear to ear.

"What about Coach Bodine?" Mrs. Eason asked. "Is Richard going to have trouble with him next year?"

"The short answer is no," Carl said. "As Miss Renfro knows, this is not Mr. Bodine's first offense. Now that we have reached an amicable settlement, I will tell you that he is no longer employed at Smoky Mountain High School. Furthermore, he has been instructed not to contact you in any way. I told Miss Renfro to let me know if he does."

Maybe I had not given Carl enough credit. He knew what he was doing by letting Richard answer his questions.

It was time to go. As we walked out to our cars, we all shook hands again. Carl and the Easons left immediately. We were the only car in the school parking lot.

On a Saturday.

Chapter Four

Jillian turned to me with a big smile. Then she put the Range Rover in gear and away we went. The mountains were majestic and the sky was a brilliant blue. The rhododendrons were in bloom. We drove in silence for a few minutes. Jillian was perhaps enjoying the drive a little too much. As we made one particularly sharp turn, I looked in the back for a helmet.

We came off the parkway, and were soon in Gatlinburg, a touristy town in a valley of several mountains. Jillian maneuvered into a parking place on the street and said, "Are you hungry? I'm starving!" Then she got out and shut her door.

"Sure, I guess I could eat. Yes, this would be fine. Let's stop," I said to an empty car.

She had parked on River Road, so named because it runs alongside the Little Pigeon River. We could see and hear the water from the sidewalk. An ornamental iron fence separated the sidewalk from the river, and about every fifty feet, colorful flowers cascaded from the baskets placed at the top of the fence.

Jillian carried a cloth bag. She stopped in front of the River Terrace, a large hotel. "I'll be right back," she said and set out over the bridge that crossed the river. "Enjoy the scenery!"

"You bet!" I said as she disappeared. I didn't know what she meant or where she went. I thought we'd be on the road back to Spruceville. But here we were in Gatlinburg. I decided to follow her advice. I discovered some well used stone steps just off the sidewalk that led down to the river. I began exploring.

I spotted four rainbow trout and several wood ducks looking for the trout. Some falling Maple leaves hit the water. The current quickly carried them around the large rocks. The ducks were quacking. Probably asking, "See any trout?" I could hear a few tourists walking on the sidewalk above. None commented on the ducks or the trout.

Jillian reappeared on the bridge. She was wearing a t-shirt, cut-off shorts and tennis shoes. She had either already been in the sun a lot or did some business at the tanning salon.

"Let me put my stuff in the car and I'll join you!" She dashed over the bridge. I resumed my exploration, and in a minute felt her hand on my shoulder. "Isn't this great?"

It was.

Chapter Five

We worked our way down River Road and crossed Main Street. "I'm taking you to my favorite lunch place in Gatlinburg," Jillian said. We walked past Calhoun's Restaurant and into an alcove of stores, stopping under a sign that said *Smoky Mountain Brewery.*

"We're here," she said.

Once inside, we walked up the stairs and got a booth next to a window that overlooked a main tourist thoroughfare. Watching tourists in a place like Gatlinburg is entertainment in and of itself. They were dressed in every way. Some wore jackets. Some wore overalls. Some wore jeans of all descriptions. Most of the younger crowd wore shorts.

"We're here for the pizza," she said. That being settled, we spent a few minutes making up stories about the people we saw walking below us.

When the pizza was first placed on the rack at our table, it did not look completely cooked. We were told to wait five minutes. Then we cut into it and I could see why it was Jillian's favorite lunch spot. The pizza was superb. "I really appreciate you coming today, Mr. Jensen. It really helped."

"Really? How so?"

"There's strength in numbers. With you there, Big Boy and Carl weren't going to patronize the cute attorney. They weren't going to stare at me if they knew you were looking at them."

I thought about that. "Cute attorney, huh?"

She took another healthy bite of pizza, getting a significant bit of it on the side of her mouth. "Uh-huh."

"And you lump Carl into this, too?"

"Yep."

"Interesting."

She wiped her mouth with a napkin and said, "He is more refined, but, believe me, he would have turned on the charm if I had come alone. He would have complimented my suit. He would have asked questions about my professional and probably personal life. Then he would have asked me to eat lunch with him."

"It would have been more complicated."

"Correct."

"But you just met Carl today. How can you tell so much about him?"

"First, Mr. Jensen, he's –"

"Please. Call me Stu."

"Oh yeah, sorry about that. Just wanted to let him know that you might be more than co-counsel, which you weren't on either count."

"True. So why are you saying all these things about poor Carl? He seemed decent enough to me."

"Number one, he's male. No offense, but men are just like that. Number two, he's a lawyer, what can you expect? Number three, experience. Are you going to eat that last piece?"

"No, it's yours. So, your intuition was correct. It helped to have someone else sitting on your side."

"You bet it did! So, how can I repay you for sacrificing a day of work on the Lodge?"

She was full of life. And she seemed to be enjoying our time together. I was glad it occurred to her that I gave up a Lodge day for her.

I thought about that. She already said I couldn't get attorney wages. Would she match what I was paid for supervision of afterschool ride waiting? I hated the assignment, but sometimes I had to take one for the team.

I almost said to forget it. Instead, I heard myself say, "I don't know. Let me think about it. By the way, you were very good in that deposition."

"Thank you. It didn't hurt to have the perfect client. I wasn't nervous about the deposition. But I was nervous about speaking in front of my old speech teacher."

Old.

"I was never your Speech teacher, but I give you an A for the day."

"Yea! By the way, what was up with your notes?"

"I was trying to look like an alert, competent attorney for the defense."

"*One?*" she asked.

"You said you'd give him to three. I was just keeping up."

She laughed. *Coach a bona fide idiot?*"

"Yeah, probably not the best thing to write."

"Especially when he's three feet away."

"I wasn't worried. I could handle him."

"Really? Just how would you have handled him?"

"If he had come any closer, I would have reached under my jacket, pulled out a big Snickers bar, and tossed it in the corner."

Jillian had made the mistake of taking a drink of her Diet Coke. She spewed it back out. "I almost choked!"

"And then when he dove for the Snickers bar, we could have run for Mt. Le Conte. By the time he finished, it would have just been him and Carl, the Ladies Man."

She started laughing again. "*The Ladies Man?*"

"Yep."

"Plus, you wrote I was still cute."

"I did."

Chapter Six

We walked out of Smoky Mountain Brewery into the pleasant June Mountain air. Jillian had eaten like she was going to the electric chair. Sweet bird of youth.

"Let's walk this way," she said. She put her arm around mine and led the way up Main Street. She showed me some of her favorite shops. We walked into a shopping area and listened to a bluegrass band play *Rocky Top.*

After we resumed our tour, she said, "This is my favorite part of town." It was called *The Village*, a collection of "Old World" brick stores along narrow brick walkways. Looked Bavarian to me, but maybe *Old World* brings more people in.

We walked past a toy store, an art store, an outfitters store, a spice store, the *Smoky Mountain Candy Kitchen*, a Christian bookstore, a store that sold only socks, *The Donut Friar* (our coffee source at the school) and a large public restroom. The restroom was in the back of *The Village*. The farther you walked, the steeper the grade.

When we reconvened after visiting the restrooms, I started to retrace our steps. Jillian turned me around, and said, "I want to show you a secret." So, instead of walking back down the incline, we walked past the bathrooms and up a steep hill. After a few hundred feet, we came to a cemetery on our left. The sign said:

White Oak Flats Cemetery
Established 1830

It was built on the side of a hill. "Come on!" Jillian said. She took my hand and began to walk up the steep cemetery. It probably wasn't a 45-degree angle, but it felt like it.

We walked for about two miles. Well, maybe two hundred feet. There was a bench at the top. She sat. So did I. We could see much of the city and the mountains that bordered it.

Jillian was soaking it in. "I love this place. I could sit here for a long time."

I needed to sit a little longer myself. I was trying to steady my breathing.

"I thought you might like it, too. I come here and think. I get a clearer perspective here than any other place."

I could see why. As my oxygen level came back up, I noticed things. Like the birds singing. And the wind blowing through the trees. And the view of the city. And the number of old markers in the cemetery.

"Many of these tombstones date back to the early 1800s," Jillian said. "This community predates the Civil War. As a matter of fact, several conscientious objectors hid in the mountains until the Civil War was over."

While she talked, she never took her eyes off the view.

"Jillian?"

"Right here, Mr. J."

"It's after 3:00. Don't you have to be back by 6:00?"

"Well, I did. But it's canceled," she said, still looking somewhere out there.

While I took that in, she added, "It was a date."

"Oh!" I didn't know exactly how to respond.

"It's okay."

"Really? What happened? Strike that. None of my business."

She turned away from the horizon and looked at me with a million watts of attention. "Today it is. You have earned a right to ask. The truth is that I went out with him the night after I found you at the Lodge.

"Okay."

"He was very intelligent. He was polite. He has a great career and is strikingly handsome."

"Oh. One of those guys. I'm sure he had a good reason."

She stared at me for several seconds. "I was the one who canceled it."

I again found myself at a loss for words again. So I didn't say anything.

She smiled and said, "I didn't realize how good today was going to be."

I let that sink in. We were both quiet. Then I asked, "When did you cancel this date?"

"Back at the bathroom."

We stared at each other. Then she put her hands on my face and kissed me. It wasn't a long kiss. But it wasn't a peck, either. She eased her face away and kept her hands on my face.

If this was a dream, I wanted to enjoy it. My eyes were still closed.

"Are you okay Mr. J?"

I nodded my head. I could feel her hands and her breath, so I knew her face was still very close to mine. I opened my eyes. She looked concerned.

I took a breath and said, "What?"

'My kiss?"

"It was the best thing that's happened to me in a long time. I may never forget it."

She smiled. "I'm glad you liked it. I'm also glad you're not having some kind of episode."

"At my age, you never know."

She nodded.

"That was a joke."

"Of course it was. I knew that. But maybe I should have warned you. Or at least know where you keep your defibrillator."

I opened my mouth to say I didn't have one. She spoke first.

"Incoming." She kissed me again. Her blue eyes were very soft. They were beautiful. Then they turned into one big eye because she was so close. "I have completely loved the whole day. Let's see how we feel about this in a few days."

I nodded again. "If we do see each other again, do you think you could quit calling me Mr. Jensen?"

Her face broke into a very large grin. "I'm not sure. That would be pretty weird."

"Weirder than kissing your old teacher in a cemetery? At the beginning of this day, I was too old, yet safe. Plus I was an attorney."

She laughed, "Yeah." She kissed me on the cheek and hopped up. "I'm not sure you were my teacher."

On the way back down, we stopped in the *Smoky Mountain Candy Kitchen*. We watched a man in a white shirt and pants and hat make taffy on a machine by the front window. If dentists want an easy way to remove an old filling, they should just have the patient chew a piece of taffy. Jillian bought some white chocolate bark, which she shared. I saw a small stuffed bear, only about as big as my hand. He looked lonely.

We walked out of the candy store into *The Village* common area. "There are only three of us who know about today. You and me and this bear," I said. I gave it to her to hold and I took her photo. "I can look at this picture whenever I think it might have been a dream."

That began a photo frenzy with her phone. I held the bear, then we both held the bear. Then she had an elderly man take our photo in front of the fountain in the middle of *The Village*.

As we walked back to the car, I took off my watch and put it on the bear's mid-section. "On second thought, maybe you should keep Mr. Bear, so you don't forget who gave you the bear. And to help you remember our *time* together in case it turns out to be just once."

I knew that was pretty corny, but it was the best I could do. She said she couldn't take my watch, but I insisted. She didn't realize it, but it was a Bass Pro model I bought on special, very cheap.

"Next time, make it an Omega."

Maybe she knew.

Chapter Seven

The Lodge was beginning to take shape. The framing was finished. We also roughed in the stairway to the second floor.

I know this early building stage gives the owner the impression that the house is moving along quickly. But at least now I could see how it was going to look.

Because it appeared like we would get some rain soon, we worked on the roof. My friends had just left. I was staring up at the roof that we finished. It was Saturday. I was tired. But I was thankful for their unselfish work.

It had been two weeks since the Gatlinburg trip. I needed a few days for the events to resonate. That was followed by panic. Had I violated some teacher code of conduct? Jillian had been in my classroom when I was a teacher and she was a student.

But that was fourteen years ago. That's 98 years to a dog. Jillian was no dog. And she was no longer a high school student. Our kiss occurred fourteen years after she graduated. That seemed like a reasonable amount of time for her to become an adult. Besides, if the school made trouble, maybe she would defend me in court.

I also thought about Richard. It was a shame that he had to endure a deposition. Yet he did so with the confidence of a Beni Hana chef at the table. He impressed me. I wondered how many adults in his life told him what a great kid he was. I'm sure his Scoutmaster did. Of course, his mom did. Maybe a teacher or two from school? A neighbor? I'd like to know.

One thing I *did* know was that I smelled pretty bad. It was going to be another night with my make-shift shower. I created a very simple one. It was a 50-gallon barrel of rainwater with a hose at the bottom. The end of the hose contained a lever to open and close the water flow. I placed the barrel on top of a deer feeder stand. The theory was that the sun would warm the water during the day.

By the end of the day, it wasn't cold water, but I didn't have to worry about getting scalded. The shower was away from the Lodge, down a little path, next to the latrine. The latrine consisted of a ditch, an old wooden ladder placed across the ditch, a small shovel, and some toilet paper.

I hit the shower. Then I cooked some hot dogs and beans on my Coleman camp stove. I had invested in a cooler that kept food cool for several days, so that's where I kept my perishables.

I looked forward to my evening campfires. There was plenty of wood, that's for sure. The smoke kept the bugs away and I spent hours sitting in a chair, by the fire, watching the stars and enjoying a night like tonight.

It also provided time to reflect on past events and future plans. I spent a few minutes thinking about that Saturday in Gatlinburg with Jillian. I wondered if I would see her again. Oddsmakers would give very low odds, as well they should. I did, too.

What a surprise and unusual course of events. I watched a satellite cross the horizon. I saluted it and put another log on the fire.

Chapter Eight

I was at a grocery store in Spruceville, stocking up on some essentials. It was the Monday of the last week of June and the plumbing contractors were finished. As I mentioned, after seeing how little I knew about building, one of my friends, Bill Linder, not only installed the plumbing, but also became the building contractor. According to Bill, in another week or so, the house would be "dried in" which meant that internal wiring could begin.

As I stared at the cereal section, I thought about Jillian. It was now over three weeks since our Gatlinburg trip. It's not often that a day would stay in my memory for the rest of my life, but that one would. I was not surprised that I did not hear from her again. Jillian had the intensity of a sparkler. But sparklers burn hot for only a short period of time. I suspected, as Hank Snow sang, *she had moved on.* Or moved back to Mr. Hallmark. Or to Zachary.

Well, I managed to get through life for this long without her. I could probably eek by a little longer. But I would always remember that day.

I had no intention of contacting Jillian. Even if I decided to be the one to reach out, I had no idea where she worked or lived. I had no phone number, no address not even an email address. Which would have been my last choice of ways to communicate with a woman. I didn't even like using email to follow up with parents about their child's speech grades.

The only problem was that I kept thinking about Richard. I did want to stay in touch with him, but, just like Jillian, I didn't have any contact information for him. Since at this point, he thought I was a lawyer, that might be a little awkward.

This meant I needed to get in touch with her, whether I wanted to or not. I certainly wasn't a lawyer, but I could pretend to be an investigator. Since I wasn't going to be back in Spruceville until the following weekend, I decided to Google *Jillian Renfro* before I went back to the Lodge. My exceptional sleuthing paid off. There she was – photo, law firm, address and email. The law firm was Jordan and Wiser. I couldn't help but notice that most of the attorneys were men.

My disdain for email made the choice simple - I went to my desk, took out a piece of plain printer paper and a fresh envelope, selected my favorite fine tipped pen and began writing. Actually, I sat there a while, trying to figure out how to make sure it sounded like my interest was for Richard alone. Finally, I scribbled this letter:

> *Dear Jillian,*
>
> *I hope you are doing well. I cannot begin to tell you just how much fun I had with you a few weeks ago.*
>
> *I am writing about Richard. With your permission and help, I would like to contact him. I want to be one of his encouragers. I realize this might be an action you don't want to happen.*
>
> *Just use the enclosed self-addressed envelope to let me know your disposition on the matter.*
>
> *If I don't hear from you, I will not pursue the issue further. I am so glad we were able to reconnect.*
>
> *I will never forget it.*
>
> *Stu*

Chapter Nine

A high school teacher's summer is like gold. You want to savor every day, because you know that in a few short weeks, you're back in the classroom. Why is it that weeks during the school year seem to drag by while weeks during vacation go by at warp speed?

This was Friday, July 1 and it was going to be a three-day weekend. Since a holiday weekend was coming up, Bill had family obligations as did most of the other guys. Fortunately, we had a very productive week. Insulation had been installed and the drywall was in. The stone fireplace was now finished and functional.

So, even though the gang was not around, I had homework to do, which was to paint the drywall with primer. That should keep me busy, especially since I had never primed a wall. But before I could prime, I had my daily job of cleanup. That took about an hour.

Then I got the primer out and pulled out a book to show me how to do this. With no internet access, I couldn't get a YouTube. I heard the gravel crunching from down below and was hoping it was a painter. It was Jillian.

As she got out of the car, she said with arms wide open, "Look at what you've done! I'm impressed!"

I smiled. "Actually, I'm the helper."

Jillian was wearing a large shirt over a t-shirt. At least that's what it looked like to me. She also had on some jeans with several holes in them.

I was standing on the newly constructed porch. She climbed up on her hood. She looked at me with a curious expression. She was holding my letter.

"Thanks for the communication," she said. "I particularly liked the way you signed it."

"Stu," I said.

"Stu," she repeated. "Plus, you indicated you had a lot of fun."

"An indescribable amount."

"And it was a day you'll never forget."

"True."

"You were glad we could reconnect."

"Very true."

"*Reconnect?*"

"I didn't want you to feel uncomfortable," I said.

"And you'll never forget our reconnection?"

"That's my prediction. I'm glad you got the letter"

"I'm quite fond of it," she said.

"Really? Get out of town."

"I don't get many – any - letters, except the kind that mention words like *sue and court* and large amounts of money."

"I left all that out."

"How come you are always alone when I come up here?" she

asked.

“Both times?”

“Yeah, where are the rest? Hiding in the trailer?”

“Camper. Nope. They have taken this three-day weekend to be with their families.”

“Wimps.”

“I know.

She smiled.

“I didn’t know if I’d see you again,” I said.

There was silence in the air for a few seconds.

“Me either,” Jillian said.

“How come you didn’t know?”

“If I’d see you again?”

“If you’d see me again,” I repeated.

“Because I wanted to think about it – to see if I wanted to see you again.”

I nodded. We both were silent. “It’s been almost a month. Has it taken you that long to decide?” I asked.

“Yes.”

“How’s Mr. Hallmark?”

“He’s Mr. History.”

“Oh. . . Your hind parts must be hot.”

She raised her eyebrows and said, "Is that a question or a statement? Never mind." She jumped off her steamy hood and did a little dance. I don't think it was for my benefit.

"Do you have a cell phone?" she asked.

"Doesn't work up here."

"Do you have a land line?"

"Don't think that's possible."

"Internet?"

"Guess."

She nodded. "Do you have a mailbox?"

"Not yet."

"Walkie talkie, smoke signals, carrier pigeons, messenger squirrels?"

"Nope."

"I never asked. Do you have a girlfriend?"

I smiled. "None."

She nodded again. "Probably a question I should have asked earlier." Then she looked at me.

"Is this a good idea?"

I paused. "Are we still talking about girlfriends or are we back to messenger squirrels?"

She sat on a sawhorse. "You – me. Are we a good idea?"

I sighed and looked at her. "Maybe we need to just spend some time together. Then we should know if it's a good idea."

She nodded some more. "I think I said that back in the cemetery."

I smiled some more. “Did you come all the way up here to ask if we are a good idea?”

She ignored my question. “So, you’re saying let’s spend some time together, get to know each other and see where that leads?”

“Unless you’ve got a preacher in the Range Rover and want to get married today.”

She put my envelope and card back in her jeans back pocket, walked over, put her arms around my neck and looked into my eyes.

“Let’s get to know each other first.”

Chapter Ten

I showed Jillian the main floor and upstairs. She liked the openness. She liked the large fireplace. She said the bedrooms were cozy.

When we walked back downstairs, she said, "I want to talk to you about Richard. Do you think I could stay here tonight?"

I felt my equilibrium shift.

"Tonight?"

"Uh-huh. Unless you have other plans. Do you have a prior engagement?"

"No prior engagement."

"What were your plans for today?"

"Do you know anything about primer?"

"I just finished priming and painting my master bedroom. I love that kind of stuff."

"You can stay."

Chapter Eleven

We finished the upstairs. Jillian was fast and efficient. She could also paint and talk. She was wearing an old shirt of mine, which came down close to her knees.

"Tell me some more about your interest in Richard."

"Okay. I've never met a teenager as mature and together as Richard. He's comfortable with who is. Not to mention smart. He has a good heart. But it seems to me he's got a big hole in his life."

"How so?" Jillian asked. She was on a stepladder in the downstairs bathroom, painting away. I was painting the opposite wall. I liked the fact that she asked me questions and allowed me to answer, without interjecting her own experience or opinion. A real art of conversation.

"He said he had no one to show him how to play team sports. So I'm guessing there's no significant male in his life. Just a hunch."

"Tell me how the fact that he doesn't know how to play football means that he doesn't have men in his life," she said, blowing a strand of hair out of her eyes. I thought about brushing it away, but my hands had primer on them, too.

"One of the things that men do is to pass on to their sons or young boys how to play sports. It's a bonding thing. Boys have a lot of energy, and they love to play outside. Get a group of them together and they will soon be playing some kind of game. And, often, it involves a ball. During the summer, it's baseball or soccer.

During the fall, it's football. During the winter, it's basketball."

"Not every boy likes football," she said.

"True. But most know how to pass one. Many have played touch football in elementary leagues. And they know enough about the game to understand what their friends are talking about.

"I had a roommate in college, Frank, who grew up kind of like Richard. Instead of Scouts, his passion was the high school band. When he got to college, he didn't know how to play a single game that used a ball."

"His father didn't teach him?" she asked, moving to the next wall.

"No, his dad, for whatever reason, did not teach him. Plus, Frank didn't want to learn about football or any other sport. Music was his passion.

"At our college, you had to have six courses in Physical Education. Frank looked at his options and signed up for tennis. I helped him buy his first pair of tennis shoes, which he kept in a shoebox. We practiced several nights a week, with Frank hitting balls against the practice wall. It took a long time for Frank to even be able to hit the ball to the wall, much less hit it off the wall. He eventually learned how to serve and hit a forehand and backhand.

"We used this same process for some of his other Phys Ed credits. Fortunately, he was able to take two that were board game classes."

"Board games?"

"I know, but it was a relief for both of us. I don't know if you even have to take Physical Education classes anymore in college, but I do know that it's helpful for males to know how to swing a bat or a tennis racquet or throw a baseball or football. It doesn't fit every boy, and maybe not Frank. But I have a feeling it fits Richard.

"I also suspect that he can use all the male encouragement he can get. I guess it's the teacher in me. Why I want to volunteer for something like this during my vacation is a mystery to me."

"Done with the bathroom," Jillian said. She surveyed my side without comment. "I get it. Your intuition tells you that Richard is capable of great things. His major roadblock is that he doesn't have many male mentors."

"Correct. What do you think?"

"We're meeting Richard tomorrow morning at ten."

Saturday?

"You talked to Richard?"

"And his mother," Jillian said. "She loves the idea."

"And you told them I was not an attorney?"

"Didn't have to. They knew."

"How could they know?"

"Mrs. Eason used to work in a men's store in Knoxville. She knows business attire."

"Oh."

"And Richard could see your notes."

"Uh-oh."

"So I told them we wanted to see them and visit. I told them it was more of a social visit."

"When did you have this conversation?"

"Last night."

I was silent for a few seconds while I processed that. "So, just to be clear, you scheduled our visit before you even drove 50 miles to find me here and asked me to explain why I wanted to see him?"

“Correct.”

“And before you asked if you and I were a good idea?

“Uh-huh.”

“And before you asked if you could spend the night.”

“Also true.”

“Wow.”

“Wow is good. Get back to work.”

Chapter Twelve

We were sitting on the edge of the porch. Jillian had primer on her shirt - my shirt. She also had it on her hands and a few smudges on her face.

I had more on me than she did.

The sun was beginning to disappear over the trees. The wind had picked up a little. We were finished priming. It had taken some work and ingenuity with the ladder, but all walls were primed.

"I have a question," she said. "You still don't have running water?"

"Not yet."

"But we have primer on us. I don't want to sleep with primer on me, Mr. – Stuart."

"Don't blame you."

"How do I get it off?"

This is where it would get interesting.

"I have what you would call a make-shift shower."

"Really? How make-shift?"

"Come with me."

We walked down the path. "The shower," I pronounced.

She looked at it, saying nothing.

"How does it work?" she asked.

I showed her.

"And this will get the primer off?"

"I have no idea. I have never had primer on. It does get rid of the other things."

"Like what?" she asked, pronouncing both words slowly.

"In my case, stink. Maybe a tick or two."

She mouthed the word *tick*.

Her eyes shifted. "What's that?"

"That is the restroom."

"That ladder?"

I nodded. "And the toilet paper."

She kept looking at it. "The shovel is a nice touch."

"This could be the fork in the road," I said.

"There's another path? Let's see it."

"Metaphorically. The other path is to get in your Range Rover and beat a trail to your hot shower and comfy commode."

"And no ticks."

"So, make your choice Jillian Renfro."

"I'm staying."

"I'm impressed."

"Don't be. I'm not getting primer on my leather seats. Plus, you're helping"

"I'm not sure I follow."

"Doesn't matter."

Chapter Thirteen

We walked back up the path. Jillian grabbed a large cloth bag from her back seat, strapped it over her shoulder and headed for the front door. The bag she packed before she asked if we were a good idea. "Don't go on a date or anything," she said and disappeared inside.

I was amazed at how much we had done. It would have taken me all weekend, and it wouldn't have been nearly as good. Jillian knew what she was doing. I wondered what she knew about installing cabinets.

The primer on me had hardened and was feeling sticky.

Jillian reappeared. She was wearing another of *my* shirts and that was all I could see. The jeans were gone. She did have some kind of rubber shoes on. Was *flip-flop* still a word? We used to call them thongs, but I haven't heard anybody call them that since *Hopalong Cassidy* rode off into the sunset.

"What are you going to wear?" she asked.

"Me?"

She looked around. "Did you think I was talking to someone else? I can't get this goop off by myself. You've got to help."

"You're serious," I said, stunned. "Taking a shower is usually a personal activity. You want us to take a shower together?"

"The operative word is *usually*. There's nothing usual about this little maneuver. Can you tell me how I can hold the trigger on that hose with one hand, hold a washcloth with the other, and use the soap, too? I want to be as clean as I can be."

I thought about that.

"I also want to make sure I have no ticks. Get your stuff, you're coming."

I spent a hurried moment in the camper. This was an unexpected development.

"Uh, what are you wearing to shower in?" I asked.

"Hurry up! A tick might be stuck in some of this primer," she said, peering into the camper. "And it's getting colder out here by the second."

"You're not going to tell me, are you?"

She said nothing about that, but asked, "You do use towels and soap out here?" She sounded hopeful.

I pulled out a bin in the camper marked *Towels.* I took out a couple of large beach towels and handed them to her.

"She smiled. Wash cloths?"

I found two.

Then I opened another bin marked *Bathroom Supplies* and took out a new bar of soap. She giggled.

"What?"

"Nothing. I just haven't used a bar of soap in a while. Is that Irish Spring?"

"It is." I handed everything to her.

"Wilderness amenities," she observed.

Chapter Fourteen

Jillian noticed my shower ensemble for the first time. I had put on a pair of gym shorts, a t-shirt and some old rubber boat shoes.

She laughed. "I'm diggin' the shoes!"

"Maybe you should call me Mr. Jensen."

We headed down the path, carrying our washcloths, towels and soap.

She looked in my direction. "Are those gym shorts from school?"

"You betcha."

She kept looking. "How old are they?"

"I'm not sure."

"Old enough to drink beer, I bet," she said.

"Waste not, want not."

"Those were old even when I was in school."

"Really? I didn't know we were making a fashion statement for the possums on our way to the shower. You do have on something under my shirt, don't you?"

She smiled.

We arrived at the shower. "Put your towel on that branch," I said.

Jillian placed her towel on the branch, unbuttoned the shirt and took it off. She was wearing a bright purple tank top and what looked like women's running shorts.

"My shorts are much shorter and newer than yours."

"I'm curious. What made you decide to bring shorts?" I asked.

She ignored that and asked, "How cold is the water going to be?"

I said. "It's not cold. It's not bad."

"I need you to hold the faucet thing. Don't you want to take off that nice t-shirt?"

"This is one of my favorite t-shirts. It's from the Rock Bottom Remainder Band. I went to hear them. See, this rendering? There's Dave Barry and Stephen King and Amy Tan and Barbara Kingsolver and –"

"I could tell it was nice because of all those holes. And because you chose it for the shower. There could be ticks under it. I'm cold. Shed the shirt and turn the water on."

I took off my shirt and she started to giggle.

"Do I even want to ask?"

"I'm sorry. I just never thought I'd be in the shower with Mr. Jensen!"

"You are beginning to make me feel self-conscious and awkward," I said.

"She gave me a hug. "Let her rip, Stu!"

I turned the water on and she screamed. Drama.

She was right. In this setting, it took two sets of hands to get the sticky mess off us. By the time we were finished, it was almost dark.

Before she dried off, Jillian said, “Could you check me for ticks?”

“Have you ever heard Brad Paisley sing that song?”

“What song?”

“A song he sang about what he’d like to do with his girlfriend.”

“Which was what?”

“He had a list and one of them was to check her for ticks.”

“Seriously?”

“Google it.”

“Hmm. Okay. Just as soon as I’m out of the tundra. Find any on this girlfriend?”

“You are clean.”

I sang it as we walked back up the path.

Cause I’d like to see you out in the moonlight
I’d like to kiss you way back in the sticks.
I’d like to walk you through a field of wildflowers
And I’d like to check you for ticks.

“Mark the last one off your bucket list,” she said.

Chapter Fifteen

I've always thought that the smell of hamburgers cooking over a fire was very fragrant. If women really wanted to attract men, they should buy a bottle of *Ode de Burger.*

We had just finished our meal. Hamburgers cooked over the campfire, with some potatoes, carrots and onions wrapped in aluminum foil and placed in the coals. We used sticks to roast marshmallows over the fire for dessert. I added another log. The temperature had dropped.

We were sitting in camp chairs. "Look at the stars!" Jillian said. "They are so bright and so many!"

I looked at them. Away from the city lights, and at our altitude, the stars were brilliant.

"It's getting colder. Do you have a jacket I can wear?" She had her jeans back on. She was wearing a different t-shirt.

"I can see how it might get a little drafty in those jeans."

"I think you like them. Go get me a jacket."

I returned from the camper with an old field jacket. She reached for it and put it on.

"Thanks. It smells like you," she said. "I like your smell.

I didn't know I had a smell, but I was glad it was good.

"Do you want to talk about sleeping arrangements?" I asked.

"I've been interested in hearing about them," she said.

"Well, I have been sleeping in the camper."

"Yeah," she said, giving the camper a careful look. "What else you got?"

"Well, if you want the real camping experience, we can sleep out here by the fire."

"Out *here?*" she said, gesturing to the trees and the ground.

"Sure. We can watch the stars and hear the wildlife."

"What kind of wildlife?"

"Oh, whatever comes our way. Owls, raccoons, possums, armadillos, deer –"

"Bear?"

"I haven't seen any since I've been here this summer."

"But there *are* bears around here, right?"

"Yes," I said.

"Plus, there are ticks."

"True."

"And they could crawl right up – what would we be sleeping in? Sleeping bags?"

"I have some if that's what you'd like. Or you can just sleep on top of a blanket and under another one."

"Wouldn't that get the blanket dirty?"

"We would put a ground cloth under the blanket. That would keep the blanket from getting wet."

"Wet? Why would it get wet?"

"We have a healthy dew each night and morning."

"Dew, huh."

"Yeah."

"Is there a third option?"

"Sure, we can sleep inside the Lodge. The windows and doors are in, which might help since it's going to be a cool night."

"Okay, good. Let's do that."

"In the Lodge."

"Yes."

I put out our campfire and we put everything back in the camper. I asked if we could take a little walk. She agreed, somewhat reluctantly, after our bear talk.

We strolled down the driveway to the road and followed it to the top of the mountain. The stars and moon lit the way. We could hear the crickets, frogs and bobwhites calling back and forth to each other. Occasionally an owl would enter in the symphony. We were on our way back down the mountain when we heard the coyotes. Jillian put her arms around me. This made walking a little more challenging, but I suffered on.

As we turned on my drive, Jillian stopped and turned me around to face her. She looked at me for a few seconds and said, "I want to remember this night. I'm trying to soak everything in. She opened her mouth to say something else. Instead, she changed her mind and kissed me. Then she apologized for not giving ample warning.

I made a fire in the fireplace. This was the first social fire made in it. It drew well and felt good. While we were bringing quilts and pillows into the house, I shared this information with Jillian.

"The first fire in the Lodge," she said. "This is an historic occasion."

I agreed.

“I’m glad you have it,” she said. “It makes this room a lot warmer.”

After a few minutes, Jillian announced, “I usually use the bathroom before I go to bed.”

“Good habit,” I said.

“I need to do that tonight,” she said.

“Do you need a flashlight?”

“I need more than a flashlight. I don’t know what’s out there. A rabid possum. A rogue bear. An angry tick.”

“We didn’t even talk about snakes,” I added.

“You’re going with me.”

I used a flashlight to get us down the trail. Jillian was on the lookout for danger of any kind and any size. When we made it to the latrine, she looked at it forlornly.

“I guess this is where it all happens,” she said.

I gave her a flashlight. She shined it on the toilet paper, then on to the shovel and the ladder that was positioned over the ditch.

“Okay, I’ll wait for you up the trail a little,” I said.

She grabbed my arm. “Wait. I’m just trying to put all the pieces together here. This is one of the strangest things I’ve ever done. This is like an episode out of *The Twilight Zone*.”

“I loved that show!” I said.

“Yeah, well, congratulations, you’re starring in this episode.”

“Are you okay?” I asked.

She was silent for several seconds. “Just before I saw you last month, do you know where I was?”

“I’ve been hoping you’d tell me,” I said.

"I was at the Ritz Carlton Central Park in New York."

"Sounds elegant."

"You have no idea. Not once did I see a hose hanging from a barrel or a ladder placed across a ditch."

"Do you want to go back?"

"Sure, I've been there many times."

"I meant back up the hill."

"Oh, no. I still have to use the bathroom."

"Okay, I'll just mosey back up the path."

"I don't know Stuart. I really don't want to get attacked in the middle of me doing my business. I think you're going to have to stay here with me."

"I don't think that's a good idea."

"I'm serious. I'll give you five hundred dollars."

I laughed.

"Five hundred dollars and a good sports jacket."

"Look," I said. "There's nothing to be afraid of. I will take thirty steps up the path and if you see anything, just yell and I'll come racing back, guns blazing."

She was quiet again. "Twenty steps and you don't have a gun. I have a gun. It's in my purse. Maybe you should go get it."

"And leave you here?"

"You're right. Listen, I do not mind you staying right where you are. I would feel much better."

"Jillian, I promise you're going to be okay."

Her voice began to crack. "You mean you won't stay?"

I took a breath. "How about this. I will walk twenty *short* steps away. I will be your alarm system. If anything comes down the path, I will let you know."

"I've really got to go," she sobbed. "Okay, twenty short steps. And if something comes down the path, I expect you to do more than give me an alarm. Promise you'll stand in harm's way. But first, give me your flashlight."

"You have one. You're holding it."

"I know. I think I need two."

"But how can you – never mind." I handed her the flashlight.

"Okay, she sniffed. "Walk. I'll count with you as you step."

"Into the darkness," I pointed out.

"Uh-huh. The animals know you."

Together we counted twenty steps. After arguing for a short time over the length of my strides, Jillian resigned herself to get on with it. I looked toward the Lodge, which I couldn't see. I stood on the trail for some time. Finally, a voice in the darkness said, "Okay, you can come back."

I turned around and walked toward the light. She was in much better spirits now.

"Thank you for putting up with me," she said.

"Adds to the memory," I said.

"You don't think I'm silly?"

"I am very glad you are here."

"Okay, your turn. Except I don't think I can walk up there like you did."

After further negotiation, she agreed to walk back up the trail, but insisted I sing so she would know "a bear hasn't silently dragged your mangled remains off beyond the ditch."

I shared a song I loved to hear Gene Watson sing, written by Larry Gatlin:

I told her to leave me alone,

that's what she's done, just what she's done.

And a house built for two ain't a home

when it's lived in by one, one, lonely one.

And I can no longer hear footsteps from right down the hall.

Here come the teardrops, the bitter they are, the harder they fall.

As we walked back up the trail, she shook her head. "I have never heard that song in my life. It's kinda weird. Why would he tell her to leave him alone if he was crying because he missed her? Did you just make that up?"

I smiled and followed the beams of her flashlights.

Chapter Sixteen

We were in the great room on the wood floor since there was no furniture yet. And we were using every blanket and sleeping bag we could find to provide some padding and cover. I had asked Jillian if she'd like to sleep in two separate rooms.

"No chance."

It was not a romantic statement.

I built up the fire. Although there was a chill outside, I didn't think we would get cold. We were also lying under about ten pounds of quilts. Jillian was surprised to learn that even in the summer, the night brings a pretty good chill in the mountains.

She was sporting an oversized baseball jersey. Where was she getting all these clothes? And how did she know she'd need them?

She peeped over at me from under the covers on her side. "How are we doing so far?"

"We are doing great, from my vantage point over here. How about over there?"

"Over here is great, as well. That might be skewed by the fact that I don't have to use the bathroom."

"You don't have any more surprises, do you?" I asked.

"Aren't they great?"

"*You* are a surprise," I said. "How do you like your night in the

Lodge?"

"I've never stayed in accommodations with no heating, plumbing or electricity before."

I laughed. "I hope this goes in *your* book of memories."

"Don't laugh too hard. When I *do* have to go to the bathroom in the middle of the night, guess who's coming with me?"

"I can do that."

"But I guess at your age, you're used to those trips."

She was correct, but I didn't see how that could help in any way to admit it.

"How long have you been divorced?" she asked

"Ten years."

"Have you dated much?"

"Some."

"What does *some* mean?" she asked.

"Two relationships. Each lasted a couple of years. Each time, we reached the point where it was time to take it to the next level."

"Getting married," she said.

"Yeah. And when I dragged my feet, the relationships ended."

"It wasn't because one of them was crazy?"

"No."

"Started getting fat?"

"No."

"Were they about your age?"

"Yes."

"Any of them my age?"

"Let me think."

"*Please!* And you had other dates during that time?"

"Yeah. A few. Those were the crazies."

"Did you ever have a date through the internet?

"Yes."

"And?"

"It was a disaster," I said.

"You can't stop there. Let's hear it."

"We agreed to meet at a restaurant."

"Was this local?"

"About an hour away. So I got there early and got a table. I watched for her to come in. In a few minutes a lady came up to my table and said, *Hello Stuart.* She looked *nothing* like her photos."

Jillian sat up. "Was it someone else's photo?"

"It was her, alright. Just at a time in her life when she was about seventy-five pounds lighter."

"Oh my goodness!" she said, laughing hard. "What did you do?"

"I didn't even recognize her. She started to cry. And I started comforting her, but then I realized this was not my fault. She had deceived me. She should have sent me a photo of the way she really looked."

"But if she had, would you have gone out with her?"

"Absolutely not! But surely she realized that a day of reckoning was coming. When we finally had a date, I would know the truth."

"She just hoped that you would see her for herself."

"Right."

"What happened?"

"We ate our meal. I was ready to go but she wasn't. So, I suggested we take a walk."

"The walk of shame. How did it end?"

"She wanted to see me again and kept pushing for us to set a date."

"I bet she did. So you just left?"

"Pretty much. I told her that it was nice to meet her. She asked me if I felt a connection and I said, *Not at this time*. She started to cry again and hugged me. It was a big hug from a big woman. I began to feel like I couldn't breathe, so I said goodbye and got in my car and left."

Jillian put her arms around her knees. "Not at this time?"

"Yeah."

"And how many times after that did you see her?"

"Funny."

"I wish I could have seen your face!" she said.

"At that time, you couldn't. It was surrounded by *a wall of human flesh*, to quote W.C. Fields. So, tell me about one of your bad dates."

She stretched and leaned back on her elbows. "I'm not familiar with W.C., but I've had several bad dates. They weren't from a computer. They were times when I was invited out and I should have declined. You live and learn." She was quiet. Thinking. "But there was one time that I truly regret."

"Let's hear it."

"It's important to remember I was pretty young – maybe in my mid-twenties."

Seven years ago.

"A friend of mine set me up with a friend of hers. I was working on a case in Maryville, so we met at a restaurant there. This guy comes in and he's gorgeous. Looked like a movie star. He lived in Birmingham but was in town on business."

"Was he a relative of Mr. Hallmark?"

"Could have been. It took about three minutes to determine that he was his favorite subject. That's all he did – talk about himself. Where he lived. What he drove. Where he went to college. Who he knew. Blah, blah, blah.

"We were in the middle of the meal. He had not asked a single question about me. He had not complimented me on my dress or earrings or anything else. He had not thanked me for agreeing to see him. He never asked a question about me. He just talked.

"So I excused myself, walked around the corner, out the front door, and left."

"You didn't tell him you were leaving?"

"I guess he figured it out after a little while."

Chapter Seventeen

We were once again in Jillian's Range Rover and once again on the Parkway to Gatlinburg. It was another sunny day.

We had freshened up after our night in the Lodge and I made some coffee using the camp stove. She didn't make a face when she drank it, but then again, it was her only option.

Jillian looked way too fresh to have showered outside and slept on the floor. Today, she was wearing some gray terry cloth shorts with UT on the side, a bright orange t-shirt with 16 on the right sleeve, and some running shoes.

"Do you remember your high school graduation?" Jillian said.

"Yeah. Why?"

"I was three years old."

"Okay. Good one."

"When you graduated from college, I was in kindergarten. I probably didn't know what college was. Probably couldn't spell it. When you got married, I was in the third grade."

"Thank you. Are you through?"

"I could have been the flower girl."

"Again, thank you. Do you mind speaking a little louder? My hearing aid batteries are running low. How did you know when I got married?"

"Just a little research."

"And how did you know I was divorced?"

She smiled. "I asked around. And guess what?"

"What?"

When you're able to draw Social Security, I'll be around your age now."

"Is this leading somewhere?" I asked.

"I'm just recognizing the facts."

"That I'm a lot older than you."

"Yes," she said. "How do you feel about that? You said you've never dated anyone this much younger than you."

Dated.

She looked at me. I didn't say anything.

"So, you don't mind dating someone a generation younger than you?"

"A generation? Isn't that hyperbole?"

"Maybe. Tell me some of your favorite songs when you were in high school. Songs that were on the radio."

"*Love Letters in the Sand* was a big one."

"See, I've never heard that song."

I looked at her. "I was kidding. Pat Boone sang that. That was even before my time."

"But you knew it," she muttered. "I'm serious. Give me a song from your era," she pursued.

"Let me think. *YMCA* was a song that came out during my high school days."

"A lot of people who like that song came out. Did you know about that?"

"I just knew the song. I had no idea who the Village People were."

"Who?"

"The guys who sang the song."

"I think I first heard that song on a kids' television show. Some vegetables sang it. Were the Beatles around when you were growing up?"

"John died when I was pretty young, but yes."

"Did you like them?"

"Yes."

"My grandmother has a Beatles album. I bet you had albums, too."

"Yes, I still play them on what we called a turntable."

"I will Google that."

"*Givin' It Up For Your Love*?"

"I beg your pardon?"

"Another good song."

"Oh good. I thought you might be having another one of those senior episodes. Never heard of it.

"Delbert McClinton sang it."

"Nope."

"*Girl, You'll be a Woman Soon?*"

"That was a song? You could have come into my toddlers' class and dedicated that to me!"

"I hope you're having as much fun as I am," I said.

"What about TV shows. Wait, did they have TV?"

"Yes."

"Cable?"

"No."

"Satellite?"

"No."

"Color?"

"Usually."

"Okay, go. What were some of your favorite TV shows when you were growing up."

"Growing up? I remember watching *The Little House on the Prairie*."

"Yes, My mother has that DVD. What else?"

"*The Rockford Files*."

"Never heard of it. Next."

"*Mork and Mindy*."

"Are you making up these names?"

"I could be and you wouldn't know."

"What about movies?"

"I remember *Piranha*."

She looked at me. "That was your favorite? A movie about flesh eating fish?"

"It was a chick flick."

She rolled her eyes.

"I don't know about favorite, but I remember it. I remember going to see *The Empire Strikes Back.*

"Was that a *Star Trek* movie?" she asked unenthusiastically.

"Star Wars."

"Did you dress up like those guys?"

"No, I never did. Never had a light saber."

"Good. I don't know what that is, but I'm glad you didn't own one. Grab that sack in the back seat."

I looked and saw a bright blue gift bag.

"Open it."

I did. Inside was a small wooden box. It contained her business card. On the back she had written her cell phone number, her home address, and her personal email. A sticky note was attached:

This is how to contact me. Keep this card with you at all times.

There was another gift box in the bag. I opened it. It was a framed photo of Jillian. She was sitting on a fence with horses in the background. She was wearing a western shirt, jeans, and cowboy boots. The sun highlighted her hair, and she was smiling. Written on the bottom of the photo was an inscription:

Stuart,

I've had the time of my life!

Love, love, love,

Jillian

Chapter Eighteen

The Easons lived a few miles from Gatlinburg in Wears Valley on Happy Hollow Road. Richard was outside, in the company of a yellow Labrador Retriever puppy. "Meet Scout," he said. "We are his foster family until he is old enough to start the guide dog program." I noticed that Richard did a double take when he saw Jillian. The last time he saw her, she was in her lawyer outfit.

We played with Scout for a few minutes and then Jillian and I went to see Richard's mom.

"Please call me Linda," she said as we sat down in the screened-in porch. The house was an attractive chalet on top of a large hill. From the porch, we could see mountains to the east and south.

It was obvious that Jillian and Linda had formed a friendship. Jillian asked how Richard was doing and if there had been any contact with Coach Bodine. Everything was going fine so far.

Richard put Scout in the fenced back yard and sat with us. He seemed glad to see us and very relaxed. After a few minutes of conversation, Jillian said, "So Richard, you know that Mr. Jensen –"

"Stuart," I said.

"You know that Stuart has volunteered to help you in any way you'd like for him to. What do you think about that?"

Richard grinned and looked at me. "So, you're not an attorney?"

I smiled. “That’s correct. I’m a Speech teacher.”

He nodded.

“He’s a person who has a lot to offer you,” Jillian said. “I’m not quite sure what that is for you yet, but you would be lucky to have someone like Stuart in your corner. And the fact that he has asked for this assignment is quite a compliment to you.”

Richard was still smiling. “I really appreciate your offer, Mr. Jensen.”

“Stuart.”

“That’s going to be hard for me to say.”

“You can. I am not your teacher. I want to be your friend. I don’t know what I can offer, either. I am impressed with you, and I want to be one of your encouragers.”

“Well, I know what we’re going to do first,” Jillian said. “Get in the car, boys.”

We said goodbye to Linda and got in the Range Rover. Jillian drove back down the road and turned right into a little park. It had a small pond, a swimming pool, picnic tables and a field for picnics and games. Jillian opened the trunk and produced a football. “It’s football time in Tennessee!” she said.

She tossed me the ball in a perfect spiral. “Richard,” she said, “I am sorry for your horrible experience with your Phys Ed teacher. You may care nothing about football, but it just might prove helpful somewhere down the line. And, I did hear you say that you wanted to learn a few of the fundamentals.

“You said that under oath,” I added.

She continued, “So, before you leave here today, you are going to learn about football.”

Then she looked at me. “I forgot to ask if you know anything about football.”

I gave her my best deadpan look, then turned to Richard. "Anything we do here today is to help you. If you don't want to do something, we don't do it. Is it okay if we talk a little about football?"

"Yes, I'd like to know."

"Great. Why don't we sit down over at the picnic table?"

"How much do you know about football?" I asked.

"Not much. Start at the beginning."

I did. I explained the basic rules of the game, the number of players, the number of downs, scoring, penalties, and a few other things. From time to time, Jillian added or simplified.

I showed Richard how to hold the ball. I showed him how to catch the ball with his hands. Then we stood about ten yards from each other and threw the ball back and forth. It didn't take him long to throw a spiral. As he got more proficient, we took backward steps and added Jillian until we were about fifteen yards from each other.

Then it was time to catch the ball on the move. We took turns running for a pass. Although the sun was bright, the humidity wasn't bad. Richard was very coordinated and had no trouble learning to pass and catch. Jillian was surprisingly agile and experienced at the sport.

Neither mentioned my football prowess, so from time to time, I would say "Good catch" or "Nice pass."

Jillian finally asked, "You are complimenting yourself?"

"Yeah."

Richard laughed.

"Don't encourage him. Next thing you know, he'll sing a crazy song by Brad Tick or Dilbert somebody."

"Brad Paisley sang about ticks, and Delbert McClinton sang, *Givin' It Up for Your Love.* You haven't heard his song yet."

She grabbed the ball and said, "I wish we could, but look at the time. Come on Richard! Let's head for the radio!"

Chapter Nineteen

We were sitting on a bench in front of Paula Deen's restaurant at a retail development in Pigeon Forge called The Island. We dropped Richard off at his home and just finished eating at Paula's. Jillian's head was resting on my shoulder.

"If you weren't here with me, where would you be?" she asked.

I thought about it. "At the Lodge."

"Doing what?"

"Sitting by the campfire, probably."

"Just you?"

"Just me."

"And what would you be doing while you were sitting by the campfire?"

"Enjoying it, mostly."

"What does that mean?"

"Enjoying the whole experience. Being outdoors. Watching the birds and the clouds. Hearing all my neighbors."

"Do you have neighbors?"

"I was referring to the wild kind."

"Like the wolves and ticks."

"Yeah, except I don't think you can hear a tick. I also enjoy hearing the wood crackle in the fire. I enjoy smelling the smoke."

"You enjoy smelling smoke?" she asked. Her head was still on my shoulder.

"Some smoke. Oak is a sweet smell. Plywood is not a pleasant smell."

"I did not know that. I've also never had a conversation about smoke before."

"You asked," I said. We were facing a very colorful, large Ferris wheel on the other side of the commons area.

"Where would you be?" I asked. "Same thing?"

She patted my arm. "Maybe in an alternate universe. Otherwise, I'd be out. At a restaurant, a theater, a concert, the gym, or maybe shopping. I wouldn't be at home or watching the sky. I enjoy being out and doing things."

"And if I weren't in the picture, would you have a date?" I asked.

"Maybe," she said. "Let's look around."

The Island offered many shops of all descriptions. I particularly liked *Emery's 5 and 10 Store.* The range of products was impressive. There were model planes from various wars, vintage soda bottles, cat clocks whose tails moved back and forth, and cookie spoons which matched the curve in an Oreo. We passed by *The Reluctant Groom Wedding Cake Topper*, featuring a bride pulling a groom across the cake. Jillian pointed out that the groom looked a lot like me.

Chapter Twenty

It was August 5th. The cabin was starting to look like a real cabin. I mean Lodge. It had running water and electricity and bathrooms that worked.

Richard and I installed handles on the cabinets in the kitchen. He spent the last two nights at the Lodge. It was hard to believe that both of us would soon be back in school. After the kitchen, we put handles on the bathroom cabinets. After lunch, we attached mirrors over the bathroom vanities. We then installed the switch and outlet plates throughout the house.

"I have a friend who lived around Gatlinburg. You might have heard of him," I said. "His name is Carl Mays."

"Oh yes. He works with the football team."

"That's right. A few years ago, his son, Carl Mays, Jr. or Two, as everyone called him, was a freshman. Carl, the dad, told Two that he could accomplish great things, but first he had to know what he wanted to accomplish.

"So, Carl asked Two what he'd like to accomplish while he was in high school. And he also told him it was okay to dream big. Two came up with several goals. Goal One was to have a perfect season in football, no losses. Goal Two, was to go to an Ivy League college. Goal Three was to get the school accredited. Goal Four was to play football in college."

"How did he do?" Richard asked.

"With his father's help, he accomplished all four goals. The team had a perfect season, the school was accredited. Two got an academic scholarship to Princeton where he played football."

Richard took all that in and said, "Impressive."

"So, here's my question to you. What do you want to accomplish in the next two years?" I told him to think about it and we'd talk about it again the next day.

The next day, Richard handed me a sheet of paper.

1. Finish the Dog Shelter (by raising an additional $100,000)
2. Become an Eagle Scout
3. Get a full college scholarship
4. Summer-long medical mission trip to in Ghana.

I read the list with interest. I knew there were more. He just didn't want to show off. We talked for a bit about the steps to take to reach each goal. He promised to prepare the action steps and show them to me.

I was concerned about a few things in life. Richard reaching his goals was not one of them.

Chapter Twenty-One

Richard was a master fire builder. I appreciated that skill. As I tried to explain to Jillian, I enjoy watching, smelling, and even listening to a campfire. We were sitting outside as the stars were coming out.

Richard placed a backlog on which to build the rest of the wood. We watched the kindling start to catch fire, and then catch the other sticks and logs ablaze. As the fire continued, some of those sticks slowly glowed and turned to red coals. He loved a good fire, too. I could tell that he had enjoyed many campfires. He understood that it's acceptable to have long gaps in conversation while the fire is appreciated.

He was also a good outdoor cook. We just finished eating his latest meal of Teriyaki Chicken, baked beans, asparagus, and fresh tomatoes, and were sitting by the fire.

"I've had a great time this summer, Stuart," he said.

"Me too," I said. "Not everyone would want to spend a part of their summer building a cabin."

"Are you kidding? I can't think of a better place to be! This has been the best summer of my life!" he said.

"I appreciate your help and your company," I said.

"I've also enjoyed the Jensen Sports Camp," he said.

In addition to football, we covered baseball and basketball. He picked up baseball quickly. Basketball was a little more challenging.

"Well, at least you know the basics."

"It's been very helpful."

We had also talked about college. Richard had an SEC school, the University of Tennessee, in his own backyard. With his GPA, test scores and volunteer record, he would have some scholarships to sort through.

"So, where is Jillian?" he asked.

"I guess she's working."

"Hard to communicate up here," he said.

"Impossible," I agreed.

"I like her," he said. "I was lucky that she was my attorney. But I'm even more glad that she's my friend."

"Well said."

"So, would I be too nosey if I asked about you and her?"

"Ask away. What do you want to know?"

"Well, it's clear you like each other."

"That's true."

"So do you think you'll get married?"

I had to give the boy credit. He was direct.

"I have no idea. It's a good question. We haven't been seeing each other that long."

"Yeah, but you've known each other a lot longer, right?"

"Well, yes, I knew her when she was a student. Then she reappeared on the radar fourteen years later, which was the beginning of the summer."

"She reappeared?"

"Yep."

"How? If you don't mind me asking."

"She showed up right here."

"Wow."

"Yeah."

"She had an interest in you before you had an interest in her."

"I suppose."

"So, she just asked you out?"

"Not exactly. Ask her for the details."

"Okay," he said with a smile. "I'll let you off the hook. Still, it must be a little difficult for you. You see each other and then you have no contact when you're away from each other."

"This is true," I said. "When I'm out here, we do not communicate."

"For how long?"

"Sometimes a week. Sometimes not quite so long. Sometimes longer."

"I know I'm just a teenager, but that would make me nervous if I were you."

"How so?"

"There she is, in town, around all those lawyer guys. She is extremely attractive. I'm sure the men notice her. If I were in your place, I would worry about that."

The fire settled some and we watched it. "It's something to think about," I said. "I guess we also have to think about summer ending and what could be an exciting new school year for you."

Richard nodded. “Bittersweet.”

Chapter Twenty-Two

The remaining days of summer vacation were active. My friends helped me move furniture to the Lodge. Richard helped me set up the beds and wash windows.

We spent a couple of days backpacking not far from Townsend. It was not far from Richard's home, yet in the national park. We climbed mountains, explored old, abandoned cabins, watched turkeys and deer, and hiked many miles.

Richard had a backpacking tent that was really a lightweight tarp. We also used his backpacking stove to cook our evening meals.

As we sat on a mountain that overlooked Cades Cove, we saw several deer eating in a pasture far below. The sky was a bright blue. We could feel a light wind. We watched three hawks sail on the thermal currents, searching for suitable prey in the meadows.

From this vantage point, it was hard to imagine we would soon be back in our respective schools. It was the kind of day you didn't want to end. And if I had my way, it wouldn't. Nevertheless, it was a perfect way to end the summer.

Chapter Twenty-Three

I wonder if students fully comprehend that some teachers do not look forward to going back to school after summer break? I wonder if they also know that some teachers make a chart of how many days are left until summer? I work with teachers who have secret charts. And they start them on Day One of each school year.

I enjoy the classroom. I enjoy teaching. It's the other stuff that drives me crazy and causes many teachers to look for other work. And a big part of the other stuff was currently happening. It's called Teacher In-Service. Not all schools have it. Some schools have it only for the new teachers. There's a boys' Catholic school not too far away from us that has Teacher In-Service for half a day. The headmaster gives each faculty member a bottle of wine on Friday and encourages him to drink it before he comes back on Monday.

Our In-Service lasts a week. It consists of department meetings, speeches, and creating student rolls for a new year of electronic record keeping. We are always changing software systems, so we are always learning a new way to enter grades, communicate with students, and submit our lesson plans. And that's the exciting part of what we do. It makes for a very long week.

This was our ninth day – or was it our second? I guess it was just Tuesday. We were currently listening to a nurse explain why we should wash our hands and not touch another person's blood. I looked around. The new teachers were listening. The veterans were reviewing materials from their school mailboxes that filled up during the summer. The coaches were reading magazines.

Some of the best people I know were sitting in the auditorium. They were professional, compassionate and encouraging to their students and peers. I was sitting next to Al Pressure. A few years ago, Frank, my truck, named in honor of my old college roommate, was in the shop. Al heard about it, walked into my classroom and tossed a set of keys on my desk. "It's the little gray two-door Nissan truck out front. Keep it until you get yours back."

A couple of the guys on my Saturday Lodge building crew were my fellow teachers. They heard about my project and volunteered. Such unselfishness was how these teachers lived their lives. It was an honor to teach with them. They taught me a lot.

I was not too bothered about the bad apples. Bad apples are everywhere you go. We had a room full of Grade-A apples. The rotten ones would never go away, but they wouldn't take over.

The nurse was through, and the insurance representatives were up. Always a breath of sunshine to hear which benefits had been cut. So, I decided to think about other things. Like Richard. I hoped that we could continue to spend some time together during the school year. We had shared a lot of time during the summer. I was quite proud of him.

Then there was Jillian. When I thought about her, I seemed to scratch my head a lot. As I explained to Richard, I did not initiate our relationship. She came to me. That, in itself, was difficult to figure out. As I reflected, it was obvious that the time we spent together had already made some of the fondest memories I'd had in quite some time. Make that ever. The key word there was *time.* Because of the Lodge, I was out of town for the summer. Because of her work, Jillian was often out of town several days each month.

Now that I was back in town, I was looking forward to more time with her. Unfortunately, she was presently out of town on a case. I received a letter from her in the mail at school. I waited until such a time as this to open it.

> *You are cordially invited to the home of Jillian Renfro this Friday evening for food, fellowship and fun! If you are smart, you'll accept.*

There was a lipstick print under it.

I was smart.

Chapter Twenty-Four

It was still early August and still summertime. I had the windows down and a CD playing. Glenn Fry was singing *New Kid in Town.* It occurred to me that this might be the story for Jillian and me. She being the kid. Or maybe it was me, being the new kid.

Johnny come lately

The new kid in town

Will she still love you

When you're not around?

I had never been to Miss Renfro's house. It was in a gated community called Birch View, a few miles from my home. She had given me the gate code and directions to her house. The houses were made of materials like old brick, fieldstone, wood, and a lot of glass. They all had circular driveways and small front yards.

I pulled into Jillian's drive. Jillian's large house had an impressive stone stairway that led from the driveway to the front door. It was a beautiful place. I was a little surprised at just how nice it was. I shut Frank's door, successfully ascended the stairs, and rang the doorbell.

She opened the door, squealed, and gave me a tight hug. Jillian was wearing a bright sky-blue sundress. She was glowing and beautiful.

"Are those for me?" she asked, pointing to the flowers in my hand.

I had momentarily forgotten about them. She went to the kitchen and put them in a vase. I was left standing in an open, airy room with a table, some couches and overstuffed chairs. There were many photographs on the narrow tables behind the couches. The photos featured Jillian in a lot of candid shots. As she walked over to me, she looked at the photos, too. "I love pictures!" she said.

I slowly made my way around the room, while Jillian explained the history and sentiment of furniture, lamps, photographs and paintings. On one of the bookshelves, I picked up a framed photograph of a handsome man and her. They were kissing. He had blonde hair and a deep tan. I looked at her, "I'm guessing this isn't your brother?"

She smiled and took the picture and placed it face down on the bookshelf. "Sorry, I forgot about that one. Old boyfriend."

"Nice looking old boyfriend," I said.

"Yeah," she said. Then with more enthusiasm, "Welcome to my home. I'm glad you get to see a little slice of my world, for a change."

I looked around and smiled. "I like this slice."

She grabbed my arm and led me to the kitchen. "Thanks. I also had a great uncle who left me some money. I had no trouble spending it on this place. It has indoor plumbing, and everything. Let's eat."

She had the makings for a salad and told me to fix it the way I wanted. Then she opened her Viking oven and placed a salmon filet on my plate, along with some potatoes and broccoli spears. She led the way to the dining table where she lit two candles. I did not have the heart to tell her that Richard and I had recently dined on broccoli on our camping trip. Hers were fresher. Ours came out of a vacuum-sealed package that stayed edible for ten years.

It had been about two weeks since we had seen each other.

"Tell me about school," she said.

I laughed. "That sounds like what my mother used to ask at supper."

She looked at me with no expression. "Do you think of me as your mother?"

"No."

"Good. Carry on."

"School In-Service," I said. "Other than that, it was great."

Nevertheless, she asked several questions and seemed to be interested in what teachers do behind closed doors. When I'd had all I could take, I asked about her two weeks.

"The first week, we were preparing a case and doing depositions in Atlanta."

"How many did it take?"

"You mean how many lawyers does it take to prepare a case? Sounds like the beginning of a joke. We had three attorneys and two paralegals. And four depositions. The second week, I was in San Francisco for a seminar."

"Was it as nice as In-Service?"

"Well, did you stay at the Four Seasons?"

"No."

"Did you receive a gift bag full of candy and drinks?"

"No. I did get a Little Debbie Oatmeal Cookie that Al Pressure didn't want."

"Mr. Pressure is still there? I love him! Did any Supreme Court Justices speak?"

"No. But the school nurse did show us a new Epi Pen video and reminded us to wash our hands often."

"I think it's safe to say it was as nice as In-Service."

"Did you do anything for fun," I asked. "We got to break into teams and answer trivia questions about American geography."

"Oh yeah," Jillian said. "There was time for shopping and touring. Some took a tour of the wine country or Alcatraz. We usually have great entertainment. This year, they had a really good band. They were not the Village People but we made do."

"You do what you can with what you have," I said. "Was this a dance band?"

She hesitated for a moment. "As a matter of fact, it turned into that. At first, we just listened. But after about the second song, everyone seemed to be on the floor. That's what good music and alcohol will do to the bar association."

"So you danced?"

"Yes," she said. I think she was blushing. "There were several men and women from my firm there and I think everyone got on the dance floor for a little bit."

"We always do that on the last day of In-Service, just before they hand out our new ID badges."

"I'd like to see that. Do you dance?"

I sighed. "No."

"Come on," she said. "I find that hard to believe."

I sighed again. "Have I ever been on a dance floor? Yes. Do I enjoy it? No. Has anyone mistaken me for a dance instructor? No."

She got up. "Let's see."

She spoke a verbal command to some electronic ghost and music began to play through speakers I couldn't see. This was not on my agenda or radar. After only a few seconds, it was obvious that Jillian *could* have been mistaken for a dance instructor. It was then I remembered she had been a cheerleader in high school. "Were you a cheerleader in college?" I asked.

"No, I was too serious a student," she said.

The ghost cranked out several songs of different genres. I should have said I had never danced. Finally, it played a slow song.

"You are a better dancer than I thought you'd be," Jillian said. Concrete evidence that she had set the bar very low.

I said, "You are good enough to be on a television show like *Soul Train*."

"Like what?"

"Kind of like *Dancing With the Stars*."

"Oh, okay, thanks."

We sat down on one of the couches and she smiled.

"What?"

She pointed to the coffee table. There was our picture in a gold frame. I remember when Richard took it at the Lodge.

"A little surprise that was waiting for me in the mail when I got home," she said.

"Richard."

"Yes, he provided the photo. I picked out the frame. Gold for pure in heart."

It was a good picture. Jillian and I were sitting on the steps to the Lodge. She had her arm around my shoulder. I was looking at the camera. She was looking at me. I liked it.

Chapter Twenty-Five

I was enjoying my screened-in porch at the Lodge. It was late August, and I was grading my first set of exams. Due to guidance counselor decisions regarding class schedules, all my students were seniors. That first exam is usually a wake-up call. For whatever reason, many of the seniors felt like they did not have to study for a Speech exam. And that's why many seniors were going to have low grades.

This class seemed to be following the annual pattern. I had graded ten exams. There was one *B*, two *Cs*, one *D*, and six *Fs*. When the grades reach the coaches, the football players would have extra laps and a few sprints. Some parents would go ballistic and take away privileges. There would be at least one parent who would want a conference with me, the guidance counselor, my department chairman and an administrator to hint that somehow this was my fault.

I had about a hundred students as usual. Most were good kids. I knew a lot of them from substituting in their classes as they were growing up. They knew me because they'd seen me in the hall since they were seventh graders. Or their brother or sister had been in my class. They also already knew about my class from former students.

They heard that I hosted Halloween, Thanksgiving, Christmas and Valentine's Day parties in my room. This drove some teachers crazy. They got so lathered up about the word *party*, they didn't ask any more questions. If they had, they would have learned that I tied the events to lessons in communication.

Halloween found us sitting around an inside simulated campfire. Each student was required to tell of a time when he or she was frightened.

Thanksgiving required research of past presidential Thanksgiving speeches, and a message of gratitude from each student.

Christmas required recounting how their families celebrated Christmas.

Valentine's Day required them to provide each person in the class with a card that included a personalized message of encouragement.

All of these served as assignments which required preparation. They received a grade. But it was a fun activity. Further proof you don't always have to grit your teeth to learn.

Meanwhile, I stayed in touch with Richard through emails. He was pleased with his classes and served as a teaching assistant in his Math class. As promised, Coach Bozo no longer taught there and had made no contact.

I saw Jillian once more since our date. She was out of town again, back in Atlanta. She thought she'd be home by next weekend. I had never been in a relationship in which I didn't see the other person very much. It felt strange. Spending that much time away from her was awkward and incomplete.

I had finished about half of the exams when Richard and his mom arrived. He asked me earlier if he could show her the Lodge. I told him that would be fine anytime. Richard walked up the steps with Linda and gave me a very enthusiastic handshake. Linda gave me a hug.

"Thank you for letting me see the *Lodge*," she said. "I've heard a lot about it. And thank you for taking such an interest in Richard even after the summer."

I smiled at her. "You are always welcome here, Linda. And it has been an honor and a lot of fun to get to know Richard."

"Do you mind if I show Mom around?" Richard asked.

"Please do," I said.

He started with where we were standing, on the porch, and gave a very detailed commentary, including his contribution to each room. Linda was entertained by his spiel. Twenty minutes later, they were back in the screened-in porch.

"I have to tell you that I am surprised!" she said. "Even though you called it a Lodge, I expected to see a deer camp shack."

"Well, it's not Dollywood, but it's something I've wanted for a long time. And thanks to the generosity and help from a lot of people, it's a dream come true for me."

"We've come to spend the night, if the offer still holds," Richard said.

"I wanted to talk to you about that," Linda said. "Richard was insistent that I pack a bag, too." I think she was blushing.

"Are you kidding?" I said. "I'm glad you came. You are welcome to stay. The only issue might be the food. The menu is very basic." That was an understatement.

"Well, I took the liberty of bringing supper, if that's okay," she said. Again, it seemed like she was blushing.

I gave her another hug. I think I almost cried.

Chapter Twenty-Six

Linda and I sat in the screened-in porch. I was finishing my grading.

She was reading an outdoor living magazine she brought. I had seen that magazine before and liked a few of the articles I'd read in it. Richard was at the table in the Great Room, working on a homework assignment.

"Done!" I finally said.

Linda smiled and put down her magazine. "I wish Richard was able to take Speech from you."

I nodded. "It's a practical class for all students to take regardless of what their career turns out to be."

"Yes, I agree. But I really meant take it from you. That would be so great. You've impacted his life in a very short period of time. You've no idea how much he looks up to you and admires you. . . I do, too."

I may have blushed that time.

"Thank you. We've become pretty close. I'm looking forward to watching him and seeing which road he takes."

Teasingly, I added, "He said you want him to be a doctor so he can make a lot of money and take care of you in your old age." "Yes, I did say that, and I hope he remembers it." she said with a laugh.

It was a nice laugh.

"Did you learn to teach Speech before or after law school?" she asked with a straight face.

I smiled. "Kind of a long story. I guess Jillian didn't tell you how I came to be there."

"She also didn't say you were a schoolteacher. I like you better as a schoolteacher."

"Thank you. You are very kind, given our awkward beginning."

"I was too nervous to be thinking about that. But thanks to Jillian, Richard is having the best year of his school life. He is intelligent and respectful and has high goals and a strong work ethic. But he also has some self-doubt. The time that you spent with him has really helped. Did you know that he's had me in the back yard to play catch with him? He's teaching me how to pass and go out for passes."

This caught me by surprise and that image was both touching and funny. "How's it going?"

"Not bad. The first thing we had to do was buy a football. I'm doing okay with it. I'm just thrilled that he is proud of that achievement. And it's not really those skills. It's the fact that you cared enough to teach him. That's what he really liked. That's why it meant so much to him."

Richard tapped on the door and walked in. "Looks like you got the tests graded."

"Yep. And your homework?"

"Finished. I was wondering if you two would mind throwing the football with me for a few minutes."

"Aw, that's sweet, Richard, but why don't you two throw the ball while I get supper squared away, if that's okay with Stuart."

"Supper can wait, Mom," Richard said in a very adult voice.

"We can help with that. I'd really like for the three of us to get outside and have some fun for just a few minutes.

Linda looked at me. "Smooth."

Chapter Twenty-Seven

Richard had improved. He could throw the football farther with a good spiral. He also had been practicing catching the ball. Linda was the surprise. Although she claimed she had never thrown a football before last week, she was able to catch Richard's passes and pass the ball almost twenty yards.

"I think you two have set me up," I said. "You look like a couple of pros!"

"Did you play football in high school?" Linda asked. She had put her hair in a ponytail. Her t-shirt said *Smoky Mountain High School.* She had a healthy look.

"Nope. I never wanted to."

"You weren't afraid the girls would only want to date the football players?"

"Yeah, I thought about it. But I wasn't going to play a sport just to impress a girl. A lot of guys did that. I thought they needed to like me for me."

She liked that answer. Probably liked Richard hearing me say it. She probably knew what I'd say and wanted me to say it because Richard was watching some of the girls salivate over the football players.

"Not all the girls were interested in the football players. They weren't then and they aren't now. The girls I found interesting were the ones who were looking for character and integrity and respect. And guess what? At our class reunion, those same girls never talked about football. They talked about who in their class showed them kindness and thoughtfulness."

I told Richard to go long. He ran twenty yards and turned around. I motioned for him to go farther. He turned around about ten yards farther and I threw it. He caught it.

Linda watched. As Richard was running back, she said, "Yeah, you could have played."

Was I trying to show off? Me?

When Richard got back, he said, "I can't believe you threw the ball that far!"

"And you caught it," I added.

As we walked back to the Lodge, Linda said quietly, "I think I have some Ben Gay in my medicine kit."

"Stay close," I said.

Chapter Twenty-Eight

We sat in the Great Room. Candles provided our light. Linda served a garden salad, lasagna and Italian bread. The night was cool enough to have a fire, so Richard built one in the fireplace.

The fire made shadows on the wall. The crackle of the seasoned wood was pleasant. The smell of the red oak was sweet.

Richard handed me a present. It was a photo of the two of us during our last camping trip. Richard had taken it, using a tripod, and Linda had it framed. "A housewarming gift," she said. I loved it and set it on the coffee table.

"Linda, I heard you used to work in a men's store. Is that what you do now?"

She stretched and looked at me. "No, I made a career change. I am the Assistant Marketing Director for Trillium Inn. Are you familiar with it?"

I was. Trillium Inn had a national reputation. It played host to a number of elite meetings. I was a big fan of it, even if I couldn't afford to stay there.

"That sounds like a great job! Did you see the article about it in *Southern Living*?"

She opened her mouth but Richard spoke first. "She set the whole thing up."

"Not exactly," Linda said with a laugh. "When the writer and photographer came to do the story, I just tagged along."

"There's more to it than that," Richard said. "She helped arrange interviews and chauffeured them around, arranged their lodging, and made sure they had everything they needed."

I smiled and this time, Linda spoke before I did.

"I do enjoy it. And I am so thankful to have the job. I look forward to going to work. It's new every day."

"I have always wanted to see Trillium Inn," I said.

"Why don't you? Why haven't you?"

"I could not afford it. Do you know how much they charge?"

She smiled. "I have a pretty good idea. You tell me when you want to come and I'll give you a tour. Tours don't cost as much."

"Deal. It is one of the places I want to stay when I become rich and famous."

"You have others?"

"As a matter of fact, yes. Not quite as fancy, but still they would be a dream come true for me."

"Care to share?" she said.

"Well, for example, I've always wanted to spend the night in a fire tower."

"Really?"

"Yes."

"Why?" she asked.

"Just the idea of being above the trees, being able to see for miles. As a kid, I remember being in the car with my parents and riding past fire towers. I wondered what it was like up there. Still do. I like the notion of being in a room far above the ground."

"That's a good dream," Richard agreed. "What do you think, Mom?"

"I agree," she said with a smile. "Anything else?"

"Here's another one," I said. "I have read that some of the best places to see stars are in national parks. I read about a park in South Dakota. They called it a 'dark sky' park. Guests bring their chairs and lean back as a ranger tells them about constellations."

"Has anyone else noticed all the stars?" Richard asked. "This is a great star watching night."

There being no objections, we walked outside and sat down on the steps of the porch. I brought a blanket for Linda.

"Thank you, Stuart," she said. "That was thoughtful."

"It's not the Trillium, but we try hard here at The Lodge," I said.

Richard took out a laser pointer from his backpack and began to point out constellations.

"The stars are so much brighter here," Linda said.

"There's no residual light," Richard explained. "The glow from Pigeon Forge carries over to our house in Wears Valley. Here there's no light around for miles and miles. It might not be a dark sky, but close."

As he talked, I looked at Linda. Her hair was black, and she wore it shoulder length. It was clear that she took care of herself. She was looking up at the constellations Richard was indicating. The stars reflected in her eyes. She was smiling. It was a good night to look at the stars.

"If you look just south of Corona Australis and east of Scorpius, you'll see six stars," Richard said. He pointed them out.

"You've been in this lecture before I presume," I whispered.

She nodded. "Wait until he gives you the spelling test." We were sitting side by side. Linda reached over and put part of the blanket around my shoulder and held it there with her hand. "Cold night at the Lodge," she whispered.

"Watch the talking," Richard said, and pointed to a group of stars with his laser. "Who can tell me what this looks like?

Linda put her mouth next to my ear, "Telescope," she whispered very softly.

"Kind of looks like a necktie," I said. Linda punched my side with her free hand.

"No, but that's one possibility, I guess. Any other thoughts."

"This might be way out there, but could it be a telescope?" I asked.

Richard turned around and looked at me. And then at his mother.

"That's correct. As a matter of fact, its name is Telescopium. It was named by Abbe Nicolas Louis de Lacalle in the mid-eighteenth century after the telescope."

"Be grateful Richard didn't bring his telescope or you'd be out here all night," Linda said.

"Very funny, Mom."

"I love this," I said. It's good to sit out here with you two, looking at the stars."

Linda hugged me with her blanket arm. "What a sweet thing to say."

Not just sweet. It was true.

Chapter Twenty-Nine

It was Wednesday. We were in the middle of Homecoming Week. This was my least favorite week of the year. Every teacher that sponsored a high school grade had to supervise the nightly homecoming preparations and activities. I was a senior class sponsor. So, that's why I was still at school as the sun went down.

It was a bad idea for the students to spend every night at school during Homecoming Week. They had trouble doing their class assignments. Teachers were cautioned about giving tests during the week. The homecoming preparation activities were stretched for an entire week.

I had made my observations known. Like I said, educators do not like change. So, we continued to do what had been done fifty years ago. If it was such a good idea, why did the students drag in each morning and fall asleep in class in the afternoon? And what about teachers who were so worn out after this week that many wanted to do anything but attend Homecoming?

Which brings me to this morning. The office sent me a message during second period that a FedEx package from Atlanta was waiting for me in the mailroom. I knew better than to open it during class, so I waited until lunch to get it and take it back to my room. Inside the shipping box was a bright orange box. Inside the orange box were several items wrapped in orange and white tissue paper.

The first item was an orange envelope containing a ticket for the University of Tennessee football game against the University of Florida Saturday in Knoxville. The second item was a UT football jersey. I held it up and saw Stu on the back where players usually have their names. There was also a souvenir program of the game.

Finally, there was an envelope with a handwritten note:

> *Stuart,*
>
> *I would like to invite you to the UT game this Saturday. Our firm has some great seats and I think it would be a lot of fun. I have also sent Richard the same package.*
>
> *Atlanta is a great town, but I'd rather be back in Spruceville with you. I know I've been out of town way too much lately and I'd like to make it up to you in this small way.*
>
> *Go Vols!*
> *Jillian*

Saturday marked the first of October. We had seen each other once in September. I received three phone calls from her while she was out of town. And one of those calls was to return my call. I learned quickly that she could not talk during the day. And she had numerous engagements at night.

That left phone texts. Usually a sentence or less. I don't like phone texts longer than a sentence or two, anyway. I take it back. I don't like phone texts period.

It was the first special delivery package I'd received at school.

Typical Jillian. She likes to do things with a splash. She's also not real big on advance notice. I'm surprised I didn't receive the package on Friday or even Saturday morning.

She obviously was used to things working out for her. That's code for getting her way.

But that's how Jillian rolls.

Go Vols.

Chapter Thirty

Jillian was all smiles on our way to get Richard for the big game. She gave me updates on her case in Atlanta, which seemed to be much more interesting than what the seniors chose for Homecoming locker decorations.

She patted my hand. "You don't know how much I've missed you! I've had no one to tell me what it was like before I was born." She smiled at me. I smiled back. Maybe I should tell her about some of the concerts I'd been to in college. Or maybe that would not help me in any way.

"I know I'm falling behind, but it occurred to me that I never asked you how your time in San Francisco was," I said. "We got stuck in Atlanta."

She smiled. "Yes, at that point, you and I had our first dance at my house."

"So, how was it?"

She kept her eyes on the road. "It was a seminar. A seminar on law. Does that tell you anything?"

"Well, what else did you do?"

"Oh, took in the sights."

"Like what?"

"You know, rode a streetcar, went to Fisherman's Wharf. Ate at some restaurants you've never heard of."

It didn't sound like my cup of tea, but then again, she wasn't real excited about my plumbing creativity at the Lodge. How could anybody not be excited to use an outdoor bathroom or take a shower in the middle of the woods?

When we picked up Richard, he came out of the house in his orange jersey. Jillian and I were wearing ours, too. Richard walked out with his souvenir program. He invited us to say hello to Scout in the backyard. Scout had really grown. His coat was a beautiful almost white color.

"Mom had to work today but says hello," Richard said.

As Richard got in the car, I looked at his jersey. His said Eason on the back. Jillian's jersey looked a lot better on her than ours did on us. Ours seemed to hang like parachutes. Hers looked tailored to make her look more like a model. Hmm. It also had 16 on the back.

Less than an hour later, we were in Knoxville. A guard let us into a parking lot that was a 30-yard pass from the field. Jillian handed us a couple of lanyards with credential badges. "Put these on."

We walked into Neyland Stadium and said hello to the other 100,000 fans there. Jillian stopped at an elevator and we got in. Shortly afterwards, Richard and I made a discovery. Our seats were not actually stadium seats. They were sky box seats. The sky box was luxury in every sense. Three rows of theater seats. An incredible view. Two video monitors of the game. And a lot of food. A large wooden sign hung on the wall, *Jordan and Wiser.*

There were several people already in this room. And most, if not all, knew Jillian. A very distinguished looking man walked up and gave Jillian a hug and stuck out his hand. "Hi. I'm Van Wiser. Welcome."

"Van is one our two founding partners," Jillian said. "Van,

this is Stuart Jensen. He is a teacher in Spruceville. And this is Richard Eason. he is a student at Smoky Mountain High School in Gatlinburg, and also a client."

"Oh yes, I'm so glad to meet you, Richard. Jillian has sung your praises."

"Thank you, Mr. Wiser. Miss Renfro did a great job of helping me. She turned a rough time into my best year ever. I don't know what would have happened without her advocacy."

Van took all that in and looked at Richard for a moment. "Thank you, Richard. I'm glad to hear that. And if you decide to become a lawyer, come talk to me." He turned to me and said, "Make yourself at home, Stuart. It's a pleasure to have you."

Jillian showed us where the bathrooms were, where the refrigerator was, and where the gourmet buffet was in the adjoining room.

"I thought the food was in here," Richard said, pointing to the stuff set up on the wet bar."

"Those are snacks. The real food is next door." She guided us to some seats on the front row. It felt like we were on a cloud, overlooking the end zone. "What do you think?" she said, turning to me.

"I'm used to standing in line with 50 other guys to go to the bathroom at a game. And standing in line to get a hot dog. And getting back to my seat fifteen minutes later, only to discover I didn't get any napkins. But I guess this will do."

She smiled. "That's a relief. I'm glad you could make it, Richard, on short notice."

Richard was in shock. He was staring at the teams below, watching the Pride of the Southland Marching Band, the cheerleaders, Smokey the blue tick hound mascot, and the Mitsubishi Diamond Vision Big Screen Video Board. He turned and said, "Incredible!"

"And how," I added.

We got up and joined the gourmet buffet line. I was relieved to see that you could get a hamburger. Somehow, I could not eat veal at a college football game. Richard followed my lead. Jillian did not. Actually, Jillian went first, so I guess you could say we didn't follow her lead. She looked at my plate and shook her head. "I'm not sure we have fries," she said. "Maybe we can find you some pork rinds."

The three of us sat down and took in the show a few thousand feet below us. Well, okay not quite that far. We seemed to be the only ones watching what was happening outside the sky box. The others were talking, laughing, eating, and doing everything but watching the pre-game activities.

"Better than the cafeteria food at your place?" Richard asked.

"I wouldn't know. I haven't set foot in there since my first year," I said. I leaned a little closer. "However, they *do* have fries on Fridays."

Richard thought that was funny. "How much do you think a place like this costs?" he asked.

Jillian answered, "With the use of the space of two sky boxes, mandatory donations to the university, food and drink expenses, personnel, extra parking, some great seats down below, and a few other things, for a three- year contract, you could buy a nice house."

Richard and I quit eating for a minute. "And you only use it for the home games during the football season?" he asked.

"Yep."

The game started and a couple of other people sat down to watch. The others maintained their standing positions in the back of the room. Some of the guests were clients. Some were family members. Some were lawyers and politicians. Money seemed close to all of them. The sky box was a great symbol of prosperity, and we were all enjoying it. Especially those of us who didn't have to share the price tag. On the other hand, if I could have afforded a sky box without thinking much about it, maybe I would have enjoyed it even more. I will never know.

I noticed that Richard was watching the game through a pair of binoculars he brought. He saw me looking. "Be prepared."

The Volunteers moved ahead of the Gators who were having another miserable year. Smokey seemed pleased. Meanwhile, Richard and I found some popcorn. Jillian ate about five kernels. She got up a few times to say hello and to introduce guests to each other.

Once when she was away, Richard said, "Not that it's any of my business, but have you noticed that Jillian is not introducing you to many people?"

It had crossed my mind, but I thought it was probably just a petty thought. "One," I said.

"Yeah, Mr. Wiser. That's it. And he started that introduction. Jillian didn't have anything to do with it."

I didn't say anything. Richard didn't either for about thirty seconds. He watched a play with his binoculars and handed them to me. As I was watching the next play, he said, "And did you hear how she introduced you to him?"

Of course I did.

"She said you were a teacher at Spruceville."

"That's accurate."

"You know what I mean. She didn't say she was dating you, or you were the love of her life or her favorite person."

"I get it," I said and handed back the binoculars.

I suspected it did her no good to say to her boss, *This is the guy I'm dating, Van. He's a schoolteacher. Might I also say that he's a senior class sponsor and occasionally substitutes in junior high classes when other teachers have to go to the dentist. As a matter of fact, and I'm just guessing here, he probably makes less than any other person in this room, with the possible exception of Richard. But give Richard time. Tell Van about the ride waiting gig, Stu.*

Perhaps if I was an orthopedic surgeon, she would have introduced me to the crowd in the back and told them how special I was to her.

Jillian drifted back to us. She gave us some complimentary hand sanitizer with *Jordan and Wiser* on the label. While Richard and I examined it and expressed our gratitude, a guy that looked like a model came up from behind and put his hands on Jillian's shoulders. She turned around and he kissed her. It was a big kiss.

She jerked her head away and said, " . . . Zachary – "

"Hello Jilly!" he said. His arm was around her waist. "Surprise! I caught an earlier flight."

Jillian's face was beet red. Richard's mouth was wide open. Jillian tried to sputter something, but nothing came out.

He stuck out his hand. "Hi I'm Zachary Taylor," he said and shook my hand, then Richard's hand. "And you must be the guests Jillian needed tickets for. The teacher from her high school and a student who is also our client. She thought I would still be in Atlanta."

I smiled and said, "I see. Yes, we are the guests. Thank you for the tickets." He was the ex-boyfriend in the photo at Jillian's house. The one where they were kissing. Although he didn't seem to get the memo about EX. He looked even better than his photo.

He was well groomed with blonde hair. His skin was tan, his teeth were quite bright. He was wearing a blue sports coat, white shirt and gray slacks. He was probably about my age. He looked at me and said, "Nice shirt."

I smiled.

Jillian was standing very still. Zachary still had his arm around her waist. Her face was still flushed. Richard's mouth was still open. We stood there for a few seconds.

Then Zachary looked at Jillian and said, "Is everything okay?"

She removed Zachary's arm and walked quickly to the door leading to the gourmet buffet. Zachary looked at me for a second and then rushed after her.

Richard looked at me. He didn't know what to say. I didn't have anything to say, either. So we sat back down and watched the game.

Chapter Thirty-One

Jillian missed the Pride of the Southland band's salute during half time to Hank Williams, Jr. That was a shame. They were very good. I especially enjoyed their rendition of *All My Rowdy Friends.* She also missed the third quarter and most of the fourth. The game was so out of hand that everyone in the suite had left except for Rowdy Richard and Ramblin' Stuart. Zachary was nowhere to be seen.

Jillian sat down beside me and stared out the window, but I don't think she saw the players. After about five minutes she turned and began to look at me. I turned and looked at her. She looked like she had been crying. Very quietly, she said, "Can I talk to you for a minute please?"

I smiled. "Sure. Richard, we'll be back in a few minutes. Just hang here and watch the game. Use that complimentary hand sanitizer if you are so inclined."

She got up. I got up and followed her into the room where the gourmet buffet was now gone. She asked me to sit down in a chair. She pulled another chair up directly in front of me. Tears began to trickle down her face. After a couple of minutes, she took a deep breath and said, "I don't know what to say."

I nodded.

"I did not know Zachary was going to be here."

"I hope not," I said.

"This may be the worst day of my life," she said.

It was probably somewhere in at least the Top Ten.

"Say something."

"Zachary works with you?"

"Yes. He's an attorney."

"A partner?"

"Yes."

"And you have been working on some cases together?"

She nodded, sniffing.

"Which might mean you were with him on your out of town . . . engagements."

She nodded again and tears began dripping.

I watched her tears. They were falling fast. "Well, I can honestly admit that I didn't see this coming. Especially during first half."

"Me neither," she choked out.

"But it explains why we haven't talked to each other very much while you've been gone."

She looked at me with red eyes and tears. She shook her head and blew her nose.

I waited. She didn't say anything. "Yeah, I don't know what to say either. But anyway, Richard's in that other room and we need to get back to him."

She nodded again.

Chapter Thirty-Two

I guess I had sensed that something was up during her time out of town. It didn't take a lawyer to figure that out.

One of the biggest surprises of my life was the day Jillian showed up at the Lodge and what developed in the next few weeks. I enjoyed every minute of it. Every minute up to Game Day. I was too old to jump into a relationship like I had, but that's what I did. And I believed that love would find a way. Sounds like a Carpenters' song. Was that *Muskrat Love*? No, I think it was that other song, *Close to You*, where birds suddenly appeared every time, she was near because just like me, they want to be close to her. Or something like that.

But, after all, I reasoned, if she didn't want to pursue a future with me, she would just tell me and move on with her life. The moving on was true. The telling me was what she forgot.

I felt sorry for Richard. Jillian and I were both his friends. He already figured out that the relationship was heading South. And he was probably making comments about how she introduced me to those people at the game to bring me along to that realization. Still, he didn't need to see the Zachary scene. It upset me because I'm sure it was upsetting to him because he knew it upset me. Circular but true.

The ride to Wears Valley seemed much longer than the trip to the game, but without further drama. Richard did most of the talking. He began telling stories. Stories about Scouting, stories about Scout the dog, stories about his year at school. As he told them it hit me that he knew that it would be awkward for either Jillian or me to talk, so he would. Intuitive and smart. We were able to respond to him and not to each other.

When we got to Richard's house, Jillian told him she was sorry for "things getting very awkward."

Richard said, "Jillian, I had a great time. You were very generous to come all this way to get me and take me home. The Sky Box was amazing. You are a wonderful friend."

She hugged him tight for several seconds. I walked with him to the door. "Well, I'm glad you didn't say it was a day you'd never forget."

"I almost did! I'm glad I caught myself!"

"Yeah, probably wouldn't have helped. Richard, I'm sorry you had to see this business today."

"I was thinking the same thing. Except I was sorry you had to see it!"

"I think we can agree that neither one of us wanted to see it. But what I really want you to know is that I'm okay. It hurt my feelings to see Jillian kiss somebody else, but I will get over it."

He nodded.

"Sometimes things just happen. Sometimes it's a result of something stupid we did. Sometimes it's the result of what somebody else did. And sometimes it just happens without anybody's help. When it happens, we just have to deal with it."

"So, if I may ask, what now?" he asked.

"I don't know. I'm as surprised as you are. If I was honest with myself, I knew the chances weren't too good from the very beginning. Jillian is a lot younger than me. She makes a lot more money than me. She is considering other places to live where there are more opportunities. And I don't think she's sold on my solitary lifestyle in the mountains."

"Plus she's a babe," he said.

"Thanks. She's that, too. So I'll be okay. It hurts but I'm not down for the count."

"I appreciate you telling me that," he said. "I know you don't want me to worry about you."

"That's true, and I also don't want you to vilify Jillian. She made no promises to me. I'll grant you, she could have handled it a little better. But nobody is perfect. If we severed our relationships with folks because they screwed up once in a while, we'd have no friends."

"I understand," he said. We stood at the door, not saying anything. "She should have told you there was another guy. And it really blew up in her face."

"Yeah, it did blow up pretty good today, didn't it?"

"You're not kidding! I didn't know what was going on when Zachary kissed her!"

"I don't think Jillian knew either," I said.

"Yeah, but I'm pretty sure she knew more than we did."

Chapter Thirty-Three

On the way back to the Range Rover, I stopped in Richard's driveway. I looked at the stars and the moon. Because of their light, I could see the mountains. I tried to collect my thoughts. Jillian still had the car running and was talking to someone on the phone. I walked over to the driver's side of the car. She put the phone down and lowered the window. Neither of us said a word.

The sun was going down behind the mountains. I could feel the air getting cooler. She put her hand on mine. I let it stay there.

"We need to talk," she said.

"You think?"

"I should have told you about Zachary. It just happened a few weeks ago."

So, I asked the obvious question. "*What* just happened?"

She shook her head.

I waited.

"I guess you could say we got back together."

"That appeared to be the case."

"I knew if I told you, I'd lose you and I didn't want to lose you."

I let that hang there and thought about it. She was right about that. Telling me she had resumed a relationship with her old boyfriend would have ended things.

"Wouldn't it have been easier to tell *Zachary* it was over with him?"

"Of course it would have."

"So, just to make sure I have this right, you and Zachary reconnected a few weeks ago. How many weeks ago exactly?"

She sighed and said, "When we were in Atlanta."

I nodded. "That was during the pre-trial work?"

She nodded.

"So when you said you danced, it was a little different than just dancing with the whole law firm. You left out the part that it was with Zachary. And while you were there, in your re-energized relationship with Zachary, you sent me an invitation to come to your house."

She sighed and nodded again.

"Where you asked me to dance."

She nodded.

"Also kind of takes the shine off this morning when you said, *You don't know how much I've missed you.*"

She was silent.

I thought of something else. "So, you were back in a relationship with him, when I was at your house. And when I saw the picture of you two kissing, you called him your –"

"Ex-boyfriend," she said. "I know. I did. I justified it by saying to myself that he was about to be."

"But that didn't happen, and the relationship continued in San Francisco. During this time, you also sent tickets and jerseys for the game to Richard and me. But you were also romantically involved with Zachary.

" You were romantically involved with Zachary and me at the same time." I opened my mouth to say more, but shut it. Then I opened it again. "I get it. Like Richard just said, you are a babe. I am flattered that you have spent the time with me that you have. I cannot express how much it has meant to me. And I am astounded that I actually let myself believe this could be something permanent." I shook my head.

She was quiet for a few seconds. "It sounds so deceitful. Okay, that's because it was. You were two of the best men I had ever met. And I wanted you both."

"Why didn't you introduce me to people today?" I asked.

"What?"

"You didn't introduce me to your lawyer friends. Why?"

"I don't know. I didn't know what to call you, I guess."

"You called me a teacher from Spruceville."

"I know," she sighed.

"Have you mentioned me to *anyone* at work?"

She slowly shook her head.

"And the reason is –"

She shook her head again.

Then I got it. "The reason you haven't said anything about me to anyone at work is because they think or know that you and Zachary *are still* a couple. So, it would be hard to tell them about me."

She said nothing.

I collected my thoughts for a few seconds. "Jillian, you are beautiful and competent and have the world by the tail. You are gaining the attention of the right people. You are living in a world where money or recognition is a scorecard. The folks you work with are racking up big scores. And you are well on your way to doing the same thing. There's nothing wrong with that.

"The only problem is that my score is low. There's nothing in it for you to align yourself with me. I'm a teacher, Jillian. I always will be. I drive an old truck. I'll never fly in early, pick up my Beamer and surprise you in the Sky Box. So, you will always have trouble introducing me.

"You didn't tell me about Zachary and you didn't tell Zachary about me. Like you said, it's because you like both of us. And it's grown serious for both Zachary and me. There is something wrong with that. Zachary may be a good guy. I know I am."

"I want to talk about this more," she said. "Get in and we can talk on the way home."

"What did Zachary have to say about today?"

She paused. "He wanted to know who you were and why I had invited you."

"And you told him that I was someone you had deep feelings for? Someone you had chosen instead of him?"

She didn't say anything.

"You told him that I was your old teacher and Richard was a client."

She slowly nodded.

"And he wanted to know if that was the case, why were you so upset?"

She slowly nodded again.

"So now he's upset with you, too. The only problem is, he's someone you work with or for. And he's a partner, which you want to be as soon as possible."

She didn't say anything. But she also didn't refute it.

"You hit the perfect storm, today, Jillian. I can't really console you. You led me on for weeks and maybe months. And I fell for it completely." I shook my head and looked out at the moon's glow on the mountains.

I paused. She was silent.

"Please correct me if I'm way off here."

She didn't say anything. Her tears started streaming again.

"You can't make things better with Zachary *and* make things better with me. Zachary is your boss. He's other things, too. Break up with me and you lose Old Mr. J. But beyond that, nothing. Break up with him and it could cost you a great deal."

I sighed and picked up a rock. I threw it toward the road. It was now too dark to see it hit, but we could hear it. I was quiet for maybe thirty seconds. "Well, I don't know about you, but I've had about all I can take for today. The last thing I want to do is to talk more about it. At least tonight. I also don't want to say anything I'll regret. So, I'm going to find my own way home."

Her head jerked up. "You're going to what? How can you find a ride from here? Get in the car, Stuart. I'm sorry for everything, and I take full responsibility, but I can't just leave you stranded. That's crazy."

"Yeah," I laughed. "You're right. But after learning that you've got another boyfriend, maybe I get to act crazy. Go, Jillian. I know that's not what you want. It's not what I want, either. But that's where we are."

She started to cry. "Is there anything I can say to change your mind?"

"By the way, who were you talking to on the phone when I walked up just now?"

She didn't say anything.

I nodded. “Zachary. Trying to somehow fix things with him, just before you knew you were going to try to do the same thing with me.

“Which clears up a question that’s been rattling around somewhere in the back of my mind since you invited me to your home. Why would you keep a photo on display of an ex who was kissing you? I’d think the last thing you’d want is a framed photo of the two of you smooching.”

She shook her head. “That did look bad. Again, we dated for several months and then it was over. But somehow, while we were working together . . .” She shook her head. “

I thought about that. I looked at her. Her tears were drying up. She was regaining her composure.

“From the way he kissed you today, Zach didn’t have any doubt about where things stood,” I observed. “The funny thing is I didn’t either. Isn’t that a kick in the pants?”

She pulled me down to her and gave me a kiss. “I am so sorry. Call me soon. Call me sooner if you can’t get home.”

She backed out of the drive and drove away.

Chapter Thirty-Four

I don't know how long I'd been staring down the road. The Range Rover was gone. I felt sick. The front door opened, and in a minute, I heard a voice in the darkness. "Sorry, we saw you out here by yourself and came to investigate," Richard said. Linda was with him. Both looked concerned.

No one said a word for a few seconds.

"I told Jillian she could leave," I said. "In hindsight, that wasn't well thought out."

Richard put his arm around me from one side. Linda hugged me from the other. If Scout had been in the driveway, he'd probably have hugged me, too.

We walked inside and sat on the couch, me in the middle. Finally, I said, "Well, here's another fine mess you've gotten us into, Stan. I hope you're satisfied."

Neither one of them got it.

"Oliver Hardy?" I asked.

Nothing.

"Stan Laurel?"

"Oh, Laurel and Hardy," Linda said. "I thought maybe you were losing it."

Richard got up, "I'll build a fire."

Linda said, "You're staying with us tonight."

"No, I couldn't do that."

She was silent for a few seconds and then said, "You don't have a car, so you probably could."

"What was I thinking?" I said to Richard who had returned with some kindling. "I apologize for involving you and your mother in my personal issue. Maybe I can call Jillian. Or maybe I can Uber to a bus stop or a motel."

Richard grinned and turned around to look at me. "For your sake, I'm sorry this happened. But I think it's pretty cool to have you spend the night. I'm not complaining. How about you, Mom?"

She took my face in her hands and turned me close to her face. "I don't know what happened. That's none of my business. But I hope you will accept our hospitality. And we are thrilled to have you in our home. We're going to do our best to be good hosts. You've obviously had something bad happen. I'm very sorry for you and for Jillian. But now you're here with us. I hope from here on, things change from bad to good."

Her hands felt good on my face. Her eyes sparkled. She kept them there and looked at me with a very warm smile. "Agreed?" she asked.

"Agreed and thank you," I said. She leaned over and kissed me on the cheek. She continued to hold my face close to hers. Then she smiled again and got up.

I looked in Richard's direction. He was lighting the kindling, which he had arranged against the backlog. "What are we having for supper, Mom?"

We heard her from the kitchen. "I'm checking. "Tacos or meat loaf? What does your friend want?"

Richard mouthed *Taco* to me. "His friend votes for Tacos," I said.

"Coming up, but everybody gets to help," she said.

Together, we fixed supper. Afterward, we played with Scout. He loved to run and catch a soft Frisbee which glowed in the dark. Then we played *Electronic Catch Phrase*. It's a game in which someone sees a word on a monitor and gives you clues. Then you guess what the word is. Linda and Richard were very good and could read each other's mind. It was not fair.

"Mom, do you think we could take the telescope out for a few minutes?" Richard asked.

"Fine with me, honey. You better ask Stuart if he's up for it."

Richard looked in my direction.

I gave him the thumbs up.

Richard got his telescope. It was quite a bit more sophisticated than I had pictured. It was in a couple of cases. He loaded it in the back of their SUV and took the driver's seat. Linda motioned for me to take the front passenger seat and got in the back.

"We need to get to top of the mountain," Richard said.

We continued up their road, taking a fork to the right, then a couple of left turns. "We have some friends who own a cabin at the very top, but they seldom use it," Linda explained.

"It's a perfect place to look at the universe," Richard said.

About ten minutes later, we were there. They were right. We were at the very top of the mountain. The road had grown steep, with some switchbacks. He parked on level ground, thankfully, on a drive that was in front of a large cabin.

Richard collected his telescope cases and Linda punched the code to an electronic lock on the front door. Then she walked inside to the wall panel and disarmed the alarm. "The Thompsons have been very generous with this house. They let Richard come up here anytime. And we try to help them by unlocking the door for service personnel. Occasionally, Lori asks me to meet the security company up here."

"We also try to keep an eye on the place for storm damage, bear damage, or water leaks," Richard added. As they talked, we walked through a beautiful Great Room with a full vault. It looked to be over twenty feet high. We walked out the back door to a large deck. The stars blanketed the evening sky. They were bright and twinkling and stretched from one mountain ridge to another. It was truly breathtaking.

"Do the Thompsons get much bear damage?" I asked.

"Used to," Linda said. "Biologists and the National Park Service estimate that over fifteen hundred bears live in the Great Smoky Mountains National Park. Everyone who lives around the area has a few bear stories. But ever since the Thompsons installed bear proof cages for the garbage cans, they haven't had any trouble. The neighbor's house has the traditional cans. They've been crunched in so many times, they look like used aluminum foil."

"Don't worry, they would have to climb pretty high to get on this second story deck," Richard said. As I looked down, I could see there was a full floor underneath us.

Richard was finished setting up his telescope. "This was my birthday and Christmas present a couple of years ago," he said.

"Mine, too," Linda added.

"It's a Celestron CPC 1100. It's a computerized catadioptric telescope with an eleven-inch aperture and GPS. I'm going to download some GPS settings I've preset. It will just take a minute."

I had no idea what that meant. "Don't ask or you'll be here with the bears all night," Linda whispered.

"I heard that," Richard said. "Don't worry, Stuart, we're just going to look at a few stars, after I tell you one more thing about this telescope. The GPS system draws information from orbiting satellites to determine the date, time and our present location."

“So, the telescope finds the stars for you?” I asked.

“Yes. Pretty cool, huh? The first constellation we’re going to see is *Aquarius.* In Greek mythology, Aquarius was associated with a beautiful Trojan youth named Ganymede, the cupbearer to the gods. The constellation is represented by a man pouring water from a bucket.” He pointed to it with his laser. “Have a look.”

I looked through the lens to see stars like I had never seen them before. They were not just bright and closer. They also were brilliant and burning and radiated colors of blue and orange and red.

“You might remember that Zeus was supposed to have carried Ganymede off to Olympus disguised as an eagle.”

“Did you remember that?” Linda asked. I smiled at her.

Richard took us through six other constellations. Each was impressive. Finally, Linda called a halt, saying she was cold and it was time to leave.

Richard packed up, Linda followed, and I followed Linda. As I walked into the Great Room, Linda pushed me back out on the deck. “Take a minute, think about things. Then pick out your favorite star and make a wish.”

Chapter Thirty-Five

"Well, Stuart, you have a choice," Linda said. We were back at their house, in the Great Room. "You can sleep with Richard in his room. He has a roll-away bed in a closet. Or you can sleep on the couch here in the Great Room."

"Or you can sleep in my room and I can sleep on the couch," Richard said.

It was past midnight and I was tired. To say the least, it had been a long day. "I'm just grateful to have somewhere to lay my head, other than beside Highway 321," I said. "Just tell me where and I'm fine."

"Okay," Linda said, taking charge. "You can sleep on the couch. Richard, would you bring in a few sticks of wood and get Stuart some bedding?"

Richard came back with wood and then a pillow and plenty of blankets. He said goodnight and disappeared up the stairs to his room. I think he was as tired as I was.

Linda reappeared from the other side of the house, which must have been where her bedroom was. "Your bathroom is around the corner," she said. "I've laid out everything I thought you'd need." She paused and said, "I didn't know what you wanted to do about pajamas, but if you want some, I think these might fit you." She plopped some men's pajamas on the chair next to the couch. "There's plenty of food, water and other drinks in the kitchen. Do you need anything else?"

"I just want to say again –"

She put her hand out with a wave. "Once is fine. Goodnight Stuart."

I normally don't wear pajamas. The ones I have are in case I have to go to the hospital. Come to think of it, I think they are only PJ pants. And, come to think of it, that's often not what you wear in the hospital, anyway.

I looked at the pajamas. They were gray and seemed made of nice silk material. The pocket of the shirt had small initials, *IG*. They looked like they came out of a time capsule. Wonder what the story was for Linda having men's pajamas? More to the point, I wondered who *IG* was. I was too tired to think about it. Since I was a guest, I elected to wear them. They were a perfect fit. In case I was rushed to the hospital, I would be a trendsetter in the Emergency Room.

I found the bathroom. Linda provided towels and washcloths, liquid and bar soap, a toothbrush, toothpaste, mouthwash, shampoo, a razor, shaving cream and a hair dryer. Impressive.

I walked back to the couch. I wanted to go over the day's events. Instead, I went to sleep.

Chapter Thirty-Six

I awoke to the smell and sizzle of bacon. Then I remembered where I was. The Great Room and the kitchen and dining area were one big room. I raised up enough to see Linda at work. She had her hair in a ponytail and wore a green V-neck sweater over some jeans. She saw me and smiled.

"Good morning!" she said. "Welcome to a beautiful fall morning in Wears Valley!"

"Thanks. It is good to be here."

"That's more like it. Do you drink coffee?"

"I do."

She poured a cup from the coffee maker and walked over. I sat up and she handed it to me.

"I see you tried the pajamas," she said. "How'd that work out?" She was smiling a little bit too much.

"As a matter of fact, they are very comfortable."

She sat on the chair next to the couch. "I forgot to ask. Are you a vegan."

"Nope."

"Good."

"Are you always this cheerful in the morning?" I asked.

She smiled some more and looked out the kitchen windows. “Well, usually. I do love the mornings. And it makes me happy that you are here with us. It’s an unexpected . . . joy.”

“That’s the best compliment I’ve received in a long time.”

She smiled again and her eyes sparkled.

I stretched and drank some coffee. “What a great way to kick off my unusual day.”

“It hasn’t even started yet, but I hope it will be out of the ordinary,” she said. “I will let you freshen up and then we can eat. Richard has gone to church, but he will be back in a couple of hours.”

“Do you usually go to church?” I asked.

“Yes, every Sunday that I’m not working.”

“And I have kept you from going. I’m sorry, Linda.”

“I could have left you a note. But I wanted to be here when you woke up.”

“Plus who would be here to guard the good silverware?”

“And that. Well, you would have been easy to spot, walking down Wears Valley Road with a silverware chest.”

“And an orange jersey,” I added.

She nodded. “Or retro silk pajamas. Along that line . . . I put out another shirt that I think will fit you if you’d rather not wear that jersey again.”

“That is the best news I’ve heard today!” I said.

“Since the sincere validation.”

“Correct.”

I shaved and showered and put on the new shirt. It was a long sleeve jersey that said *Great Smoky Mountains Half Marathon.* It fit. There was also a pair of men's boxers, still in the package. They also fit. Why did she happen to have them? I was not in a position to look a gift horse in the mouth.

I walked into the kitchen feeling refreshed. I admit I hurried the freshening up. I was hungry.

"Yea! You didn't run away." Linda said. "Come help yourself!" The food was lined up on the island, which had bar chairs on one side. I didn't want to hurt her feelings, so I helped myself to bacon, eggs, biscuits and jelly. She poured a fresh cup of coffee and sat down beside me.

"You didn't tell me my hair was sticking up in all directions when you gave me the coffee on the couch," I said.

She tried to suppress a laugh. It didn't work. "No, I didn't. It was pretty funny."

"Well, thank you for not laughing out loud."

"You've hosed off well," she said. "How was the couch?"

"I fell asleep as soon as I hit the pillow. My next memory was waking up to you and bacon."

"I remember that head popping up," she said. As we talked, I looked out the kitchen window. She was right. It was going to be a beautiful day.

"It looks like the shirt fits," she assessed.

"Yes, the boxers, too."

She smiled. "Good to know."

She didn't offer an explanation. I didn't ask. At least at first. "Care to spill the beans?"

"You want to know why I have men's clothes at the ready?"

"It did enter my mind."

She crossed her legs and said, "The running shirt was to be a present for someone who never received it. The pajamas came from a dear friend whom I love with all my heart. And the boxers . . . You might not want to know."

"Okay."

"Any questions?"

I thought about that for a second. She also left out the part about the shaving cream and razor. So, I asked, "Are you a runner?"

She smiled. "Very diplomatic. Yes, I like to run. How about you?"

"I wouldn't call myself a runner. I like to walk and run but much shorter distances than half a marathon."

She nodded. "Running around here gives me a chance to enjoy God's incredible creation."

With the steep hills, it would give me a chance to meet the paramedics.

"I'm able to clear my mind and simply enjoy the moment. It's not always fun, but it is a ritual."

"How often do you run?"

"I try to run at least two days a week after work and a little longer on the weekend." She picked up her plate and took it to the sink. I followed with mine. "I'd like to show you something," she said. "Follow me."

I followed her up the stairs to a landing. There was a beautiful area rug over the wood floor. It was a scene of animals and birds in the woods. I stopped to admire it.

She looked at it, too. "It's a Claire Murray. Hand hooked. I love this scene."

The landing led into another room. A desk was on one side

of the room. Beside it was a large painting of snow falling in a meadow. Cardinals were perched on a wooden fence, surveying the majestic beauty all around. Bookshelves filled two walls. On the bookshelves were books, photographs and mementos. A wooden table was in the middle of the room with a library lamp in the middle.

"Richard's domain," Linda explained. We walked through the room to a door on the other side of the large room. "This is Richard's bedroom." We walked into the bedroom. The bed was made. It was as neat as any bedroom I'd ever been in. No clothes on the floor. No candy wrappers. No DVDs on the dresser. As a matter of fact, there was no television in either room.

"I knew it would look like this. It always looks like this," she said.

This room was also large, with two built-in bookcases on either side of a window. The headboard on Richard's bed was also a bookcase. On the wall were large photos of Smoky Mountain vistas. An old, weathered wooden sign said *Great Smoky Mountains National Park.* Linda pointed to the headboard bookcase. On the top of it were four framed photographs. One was a photo of Richard and Scout; one was a photo of Richard and Linda; another was a photo of his Scout troop; and the last was a photo of Richard and me.

I looked at the picture. We had our arms around each other's shoulders in front of the Lodge. It was a good photo. Then I looked up at Linda. She was smiling widely. There were tears in her eyes.

Chapter Thirty-Seven

I was in the Great Room checking my phone messages. Linda was on the phone in another room. I had three voicemails from Jillian. One from last night. Two this morning. I had six texts from Jillian. They varied. She wanted to know if I was still in the driveway where she left me, or walking back home, or in a homeless shelter. But they all ended with a plea to talk.

Linda came in and I put the phone in my pocket. "That was Richard. He has been invited to spend the afternoon with a friend, but he wanted to make sure that wouldn't interrupt anything we're doing."

"Good for him. Are we doing something?"

"Well, unless you want to give up your teaching job and stay here on the couch, we need to get you back home sooner or later."

"True."

"Are you in a hurry to leave?"

I had no desire to leave, yet. This was a good place to be. "Not at all."

"You don't need to grade some papers? Wash some clothes? See somebody?"

"No."

"Good, then consider yourself booked for the next few hours.

Grab your stuff and let's take off. Oh yeah, you don't have any stuff," she said with a smile.

I smiled back and followed.

She smiled and disappeared in the direction of what I still assumed was her bedroom. She returned and tossed a jacket to me. "You'll need this." Whose jacket was that? The dude she loved with all her heart?

We got into her Jeep Cherokee and headed towards Townsend. Before we got there, she turned left onto a narrow road. A couple of miles down, she stopped and unlocked a farm gate on the right. When she passed through, I locked it back. "This property belongs to some friends of mine," she explained.

We followed some dirt tracks for a few hundred yards and stopped at the base of a mountain. "End of the line for vehicles," she said.

She grabbed a daypack from the backseat and we hiked into the woods. "The land borders the park," she said. "Only a handful of people know about it, and even fewer have permission to use it."

Linda led the way. She was wearing a vest over a long sleeve shirt, hiking pants with some cool brown and gray hiking shoes. She also wore a khaki Trillium Inn cap. I liked that cap a lot. I hoped she had more. She set a fast pace and talked the whole time.

"I started hiking when Richard was in Cub Scouts. When he entered Boy Scouts, I volunteered for every hike I could. Trillium has been wonderful in letting us hike on its property."

"Is there enough of it to make for a good hike?" I asked.

"Yeah, around 5,000 acres."

That was enough.

It seemed to me that we were hiking straight up, but I guess that's impossible. "This is where the National Park begins," she said, pointing to a very old sign that said *Smoky Mountains National*

Park. We continued walking on the trail for about forty-five minutes. She took a side path for another five minutes that led to a rock bluff. From its vantage point, we could see the panorama of Wears Valley far below us.

Together, we took in the scene. A valley framed by mountains. A tractor plodded across a field. Birds flew below us. The wind was stronger up where we were, and Linda pushed her cap down on her head.

"This is one of my favorite places," she said. "I like to use this place to talk to God. Being up here reminds me of God's touch. I mean, look at this!" She gestured toward the fields and the mountains. "I see God's work. God made those mountains. And those fields. And those birds. And that man driving that tractor.

"From this spot, I gain perspective. I get a sense of being removed from what is happening down there. And I feel like God is right here, listening to everything I say."

Chapter Thirty-Eight

Linda opened her pack and took out a blanket. She unrolled it and placed it at the edge of the bluff. She sat on it and motioned for me to join her. "If you decide to go to sleep, I recommend moving away from the ledge," she said.

I nodded.

"Would you mind if I asked you some things that might be personal?"

"Nope," I said and leaned back on my elbow. "Free loading boarders are fair game. Shoot."

"Tell me about your first marriage."

I did. The good and the bad. I married a wonderful woman who realized too late that I wasn't the one she loved.

Then she told me about hers. Her husband left shortly after Richard was born. "He claimed he loved me," she said. "But apparently that wasn't enough. He wanted a lot more than a wife and son. The day he walked out was the last time I saw him."

"He offered no financial help for Richard?"

"None."

"So Richard has no memories of him?"

"No."

"You have dated at least two men since then. And you withheld presents from them."

She smiled. "I thought I was asking you the personal questions."

I shrugged. "Danger of the territory. Have there been any serious relationships?"

She turned toward me and leaned back on her elbow. "At the time, I thought they were serious. There were three. But each time, I ended them. The reality was that I didn't think they were right for Richard."

I thought about that. "How did Richard like the men?"

"He was eager for male companionship, but they were not as eager for the companionship of a little boy."

I nodded.

"So, why did Jillian leave you?"

"Yesterday?"

"Yes. Unless there are more times besides yesterday."

"No. Once is it. And once is enough. Not that she did."

"Leave you?"

"Correct."

"Kinda looked like it from where I was standing."

"You were watching?"

"Absolutely."

"Well, I *did* tell her to leave. She didn't want to, especially since it was a long way from home."

"Okay. That's understandable."

"Has Richard told you about events in the Sky Box?"

"Yes, at my request. But I'd like to hear your take on what happened."

So, I told her. I told her about receiving the same invitation that Richard did. I described our entry into the Sky Box. I told her about Zachary walking in, and the drama that ensued. I told her that Jillian was very upset and wanted to talk about it some more, but I didn't.

I did not tell her anything regarding what I said to Jillian. I did not tell her my analysis of the events. I did not itemize the way Jillian deceived both me and Zachary.

Linda listened, saying nothing. She looked at me with intensity. She nodded occasionally. Beyond that, she was still, completely focused on me.

When I finished, she sat up. "Wow! What a night for all of you."

"Yeah, I'm so sorry that Richard had to see the drama."

She smiled and said, "You don't have to worry about that. He is as cool as they come. You saw how he was at the deposition. His only concern about last night was for you . . . and Jillian."

I thought about that for a second. That's a lot of maturity for a teenager. Or anyone, come to think about it.

"I have listened to Richard tell of his time with you and I have observed and listened to you while we've spent a little time together. I have my opinions. But I really have a lot to learn about you. So, we are getting to know each other.

"I'm going to save you a little time in getting to know me. I'm cheerful. I'm fun to be around. I'm organized and goal oriented. I get things done. I take care of myself. I have provided the best environment I could for Richard and we enjoy each other's company."

I opened my mouth to say something. She put her finger on my lips. "I'm also very intentional when it comes to whom I spend my time with. And I'm very protective about who spends time with Richard.

"I guess we are sitting where we are because I want you to confirm that you are the man that I hope you are. I know you're not perfect. I'm asking questions to learn about your character, your heart.

She had taken her finger off my mouth, so I thought I could talk. But when I opened my mouth, she put her finger back.

"I don't know what the deal is with you and Jillian. If you have something going and it's a good thing, then I am glad for you. And her. You and she have been good for Richard and for me. And if things are not working out, I'm sorry."

She paused. "Now that I've said what I've said, you can respond or you can make a break for it and catch a ride back to Spruceville on one of those huge RVs down there, which are much too large to be on that road."

"Or jump," I added.

"Or that," she said, with no smile.

Since a little slice of my life partially occurred in her driveway, I felt obligated to tell her more. Plus, I trusted her.

I began with Jillian's first visit to the Lodge under construction. I told her about Jillian's request for me to accompany her to the deposition and ended with yesterday's surprise visit from Zachary.

When I finished, Linda said, "Just to make sure I understand, Jillian came to see you? I mean, she sought you out?"

"Yes. Funny, Richard asked the same thing."

She nodded. "She just showed up? Just like that?"

"As far as I know. Jillian is impulsive and so it does fit with her personality."

"And when you came with her to school, that was the first time you two had done anything together?"

"Yep."

She was quiet for a few seconds. Thinking.

So how do you feel about things with Jillian now?"

"I don't know. I feel disappointed. In her. And me. I should have picked up on the signs. I should have known something was up. I'm almost fifty years old and- "

"*Fifty!*" Linda repeated. "You're fifty?"

"Well, I'm forty-eight. I know. That's way too old for her."

"That's not why I reacted," she said. "You are well preserved."

"How old are you, if I might ask?"

"Thirty-eight."

I shook my head. "I thought you were the same age as Jillian."

That brought a smile. "Continue."

"Being close to the fifty-yard line, I knew dating someone that young would have issues. I will admit, I've been blind to most of them."

"Blind trust," Linda said.

"But blind, nevertheless. Anyway, I think it's water under the bridge."

Linda let that one hang for a minute as we soaked in the sun and the view. "Perhaps. But let's say she hasn't decided. What do you want to do?"

She was very astute.

"I think Jillian probably loves me, but not *just* me."

"That's not what I asked," she said. "What do *you* want to do?"

I thought about that. "It's a good question. I honestly don't know. Any words of wisdom?"

"About you and Jillian?" she asked.

Behind her were the rolling hills and mountains. "Yes."

She shut her eyes for a moment. Was she praying?

"I don't know if I should get involved in that."

"I'd welcome any feedback. I am going to have to decide sooner or later. I know you don't know me too well, like you said. That might help, in this case. Just tell me what has gone through your mind."

She smiled for a few seconds. What did that mean? Then she said, "Okay, I can share a few thoughts. You have some options.

"Option A. Do everything in your power to make it work with Jillian. Or at least pursue the possibilities. You've spent a lot of time with her. It was a good time. I know her pretty well and I don't think she has *tried* to deceive you. Or Zachary. She saw two good men and was trying to decide which one to choose. That doesn't make her a bad person. I think she's a catch.

"Yes, she could have handled it better. Have you ever screwed up? Cut her some slack. She deserves that much. Talk to her. See what happens. Doesn't mean things will work out. But it doesn't mean they won't. At the very least, she should be your friend, and you hers.

"Option B. Deuteronomy 31:8 says, *He will be with you. He won't abandon you or leave you. So don't be afraid or terrified.* Even Jesus got up early to be alone and pray.

In other words, go hibernate at the Lodge. You love it there. It's a great place to sit by the fire, walk in the woods, think about life. Be alone as much as you can for the time being. And if you haven't tried it, talk to God and ask for His direction. There's a lot to be said for that. That means take a break from women.

That might lead back to Jillian. Probably not. She has too much to offer without some other man or men pursuing her. She will move on.

"Option C. Take some time and then look for someone else. You are handsome and virtuous. That's rare. If you let women know you are open to a relationship, you won't have any trouble getting opportunities. It can be fun. If things don't work out with Jillian, there are plenty of other beautiful women who would love to be with someone like you. Be yourself, don't feel like a victim, and continue to ask God for help. He will lead you to just the right woman."

Chapter Thirty-Nine

"Those are your choices, in my opinion," Linda said. "Do you see any others?"

I played over the options she listed. "No."

"I know there's nothing original about anything I've said. I didn't say anything you didn't already know. But, you asked. I'm certainly not a relationship guru. But I am a good sounding board if you ever need to talk."

"Yes. You are."

She was quiet. Looking intently at me.

"Did anyone tell you that you are very direct?" I asked.

She opened her mouth, I think to rebut or rebuke that comment. But then she shut it and started again. "Yes, a few times."

"Are you always this direct?"

"No."

"Okay."

"I'm direct when I have skin in the game. I'm direct when Richard is involved."

"Okay. Fair enough. You are a good listener and I'm sure I'll call on your services."

"I would be honored. So, just to take this a little further. I have a question. Jillian is certainly a talented attorney, a charismatic personality and a real beauty. What was it that got your attention?"

I took a few seconds to think about it. "Jillian reawakened something in me. She saw something in me that I guess I didn't. Or at least hadn't for some time. She saw me for who I was, better than anyone ever has before. I think she loves me and she gets me. We have had many good times together.

"She is beautiful. She is energetic. She enjoys spending time with me. She invents fun. "

Linda opened her mouth. I put my finger on her lips. "Believe it or not, I need more. I need someone who can't wait to be with me. *Just* me. I need someone who is so proud of me, she is about to pop with pride, and can't wait to introduce me to others. I need someone who is not looking around to see what her other options are.

"I get it. What you said. She happened to meet, at about the same time, two guys she really liked. She was trying to figure out which one she liked more. Nothing wrong with that. And she certainly didn't have to tell me that she was dating someone else. But she sure did make it seem like it was me, and only me. She caused me to take a plunge that I wouldn't have taken had I known that she was just as interested in someone else. Out of sight should not be out of mind."

I took my finger off her lips. She waited and opened her mouth. I put it back on them. "I do enjoy quiet. I enjoy simple. Sometimes I enjoy taking a step back and being by myself. I like to think about where I've been, where I'm going and where I'm at. That's why I built the Lodge.

"But that doesn't mean I want to be alone all the time. I love shared experiences with those I hold most dear. To me, shared experiences are the best kind. "

I let out a sigh. Then a chuckle. "Until yesterday, I was in what

I thought could be a lifetime relationship with Jillian. Maybe I still am.

"If it's okay with you, I'd rather not talk about it anymore right now. Could we just enjoy the view?" I took my finger off her lips.

Linda smiled. Together, we enjoyed the view.

Chapter Forty

It was Friday. The students were taking an exam, so beyond making sure no one cheated, I had plenty of time to think. I thought about what Linda told me on the way to my house last Sunday night.

She encouraged me to talk to Jillian. She repeated that Jillian deserved to be heard.

I called Jillian on Tuesday. I got her voicemail, of course, but she called me back the same night. Our conversation had been short. She was in the middle of something at work. I told her I wanted to see her.

She said, "Oh good! I can't wait to see you, too. How about Friday?"

She can't wait.

And I'm dreading it.

Chapter Forty-One

When I walked out to Frank in the school parking lot on Friday afternoon, I found an envelope under the windshield wiper.

Dear Stuart,

By the time you read this, I will already be at the Lodge.

See you there!

Love J

Just like Jillian. We can't really discuss where to meet if she's already there. I wondered what she had cooked up.

I went home to change and made the hour trek.

The first thing I saw was a very large sign stretched across the porch. It looked like it was made of wide butcher paper. With large blue letters about four feet tall, it said:

BELIEVE

I stooped and walked under it and opened the front door. Jillian was sitting on the couch. She wore a sweatshirt with a hood and some sweatpants. Candles were everywhere. She was smiling brightly.

I stood there for a moment to take it in. There were two poster boards on the wall. Music was playing in the background.

Jillian stood and said, "Hi Stuart."

I smiled back. "Hi Jillian."

"Welcome home," she said.

"Thanks," I said.

"I'm so glad we get to talk. Thanks."

I nodded. I still hadn't moved. Neither had she.

She looked around and said, "I seriously thought about having a big production. I wanted you to know just how I felt." She paused and smiled. "But I toned it down. So no marching band."

"Seriously?"

"Yeah. No string quartet. No gourmet cooks. No cheerleaders. No fireworks. No celebrity endorsements. No choreographed dance. Heck, I even thought about borrowing a Titans cheerleader's uniform, complete with the pompons."

I shut my mouth when I realized it was open.

"I just want to talk. No glitz. Just you and me."

I nodded.

"I'd like to talk about what happened at the game. But not for long, I hope." She closed her eyes for a second and continued. "The fact of the matter is that I happened to get to know the two best men I have ever met and probably ever will meet. Zachary is above reproach in every sense of the word. He is a gentleman. As are you. I hope you know how I feel about you."

I didn't say anything. I simply watched her, silhouetted by the candlelight, and listened to what she was saying. "I knew you were great even back when I was in high school. Now, years later, I have feelings for you stronger than for any other man I've ever known.

"It was no accident that I came here to see you in June. I had heard little bits and pieces about your life. I heard you were still just as passionate about teaching. I heard you were divorced. And

I heard that you were still handsome.

"When I had this case with Richard, you immediately came to mind. I really did need someone in my corner. You really were perfect for that. I guess I wanted to find out for myself just where you were and what you were doing. And . . . if I had . . . feelings for you. Call it crazy. Or intuition. Through the years, I thought about you from time to time, wondering how things were going. So, I found you. Finally. It wasn't easy.

"I had no idea it would lead to what we have now. But I have absolutely loved it."

She stopped, looked around at the candles, and said, "If I knew how to build a fire without possibly incinerating the Lodge, I would have made one." She was quiet for a bit.

"As you know, I met Zachary before you, and we began to see each other. We decided to end our relationship before I ever came to see you that first time. It was mutual.

"When I went to Atlanta, the last thing on my mind was Zachary. While we were there, he invited me to dinner. Maybe I shouldn't have gone, but I felt like we could still be friends. During that night, he told me that he had time to think about things. He said I was the best thing that had ever happened to him.

"I told him that I was not interested. I had moved on. No, I did not mention your name. I did not mention that I was in another relationship.

"He said he would simply like to spend time with me while we were in Atlanta, no strings attached. He hoped in this no-pressure atmosphere, I would want to renew things with him. But if I didn't, he would certainly understand.

"During that time, there was no romance. There were no long, passionate kisses. We did a lot of talking."

I thought about that. "Do you think things can be romantic without long, passionate kisses?" I asked.

She made a smile of acknowledgement. "Yes. I do. So, I guess it was romantic I know, the question is, why did I even spend time with him? I decided that I owed it to him, and maybe to me, to see if there was still something between us that needed to be recognized or resolved. We were both there anyway. In my mind, it was about closure."

She paused and looked at me. I looked back at her.

"More questions?" she asked.

I hesitated, then asked. "During this time in Atlanta, he was one of the three attorneys preparing the case?"

"Yes."

"So your time with Zachary included all day and the evenings, too?"

"We went to dinner on the third night."

"Okay. You went out to eat and did other things, too. Like what?"

She paused to think and said, "Well, we did take some walks, and went on a carriage ride."

That opened the door for a lot of romantic time for them, but I let it go. "Okay, so are you saying during this time, it was simply emotional?"

She paused for several seconds. "No. There was some physical."

"So, hugs, maybe hand holding."

She nodded.

"You said no long kisses. Were there short kisses?"

She slowly nodded.

I was growing uncomfortable and tired of the conversation.

"Doesn't sound too much like closure to me. And you obviously decided not to tell me anything about it."

She opened her mouth to respond, but instead just nodded.

We let the silence take over for a bit. Finally, I said, "At that point, you were in relationships with both of us."

She didn't even nod this time.

"Okay, so now you move to San Francisco where you stay the next week. Anything you want to tell me about that?"

She paused even longer. She took a drink, looked at me and looked at the photo of Richard and me. She looked at it for some time. Then she looked at me.

"We had meals together. We rode the street cars. We walked by the Bay. It was romantic. Like I said, I was with him before I was with you." She shrugged. "It felt natural and easy. Like putting on an old pair of gloves."

She was quiet. I think she was going over the events. This was not a rehearsed speech.

"I knew you were back home. I knew that I loved you. But I also had very strong feelings for Zachary. I did not know what to do."

"Did you talk it over with anyone?" I asked.

"No."

She was quiet again. I waited.

"Was it wrong for me to be with Zachary? Maybe. But I wasn't trying to go behind your back, or to hide you from Zachary. I was trying to determine which one of you I wanted to be with for the rest of my life. When I knew, I would certainly have spoken up."

I thought about that. "How would that work? You would say to the loser, *Sorry, I know I didn't tell you, unknown to you, I've been seeing someone else, and, well, he's in and you're out. But please know how much I care about you, too. Can we still be friends?*"

She didn't say anything.

"I know. I can't defend what I did. I'm just trying to tell you what I did."

I let that sink in, took a breath, and said, "It sounds like Zachary is a good guy. And I'm a good guy. And you like both of us. And you've been hanging out with both of us, without either of us knowing. Then it blew up when Zachary surprised us at the game."

She didn't say anything. She was looking at me, still from across the room.

"And now we're talking about everything that happened and I'm assuming that you're about to tell me that you've picked me. Otherwise, why would you have made that sign? And why would you even be here?

"So, if that's the case, now you have the challenge of convincing me that you can be trusted. That this won't happen again. . . and again."

She nodded.

I waited.

She didn't say anything, so I did. "Jillian, from what you just said, I think you'd be happy with either one of us. That bothers me. It shouldn't be that difficult to decide if I'm the one or not. And, so far, I'm not convinced, I *am* the guy. Zachary has a lot going for him. And I think you have much more in common with him, both now and in the future."

She slowly walked over to a poster board that was on the wall. She took a marker from a table in front of it and wrote *Zachary* at the top.

"You're right, she said. I guess it does look that way. He's my boss. We do have some history. He does have money and a future with the firm."

As she made those observations, she wrote them on the poster. "What else?"

I shrugged. I would go along with her. "He's handsome," I said. She wrote *handsome.*

"Plus, he is a gentleman," I said. She added *gentleman* to the list.

"And you share a future of law . . . stuff."

She wrote *Law Stuff Future.*

"So," I said, "how could I compete with that?" He comes out ahead on many levels."

She continued to look at the poster. "Yes, I cannot deny he is all those things, and much more."

"Plus he plans very good dates," I said.

She nodded.

"All over the country," I added.

She nodded again.

She slowly walked over to the other poster and wrote *Stuart.* "So how can you compete?" she asked.

"And why are you even here?" I added.

She looked in a cloth bag that was on a chair next to the poster. She pulled out a bent nail and taped it at the top of the poster. "The first time I came here, you were sweeping. I picked this up and took it with me."

"Were your pants loose enough to stick a nail in a pocket?" I asked.

"I stuck one in my purse while you were gawking."

"I don't remember you bringing a purse."

"I rest my case. But you remembered my name after fourteen years."

"I did."

"That day was the start," she said.

She reached in the bag again and secured another item to the poster. It was the sheet of paper containing my notes at the deposition. I looked at it for a moment. I particularly liked the part that said, *Gimlet Eye ineffective.*

"That was the beginning of me falling in love with you. It was a great day with many memories."

I agreed. That's when she canceled her date. Was that something I should have been impressed with or concerned about?

After poking around in the bag for a few seconds, she came out with an envelope. It was my letter to her regarding Richard.

She attached it to the poster and smiled. "I must have read it 100 times," she said. "You didn't address how blown away you were that a beautiful woman kissed you. You simply wanted to know how you could get in touch with Richard."

I nodded. "Whatever happened to the self-addressed stamped envelope?" I asked.

"I'm saving it for a special occasion," she replied.

She next put a piece of toilet paper on the board.

"From my subsequent trip to the Lodge," she said. "Perhaps it needs no comment."

"I remember standing in the dark, waiting, for the all clear signal that night." I said.

She nodded. "One of the best of my life."

She took a step back and looked at both boards. With a bent nail and a piece of toilet paper as the shining evidence for why me, I thought she did an excellent job of representing Zachary as the best man.

"I agree that you have never been described as dapper or rich. But you are a good man with a good heart who makes my heart skip a beat.

"It's not how many times our hearts beat. It's how many times they skip a beat. Or beat faster."

Unless you're at the cardiologist, I thought but didn't say.

"I believe in you. I think life with you would be an adventure. Oh, I'm not saying we won't have bumps in the road. But I *believe* we would have many more happy, memorable times.

She wrote:

Adventure
Memories
Heart skipping

"Now, how can I persuade you to reinvest your faith in me?" She paused. Looked right at me. Took a breath, exhaled and said, "I can't. The lawyer in me wants to try. But I know I can't. That part is up to you.

"What I can promise is to make your life richer and happier than it could ever be otherwise. I can promise that you would look forward to our time together and *remember* each adventure with fondness. But that's up for you to decide.

"Look at the two boards. The difference is *memories.* Zachary's board is full of," she paused, searching for the word, "facts." Your board is full of memories. Memories of us. That's why I choose us. That's why I *believe* in us. And that's why I think you should, too. You and I have many memories."

She wrote *BELIEVE!* at the bottom.

She sat on the couch, took another deep breath, and blew it out, just like she had finished four quarters of football, or maybe courtroom final summation.

I was silent, too. I did not know what to say.

"I don't expect you to even comment on all of this tonight," she said. "I did take the liberty of bringing some hamburger patties to grill and some other stuff to go along with it. I'm hoping we can just have a good time. Then when you are ready, you can tell me what you want to do. But not tonight. And, if you don't want to share a meal with me, I'll leave right now."

I looked at her. She looked at me. I looked at the photo of us in Gatlinburg with the bear. I closed my eyes for a moment. When I opened them, she was still looking.

"If you left, would you take the hamburger patties with you?"

"Yes," she said, without a blink.

"Let's eat," I said.

We ate the hamburgers and other stuff, in front of a fire we both made in the fireplace. Always the teacher.

When we finished, Jillian stood up and pulled me up and led me to the porch, under the BELIEVE sign and onto the driveway. "Don't move," she said, and went over to her car, rolled the windows down, and rushed back to me.

"Tonight, the key word is that," she said, and pointed to the big sign. "We both must decide whether we believe in us. She took my hands, just as Vince Gill began singing from inside her car.

Everybody wants a little piece of my time
But still I put you at the end of the line
How it breaks my heart to cause you this pain
To see the tears you cry fallin' like rain
Give me the chance to prove
And I'll make it up to you

I still believe in you
With a love that will always be
Standing so strong and true
Baby I still believe in you and me

As the song played, she took my hand and began to dance. I looked at the stars overhead. I felt a gentle breeze. Its sound blended with the music. I looked at the sign. *BELIEVE.*

Then I felt her tears.

Chapter Forty-Two

I should not have been surprised that Jillian was up before me. I could smell cinnamon rolls in the oven and coffee brewing . Today, she was back to jeans and a sweater. She had an apron on over her jeans. She was wearing hiking shoes.

I'm pretty sure she had showered and washed her hair. I wonder when she got up?

She offered to leave last night. I assured her it was fine, not to mention much safer, for her to spend the night. She was delighted to stay. As a matter of fact, she had put her stuff in the guest room before I even got there.

When she saw me, her face broke into a smile. "Good morning!'

I smiled back.

She poured a cup of coffee and handed it to me. "It's another beautiful day here at the Lodge!" she chirped. "I can't think of another place I'd rather be."

I drank some coffee.

"Not The Million Dollar Mile, Not Ghirardelli Square, Not Saks Fifth Avenue, Not Macys, but right here at the Lodge. This is exactly where I want to be."

"I get it," I said.

"Good." She took the cinnamon rolls out and handed me one. Then poured coffee for herself and added some flavored cream. We sat down at the table. "How'd you sleep?"

"It took a while. I had some thinking to do."

She was holding her coffee cup with both hands, peering at me over it.

"I want to thank you again for last night, Jillian."

She let that hang for a few seconds. "Is there a *but* coming?" she asked.

I was silent for some time. She was frozen, fixing me with her gaze. "This coffee is good," I said. "Did you bring it from San Francisco?"

"*Stuart!* Is there a *but* coming?"

I sighed. "It means that I've changed my mind about how to respond to what happened."

I think she let out a sigh. Maybe of relief. Maybe of exasperation. "Okay," she said slowly. "Can you give me a little insight into what that means?"

"It means there's not a *but*. You screwed up. Royally. And you said you were sorry. And you've asked for a second chance. It seems dishonorable and hypocritical not to do that."

We sat there, looking across the table at each other.

She was smiling again. A big smile. "Would it be dishonorable to give you a kiss?" she asked.

I smiled this time. "No."

She did.

We spent the rest of the morning hiking. There were many trails that I wanted to explore. And Jillian was up for it. She was in great shape and seemed to enjoy the trek as much as I did. That was surprising. I did not picture her enjoying a hike. The air was cool and her face slightly pink.

We sat on the edge of the porch. It was about noon. "This has been so much fun!" she said. "I'd love for us to go on some more hikes."

"One of my favorite things to do," I said. "I'm glad you like it."

"I do. And thank you for this morning. I know you did not sanction a conversation at the Lodge. And here I am, into the second day. So, I am going to leave.

"Last Saturday was the worst day of my life. This Saturday might be the best. I don't know what happens after I leave here. But I want you to know how precious this time has been. I have made the best case I can. I heard you say that you would give me a second chance. I don't really know what that means. I know what I hope it means. I'm not going to pressure you. The next step is yours."

We took down the banner. She gathered up her stuff, and, after another hug and kiss, got in the Range Rover.

"I want you to know that I will always remember this visit," I said. "Every time I think of you, I think Wow! You are Wow to me. From the first time you walked up to the Lodge and told me you were here 'because I was safe,' I breathed faster and my heart beat quicker. It still does."

She smiled brightly. "Good to hear. Still no buts?"

"Nope."

"Good! Great! I love you, Stuart. Don't forget that."

As she began to drive away, she said, "Oh yeah, I left something for you on my bed. Well, the guest bed. Take care of that heart."

I watched her drive away and felt the absence.

Oh boy.

Chapter Forty-Three

Even with her past indiscretion, maybe indiscretions, Jillian had been very straightforward. It is hard to be mad at someone who is telling you she loves you. Especially if that person is someone *you* love. Linda's counsel helped me. Maybe I should have told Jillian about that.

After she left, I sat on the porch and stared down the driveway. The dust from the Range Rover had settled. I felt a slight breeze and heard the leaves rustle. A few fluttered to the ground. Two sparrows flew on the porch very close to me to inspect a bug. One grabbed it and flew off, the other in hot pursuit. I shook my head and laughed out loud. At my age, I thought I had seen everything. But I had never experienced Jillian. And now that she was gone, I felt alone. I didn't like that feeling.

This was a little too much. I decided to see what Jillian left on the bed. It was a DVD. I took it downstairs to watch. The image on the screen was Jillian, sitting on a bench. It took a second to place where she was. I knew it looked familiar. It was the bench from the *White Oak Flats Cemetery* in Gatlinburg. She was wearing a leather jacket over a turtle neck sweater, tan pants and brown boots.

Hello Stuart, I'm speaking to you from where we kissed for the first time. Do you remember? You went from safe to what? I'll just say from safe to kissable. I told you that sometimes I like to come here to think. Well, that's what I'm doing today. I'm thinking. I'm thinking about the mess I've made and if there's something –

anything – I can do to fix it.

Today is Tuesday, so I don't know. I'm in the process of preparing for a date with you this Friday night. A date you don't know about."

She paused and looked at her view. I remembered the view. She could see the whole city from there. Then she looked back at the camera.

I can't sleep at night. I can't eat during the day. I intended to end things with Zachary before last weekend, but I didn't. I was going to tell him about you and explain that I was in love with you and sorry for being dishonest with him. Obviously, that's not what happened. So, I planned to talk to him on Monday when he got back in town. But, as you know, he came back early.

The fault lies with me. Don't blame Zachary. I don't know if you've ever been attracted to two women at the same time, but that's what happened. I had the misfortune or fortune of knowing two very good men.

I know I haven't made things easy. Last weekend aside, I am gone for long periods of time. I haven't called you as often as I should. And I spend a lot of time at work. I can only say that I realize that, and I am willing to change anything that gets in the way of you and me.

If you are watching this version, it means that things went well Friday night. I really hope you are watching this one. The other was incredibly sad. I sobbed the whole way through. It took me a bit to compose. But it's also getting cold up here, so I moved on to the happier message.

In case you didn't know, I painted the banner myself. At least I hope it's finished by Friday. It is stretched out in my garage right now. It bled through the first time. So I had to create it again. BELIEVE now permanently decorates my garage floor.

She crossed her legs and looked out again. When she looked

back, her eyes were full of tears. I don't know if you will give me another chance, so you may never see this video. But if you do, I want to say thank you again. I'm sure there have been many thank yous already.

The question now is where do we go from here? I understand you are not going to open your arms and say let's start over. I mean if you want to, I'm game. But I also know we're talking about serious, life-altering matters. So here's my proposition.

Let's take a little time to see how things go. If you are satisfied, we'll continue. If not, we won't. I know, that's how we started our relationship.

It's up to you if you even want to give this a go. You'll have to initiate it by getting in touch with me and suggesting something. I will be receptive. I will not contact you, or just show up, so don't worry. Of course, I hope you will call me quickly.

She looked past the camera and paused.

I look at these markers in the cemetery and I see husbands and wives who lived together and were buried together. That's what I want for you and me. Okay, I hope that didn't sound as creepy as it just did to me. But I think you know what I mean. I'm talking about a forever deal, here.

Yes, I did come all this way up here to think. And to make a video. It's worth it to me.

One more thing. I don't know what happened after I left you on Linda's doorstep Saturday. But I'll admit I drove by your house more than once Saturday night and Sunday morning.

Just give me a chance. That's all I'm asking. Maybe I'm reading too much into your stay, but if you happen to decide that Linda's the one, I'll sit at your wedding and throw rice. Well, maybe not. You may decide I'm not the one and eventually hook up with someone else. I don't want to hear that, but I will survive. And then one day you'll be sorry and it will be too late. And you'll wander aimlessly for the rest of your pitiful life.

She laughed. *Sorry. That was a little joke here in the cemetery. I know this whole video is crazy. But so am I. At least when it comes to you. Goodbye Stuart. I'll see if I can find us a plot.*

She smiled. *More humor. I love you.*

Chapter Forty-Four

I was back at my house on Sunday night.

In reflecting on my time with Jillian, I was more than a little surprised to hear what she said about Linda. I must admit, Linda was very attractive and would be a wonderful person to spend time with. Do women have some kind of antenna that men don't know about? Of course they do.

Back at the Lodge, I found that Jillian also left a framed photo of herself, holding the little stuffed bear with my watch around him. I placed it on my bedside table. I remember taking that photo at the Village on the day things changed. Attached was a note:

Our mutual friend wanted me to remind you that I am not a dream. I'm real. And I want to take advantage of our time while your ticker is strong.

The other item on the bed was a box of fudge from the Smoky Mountain Candy Kitchen in the Village in Gatlinburg. I noticed it was missing a piece.

I had some serious thinking to do. I wondered if The White Oak Flats Cemetery was open at night.

Chapter Forty-Five

School was once again in session. Fall Break was a little over a week away. Jillian was in town. I saw her on Wednesday. It was a very pleasant time. We took a long walk in the evening. She asked if I'd like to do something for Fall Break. I told her that sounded good. She said it was my turn to plan.

When I came home Wednesday evening, there was a FedEx package at my door. It was from Linda. Inside the package was a letter and a gift. I read the letter first.

Dear Stuart,

Thank you for listening to my speech on the bluff. I can get a little intense. I think I hit a personal high that day. You were patient, kind and considerate. Especially given what happened the day before. I'm glad you didn't jump.

I am very confident that Jillian didn't just say goodbye. She wants you. I don't blame her.

You're doing the right thing to explore, ask questions and make decisions about your relationship. By the way, Richard includes you in all his prayers before meals.

Your second biggest fan in Wears Valley,

Linda

I opened the package. It was a khaki *Trillium Inn* cap, just like hers, and a white, long sleeve Trillium Inn jersey. She was playing dirty. I put the cap on right away. Good fit.

Chapter Forty-Six

If you weigh two hundred and fifty pounds, you don't wear a jacket in Speech class, even if it is your letter jacket. Slender girls get cold in class including the spring. Big guys complain about the warm temperature all year long. That was my first clue that Nathan was cheating.

I heard from students that he had cheated on past tests, but I had not observed it. Today I did. He had some lists written down. They were on a sheet of paper up his jacket sleeve. It was easy to see him pull them out.

After class was over, I asked him to stay.

Nathan was a good kid. He was on the football team, well-liked by his friends and teachers. He was a junior and already had college scouts expressing interest in him because of his speed and size. Something like this could hurt his chances.

I asked Nathan if he had anything he wanted to tell me. He said he didn't.

I gave him the silent treatment for about two minutes. He just sat, squeezed in the desk in front of my desk. I looked at him again. "Nathan, you're in a hard spot. You've made a mistake. I am going to give you thirty seconds to admit it."

We both looked at the clock on the wall. He didn't say anything. I went over and pushed the button on the intercom.

"Yes?" Faye Clegg answered. She was the secretary in the principal's office.

"Could you please send an administrator to my room please?"

"I certainly will, Mr. Jensen. Is that all?"

"That's all I need at this time. Thank you, Mrs. Clegg."

Administrators know that a lot of things can happen on a student's trip down to see the principal. For one, cheat sheets can disappear. So, it's better to let the teacher keep an eye on the kid while the administrator makes the walk.

Mrs. Clegg also asked me, by code, if everything was okay. The way I answered would let her know if she needed to have security come down to the room. I didn't need security. But Nathan would when his coaches found out.

I felt sorry for Nathan. Even if he had confessed, I wouldn't have been able to let things slide. I couldn't handle it in a private way, just between him and me. That could open the school up to a lawsuit if other students felt they were not given the same privilege by me or another teacher.

Cheating didn't happen often in my room. But when it did, I always asked the student to admit that he or she did it. It was a teachable moment. If they did, I would give them the two-minute talk about making mistakes, taking responsibility for them, and how to recover. I would also go to bat for the student and be an advocate in any way possible. But when they wouldn't admit that they cheated, it became a matter for someone over my pay grade, which, I think, was just about everybody.

There was one of four administrators who could come down. Whoever happened to be the Administrator on Call. That administrator would own the incident and follow it through to the penalty phase. I knew who Nathan's best hope would be. And I knew who would follow the letter of the law, with no leniency. The door opened and in walked Mr. Dill. Nathan should have talked to me.

Mr. Dill knew Nathan and said hello. He asked, "What seems to be the trouble, Mr. Jensen?"

"I caught Nathan cheating."

Mr. Dill looked back at Nathan. "Nathan, do you have anything to say about that?"

Nathan didn't say a word. He also hadn't moved a muscle since he sat down.

"It's in his left jacket sleeve," I said.

Mr. Dill said, "Nathan?"

Nathan pulled it out and handed it to Mr. Dill.

Mr. Dill looked at me. "Anything you'd like to say at this time, Mr. Jensen?" I gave him a brief description of what I observed. We both knew I had a written report that would be due by the end of the day. I would have to explain in writing what I saw.

Mr. Dill examined the cheat sheet while I was talking. He handed it to me. There were only a few items the students had to know and define for this test. Things like the four types of space – Public, Social, Personal, and Intimate. You had to do a little bit of study, but thirty minutes would have been enough. It was a regular chapter exam. I gave them every other Friday. I handed the sheet back to Mr. Dill. "That's for this test," I said.

"Okay, Nathan. You need to get your books and come with me." Mr. Dill was a big guy, too. They lumbered out of my class and down the hall. I knew the drill. Nathan would spend the rest of the day in Mr. Dill's area. His parents would be called. His teachers would receive an email. His coaches would be notified. He would be suspended for up to three days. Any tests or grades due in any class during these days would be marked as an F. There would be conferences with parents, administrators, teachers and coaches. He would not be able to play in this week's game, which was a big one.

Some college scouts would probably be there.

I shook my head. All he had to do was to tell me he wasn't ready for the test. I never refused a student who asked for more time. And I let them know they were free to ask. He didn't. He cheated. He got caught. He was paying a big price. A price that was still being calculated.

Chapter Forty-Seven

Since it was Friday, I arranged to get together with Jillian. I decided to treat her to supper at my place.

I drove over to pick her up. When she opened the door, she jumped into my arms and kissed me. "How are you tonight, Mr. Jensen?"

She wore a jacket and some type of stretch pants that looked like jeans.

I held the door open for her as she got in the truck.

"Hello Frank," I heard her say as I shut the door.

She asked me about my day. I didn't really want to talk about Nathan, but she kept asking for specifics, so I did. She showed interest. She asked how I knew Nathan was cheating. She also wanted to hear about the protocol, and penalties.

She continued to ask questions about Nathan as we approached the front door. When she stopped for a breath, I said, "Sorry, they were all out of banners at the banner store," I said.

"If you buy them, it doesn't count. You have to make them."

"I want to see your garage floor for verification."

We walked inside and she handed me her jacket.

I couldn't decide if she was wearing a long underwear top or if it was supposed to look that way. I'm kidding. Jillian did not own long underwear. She caught me examining it.

"What do you think?"

"I like it. What would you call something like that?"

"It's a Thermal Henley Sweater."

Trying to sound up to date on fashion, I said, "So it might be a relative of long johns."

She smiled. "Got it down at the *Tractor Supply Store*."

Maybe I should have just smiled and not inquired.

We walked into the kitchen. I said, "Open the fridge and let's get this party started."

I thought it might be fun to make a pizza. Jillian seemed happy about the decision. I had the ingredients from the grocery store. Luckily, Jillian had made a pizza before. We put everything out on my counter.

"Did you know this is the first time we've ever eaten over here?" Jillian asked.

"As a matter of fact, I did know that which is why we're here. And to celebrate that fact, I have something for you to wear so you don't stain your *John Deere* garment." I went to the closet and said, "Close your eyes until I tell you to open them." She did and I took something out of the closet and placed it around her neck and her waist. "Okay, open your eyes."

She looked down. Being a male, I did not have mirrors every ten feet in my house. So, she ran to the bathroom to look. And then she squealed. She eventually came out. "I love this!" What she loved was an apron that covered her sweater and waist. On it was an image of her as a cheerleader in elementary school.

"Research," I said.

She hugged me and thanked me. Then she said, "What about

you? You need something, too."

"Oh, yeah. You're right." I reached into a drawer and donned my apron. Again, there were screams in the house. My apron had an image of Jillian in a Homecoming Court in junior high.

"That is too funny! I want them both. Can I have them?"

"I don't know, I'm kind of fond of them. We'll see. Let's get started on the pizza."

"I can get you a discount on fertilizer down at the store," she said.

"We'll talk."

Jillian began to give instructions and I turned on the stereo. The song was *Let's Get the Party Started* by Pink. Jillian sang with it as she rolled out the dough. "I remember this in college. We had a dance for it."

"Show me. It wasn't that long ago."

She did. It was impressive.

The next song that came on was *Complicated* by Avril Lavigne. She sang and gyrated to it, too. The next was *Cry Me a River* by Justin Timberlake.

She stopped and looked at me. "Do you know any of these songs?"

"Nope."

"But I do. I used to sing them as a teenager."

"Really?"

She smiled. "A gold star, Mr. J!"

We added some Canadian bacon and pepperonis and mushrooms, and then a few black olives and some other ingredients while *This One's for the Girls* by Martina McBride came on.

We finished things up as *Brokenheartsville* by Joe Nichols came on. I knew that one.

Jillian popped the pizza in the oven and said, "Let's dance to Joe while we wait. We danced, apron to apron.

The words were ironic, not to mention a little awkward, but we made it work.

Here's to the girl, who wrecked my world
That angel who did me in.
I think the devil drives a Coupe De Ville
I watched 'em drive away over the hill
Not against her will, an' I've got time to kill
Down in Brokenheartsville.
Here's to the past, they can kiss my glass.
I hope she's happy with him.

With four minutes on the oven timer, the last song came on. Girl You're a Woman Now by Gary Puckett and the Union Gap.

She looked at me and said, "I remember. A little before my time, maybe. You should have sung it to me when I graduated from high school."

"Timing is everything," I said

Chapter Forty-Eight

Fall Break finally arrived. The only problem was that Jillian had to go to Los Angeles for some pre-trial work on a large case. She asked if I wanted to come out to the coast. She got credit for that. But she was traveling with other lawyers and would be working long hours. If I was going to be on my own, I'd rather be on my own at the Lodge, which was where I was.

She made sure I knew that Zachary would not be on this trip. I was relieved to know that. And hoped that would be the last time I would hear Zachary Taylor's name. But I did hear his name, in fact I heard directly from him. It was in the form of a letter, delivered to school. The letterhead said Jordan and Wiser.

Dear Stuart,

Jillian and I had quite an interesting conversation a few weeks back. It was a couple of days after the UT game. She explained that, in fact, I was not the love of her life. You were.

She also apologized for her lack of judgment in renewing a relationship with me when she already had one with you. In light of this revelation, I can only tell you how sorry I am for my display of affection for Jillian in front of you.

I am embarrassed on my part and angry towards Jillian for what she subjected you to endure. She was dishonest with both of us.

Jillian made a mistake. A rather large one in my opinion. But she did have the courage to come and talk to me about it. She knew that such a move could jeopardize her future.

I have no idea what your intentions are with Jillian, at this point. But I did want you to know that neither you nor I knew what was taking place on the other's part.

Finally and ironically, I must say that while I am disappointed and hurt, I have made mistakes in my life, too. And I am grateful that I was given the opportunity for a second chance. It seems that we both, in our own ways, have been given that opportunity to forgive Jillian.

Jillian simply asked if I would write you a letter and say whatever I pleased. She is unaware of its contents. Pretty gutsy. As far as I'm concerned, the issue with Jillian is a private matter and I will handle it as such. She has much talent and I will treat her fairly and kindly.

Please feel free to contact me if you desire further conversation,

Personal regards,

Zachary Taylor

Chapter Forty-Nine

I was currently putting together the bird feeder I've had in storage for several years. Fortunately, it was fairly easy to construct. The metal pole was about six feet high with the bird feeder mounted on top. The feeder was pressure sensitive, meaning if a squirrel stepped on the ledge, the glass would come down and prevent the little thief from eating all the feed.

It was a beautiful October Monday in the Smokies. I thought it was too pretty to sit inside, so I found Frank pointed toward Gatlinburg. The next thing I knew, I was walking past the Village and up through White Oak Flats Cemetery to the bench. Although the sun was shining, the bench was not warm. And it quickly permeated my jeans. My ski parka and flannel shirt kept the rest of me warm. I was good for the time being. Since few people knew about the cemetery, I was by myself.

Jillian was right. It was a good place to think. I would not be making a video, though. Since the cemetery was on a hill, and the bench was at the top, I was able to look down on the many gravestones. Some were well over a hundred years old. Some were recent. It was a harsh reminder that life here on earth does not go on forever. Whatever it is we want to do in life, we need to get with it while there is still time.

On my way up the steep cemetery, I stopped to read a stone monument. The husband had died. He was eighteen years older than his wife. The wife's name was written on the marker, too, but she was still alive. I looked at the marker some more.

If I married Jillian, chances are I would go first. So, would she put her name on the stone in advance, or hold out for a better offer?

I reflected on that as I enjoyed the view. Jillian wanted me to trust her. She wanted a second chance. She made that abundantly clear. Could she be trusted? Was I going to find out the hard way?

And what of her comments about Linda? It's easy to be honest in a cemetery, I found. And if I was being honest, I thought Linda was very attractive in many ways.

I also had another thought about Jillian. She said that she could adapt to my somewhat simple lifestyle. Could she?

I vacated the bench and walked back down the hill. I had no answer to my dilemma. So, I did what any sensitive male would do. I stopped at the public restroom. Then I walked down the cobblestones to the Smoky Mountain Candy Kitchen. I bought a box of Rocky Road and a box of assorted chocolates and left.

Chapter Fifty

To get to the Lodge, I drove through Wears Valley. I turned on Happy Hollow Road. It was almost five o'clock. I wasn't sure what time Linda got home. And I didn't know what she would think about me dropping in unannounced.

When Frank and I pulled in the drive, I did not see Linda's car. I rang the doorbell. No one answered. I walked back to Frank and heard "*Stuart!*"

It was Richard. He was rounding the corner of the house. About that time, a yellow streak shot past him and came straight at me.

"Hello Scout!" I said as he collided into me. Richard threw a Frisbee to me. It had a lot of Scout's slobber on it. I threw it for Scout to chase.

Richard said, "It's great to see you! Boy, will Mom be surprised!"

Scout came back for another toss. He dropped the Frisbee at my feet and took a couple of steps back. His tail was wagging. Actually, the entire back part of his body was wagging. I gave the Frisbee a long toss.

"Yeah, this is definitely a surprise visit. But I wanted to stop, if even for just a minute."

Richard picked up on my uncertainty. "Oh don't worry. This is a good surprise. You'll see."

I didn't know how much Richard knew about what was going on. I guessed he knew everything. We played with Scout, who loved every minute of it. And then Linda drove up.

She parked in the carport and walked over to us. She was wearing a blue parka that said *Trillium Inn* on it. She was also wearing jeans and boots.

Her smile was evident from across the yard. She was walking pretty fast. Not as fast as Scout but not too much slower. She collided with me, too, put her arms around me and gave me a very tight hug. Still holding me, she looked into my eyes. "You smell like candy," she said.

I looked at Richard. He was grinning.

I think I was, too.

Chapter Fifty-One

Linda knew it was Fall Break week. But she didn't know what my plans were. As a matter of fact, she didn't know anything about me since the last time we were together.

We played with Scout a little more, then Richard took him to eat. All he had to do was say, "Are you ready to eat?" Scout made a beeline for the supper dish.

Linda put her arm around me and led me toward the house. "I did not expect to see you today," she said.

"I know," I said.

"Well, I am glad to see you. I have missed you."

"Surprise," I said.

She laughed. "Surprise. You get to help fix supper."

The meal was spaghetti. It was good. The sauce was even better. I went out to Frank and brought back the assorted chocolate box. As Linda had detected, the Rocky Road box had been opened. We each took a bite from an assorted piece and showed each other the mystery centers.

Richard announced that he had to leave for a troop meeting. "Stuart, will you be here when I get back?" he asked.

"Yes," Linda said. "We'll see you soon."

We sat on the couch in front of the fire, with a little distance between us. It was easier to see each other that way. I didn't like to sit four inches away from someone and try to hold a conversation. It violated the other person's Intimate Space. That's four to eighteen inches, Nathan. It also made the other person look fuzzy and distorted.

So there we were, in our Personal Space, which was eighteen inches to four feet. Linda put her hand on my shoulder. She was now in my *Intimate Space*, but I didn't call her on it. She had changed from her work attire into a Smoky Mountain High School sweatshirt and a pair of jeans with holes in the knees.

"Thank you for my care package," I said.

She smiled.

"I was not looking forward to slipping in here and stealing your cap," I said. "And the jersey is great, too."

"I'm glad you like them."

"Things are – well they are more complicated than I thought. I could use your counsel."

She smiled and said she wanted to hear it. For the next twenty minutes, I told her. I didn't leave much out. I included the time at the Lodge with Jillian. The banner, the video and on down the line. I told her about Jillian's proposal for another chance. I also told her that we had seen each other some more and gave some of the details. I may have omitted some kissing segments, but I did include the part about our dances. I felt awkward in telling her. I needed someone to tell. But was she the right one to tell?

Does aspirin go with Rocky Road?

Chapter Fifty-Two

When Richard arrived, we caught up on the previous weeks. This was his best year by far at school. Although things are never perfect, it was much better than last year.

He was also making progress on his Eagle Scout project. He had enlisted several members of the community to aid in the construction of the new training facility for guide dogs. This included professional individuals and corporations that built buildings for a living. Word of his project spread to the state capitol in Nashville. He had been invited to participate in a Young Leaders Institute during the break. He would leave tomorrow to spend the rest of the week there.

"You may feel like the fly that flew into the spider's web, but they have asked me to give a presentation on the training facility," he said. "I could really use your help."

I was happy to help and sorry he had not taken my class. It would have made things a lot easier. So, I gave him Speech 911. I explained how to create and organize a speech. I showed him how to practice. I gave him suggestions on when and how to use visuals.

He brought his laptop down and we constructed a presentation. We did a walk-through a couple of times and he excused himself to go pack. He promised to practice and do a practice presentation in the morning.

After a few minutes more, Linda came in with bed supplies and a pillow. She sat down in a leather chair and smiled. "Richard is on Cloud Nine. Thanks so much for your help. The speech opportunity was a last-minute invitation. He was very nervous about it."

"He will do a practice speech before he leaves in the morning," I said. "I wish you could be here for it."

"I will be," she said.

"What about work?"

"I have rearranged my schedule. I will be here tomorrow." She looked at her watch. "I can't tell you what it means to me for you to come here today." Her eyes were moist. "And how providential it is that you came at the very time Richard needed help with a speech. I need to go spend a little time with him. Then I have some more work to do." She looked at the blankets. "Please make yourself at home. Your toiletries are in the top drawer of the bathroom vanity. I will see you bright and early tomorrow morning. Dress is casual."

That was good since I had nothing but what I had on. She came over and I stood. She hugged me for a long time. Then she left.

I found all the necessities that I needed in the top drawer of the bathroom vanity, just like last time. I also found a note on stationary that said,

> *Welcome back, Stuart! In the next drawers, there are other things you might need.*

I found the PJs, more boxers, t-shirts and some socks in the other drawers. Where did that stuff come from?

I was not sure how providential my timing was. How does that work? And what does it mean? Do the stars line up to determine an event? Does God monitor events on earth that closely? Did He pay Richard and Linda particular attention? I didn't know, but I was glad it worked out.

Chapter Fifty-Three

Richard practiced several times before we heard him. He took my suggestions to heart. His practice presentation went well. I'm not always a fan of Power point, but in his case, Richard could show photos of the old training facility and construction of the new. He could also show a video of Scout in training. Linda was visibly surprised and impressed. So was I.

As part of the Fall Break experience, Richard was picked up by his local Representative of the Tennessee State Legislature. Linda took photos, gave hugs, and wiped away a tear as she waved goodbye.

We walked back inside and sat at the dining table. She poured us cups of coffee. The sun's rays highlighted her hair. I could smell her perfume. Her skin glowed. She looked at me as she drank the coffee. She was wearing a light blue oxford shirt over some gray leggings.

Thanks to Linda and her stash of male clothing, I was wearing a brown t-shirt today that had a little bear logo on it. I found it folded up next to the PJs. I'm sure she had noticed it but hadn't commented on it. Until now.

"It might be in your best interest to leave a change of clothes here."

"Thank you. I will take that offer as a compliment."

"It is a large compliment. And a first invitation of its kind." She put the cups in the dishwasher and said, "If it's alright with you, I'd like to take you somewhere."

Chapter Fifty-Four

I put my parka on and off we went. When we got down to Wears Valley Road, Linda turned right.

As we drove, we passed pastures with cows having a high old time, munching on hay and soaking up the sun. On the other side of the pastures were mountains which appeared purple today. The traffic was light. I watched the cows and listened to Linda.

"Since we have some time, I thought maybe you'd like to see a little bit more of Richard's life. The more you know about him, the better a friend you can be."

She kept her eyes on the narrow road, which was beginning to curve and descend. And then ascend.

"Does that make sense?" she asked.

I nodded.

"And you *do* want to learn more about Richard?"

"Absolutely."

About five minutes later, we turned left down an even narrower road. She turned into a parking lot in front of an attractive large brick and wood building. The sign said, *The Harvest*.

"This is our church," Linda said. "Since church plays a big role in Richard's life, you need to see it."

We got out of the Jeep and walked inside. "We have a coffee

shop that's open every day," she explained. "It's open to the community. I just wanted to stop in and give you a peek."

It was a short walk to a room that said, *Coffee Shop*. I wondered if I was dressed appropriately. But Linda wasn't dressed up either. The large room consisted of several tables, a couple of refrigerators, sinks, commercial stoves and some couches and chairs. Commercial coffee pots were brewing, and all kinds of pastries and fruits were on the counter. At least twenty people sat and stood, talking and laughing. I wanted to inspect the food more closely, but that's when the people saw Linda.

One lady shrieked, *Linda!* Some ran up and hugged her. Maybe all of them. She was one big smile. She introduced me to everyone eventually.

Finally, a wise, generous soul asked if I would like some food. I informed her that I would like a plate to eat right now and a box for the ride home. Well, I didn't say it, but I thought it. There were pies, homemade loaves of bread, brownies, cheese and crackers, pastries, fruit and more.

We sat down, and the hoopla began to play out. Maybe they treated every person that walked through the doors like that. I don't think so. As we sat and I ate, various people came up to talk to Linda, and, therefore, to me. They struck me as very genuine.

Several were senior citizens. But not all. Some of the hostesses were younger than me. Some of the ladies used a cane. Some of the men wore overalls. I learned that church members made the food and took turns bringing it. They also took turns playing host which meant, as far as I could tell, making sure the coffee was fresh, the food was out, and everybody was having a good time.

Linda was having a great time. She was proud of her church and wanted me to meet these friends who knew her and, therefore, Richard. She also evidently wanted her church friends to know who I was.

Score one for Linda. This was not a calculated move. This was

Linda. And Linda was not hiding anything.

A man perhaps in his forties sat down with us at the table. He gave Linda a hug and she hugged him back. "Jimmy, this is Stuart. Stuart this is Jimmy, our pastor."

Jimmy stood up, so I did, too. He shook my hand enthusiastically. "Stuart, I am so glad to finally meet you. I have heard about you from Linda and from Richard. I want to thank you for your interest in Richard. I think you have made a big difference in his life already."

I thanked him. The pastor was a handsome man. I saw no ring on his finger. Do pastors get married? I thought so. I did not know what kind of denomination this was, but if he could, why wasn't he chasing after Linda?

And then there was the issue of Linda talking about me. I wasn't concerned. Just surprised. Linda was telling those most dear to her about me. Jillian, on the other hand, had not mentioned me to anybody.

Jimmy asked me if we could stay for the morning devotional. I looked at Linda. She had a hopeful look in her eye. "It's over before you know it," he said with a wink. And so we stayed.

One of the hosts asked everyone in the Coffee Shop to settle down. Then a woman stood up and asked "if anyone needed to be added to the prayer list." Several mentioned the names of people who were in the hospital, nursing home, hospice or just weren't doing well for one reason or another. At the end of that, an older man asked everyone to bow their heads as he led a prayer. He asked God to be with those who had been mentioned. He also asked God to be with the "homeless, the orphans, those who were having financial difficulties, the broken and the broken hearted." He was sincere and kind in his petitions. His prayer also wasn't long.

Jimmy stood up and welcomed everyone to the Coffee Shop. He expressed his concern for those who weren't there. He welcomed an older lady, Cecil May Turnbow, who was back in the saddle at the Coffee Shop after having a cold for the last week.

"We also want to welcome our special guest, Stuart Jensen. Stuart we are glad to have you here and we hope you will come back soon. Linda is one of our favorites and if you have her attention, you are indeed a fortunate man. May God bless you as you continue to get to know Richard and Linda."

I was a little unnerved about his comment, but he didn't hang me out to dry. His words struck me as the real thing. I liked him.

His message was about those who are "poor in spirit." He explained that *poor in spirit* meant understanding your need for the Lord. He said Jesus was saying to his audience that day on the mountain two thousand years ago and to us today that we could only have a true relationship with Him when we understood our need for Him.

He gave an easy-to-understand example. He kept it light. Plus, he was true to his word. He finished in less than ten minutes. He ended by saying, "The truth is, unless the Lord returns, none of us is getting off this old world alive. Sooner or later, you and I will pass away. But isn't it good news that those who understand this idea of poor in spirit don't have to fear death anymore? Rather, we can look forward to the day that we take the party upstairs."

They laughed, he smiled. And he was through.

Chapter Fifty-Five

We spent a few more minutes visiting with anyone who wanted to talk. Which was everybody, I think. Then Linda wanted to show me around. She explained that *The Harvest* was a community church. She said it was independent, started about ten years ago. Anyone could worship there.

Before we left, Jimmy walked up and said, "I'm glad to meet you, Stuart."

I told him I enjoyed being there. "What can you tell me about Richard?"

He thought about it and said, "He loves the Lord. He is an achiever. He is a poster boy for Boy Scouts. He is a leader. He is compassionate. He has no ego. He is very intelligent. He loves to learn. He has a great life with his mom. What I think he needs is more males in his life. He has the Scouts. But he could still use more male influence. That's why I was glad to meet you."

"Suggestions on what I should do?" I asked.

He smiled. "You're a teacher. You know kids. Your intuition will guide you. Just spend time with him. He'll let you know what he needs."

As we walked to the car, Linda grabbed my arm and repeated, "Like I said, this is a big part of our life, and you need to know more about that to better understand Richard."

"And you."

"True. So, what are your first impressions? Be truthful. Don't worry about hurting my feelings."

"Is the food always that good?

"Yes."

"Do you think Sister Turnbow was contagious?"

"No."

"I like it."

"Would you consider going with us to church sometime?"

"I would."

"How about this Sunday?"

"Okay."

Chapter Fifty-Six

I received two phone calls from Jillian since she left on Saturday. Also a few texts. It was a big case. They were working with William Whitsitt, a lawyer who formerly worked with Jordan and Wiser. He left a few years ago to form a law firm with two other lawyers. It had grown to thirty lawyers. The reason that Jillian and her cohorts were there in LA was because Billy had more business than he could say grace over. So he contracted it out to Jordan and Wiser.

The case had to do with sexual harassment. Whitsitt's firm was representing three women who were filing suit against the Chief Operating Officer of a multi-billion-dollar company. The stakes were high on both sides.

There had still been time to go to a Lakers game, she said, thanks to Whitsitt. She reminded me that *you-know-who* was not on this trip. She also said that she couldn't wait to get back to see me, but she wasn't sure when that might be.

I called her the night before. In the course of the conversation, I told her that I was spending part of my Fall Break at Linda's house. She was quiet for a while and then said, "Thank you for being honest about that. Richard is lucky to have someone like you.

"I don't know what to say about you staying there. It makes me uneasy. But I am asking you to trust me, so I need to trust you. Linda is a good woman. Tell her I said hello. And tell the Lodge hello for me as soon as you get there, which I hope is soon."

Meanwhile, Linda and I were back in the car. I was thinking about an apple strudel I'd eaten at *The Harvest* that someone had made. It was very good. I wished I had taken one for the road.

We were heading to another place Linda wanted me to see. I hoped they had food, too. She seemed happy.

I thanked her for showing me her church. "You're right. It helps me understand more about Richard. And you. And I appreciate you introducing me to all those folks."

She smiled. "You're welcome. It was fun. I'm glad it worked out."

She was happy. It was a beautiful day. We were in the middle of the mountains. I was smiling.

"Were you concerned that people might think you were introducing them to your new boyfriend?"

She smiled even wider. "Were you concerned?"

"You know what I mean. Here you walk in, and all eyes are on you. Then me. They make assumptions. You didn't feel the need to explain who I was in your life?"

She laughed and said, "Who you are in my life? When I figure that out, I'll tell them. But it doesn't matter what role you play. If I didn't want to introduce you to my friends and family, something's wrong. I'm hiding something or someone, or I'm ashamed of you."

I thought about that. It made a lot of sense. And very timely.

"We're here," she said. We had turned off Wears Valley Road and up to a gate. Linda punched a code and the gate opened. We drove through a subdivision of upscale houses. The farther we drove, the higher on the mountain we traveled. We got to the end of a street and pulled in a driveway. Linda stopped the car and said, "Show time."

We walked to the front door and were met by a woman about

Linda's age. She was very attractive with blonde hair, slender build, and beautiful skin. They hugged and Linda introduced me to Nestle. "My best friend."

Nestle hugged me and said, "I've heard a lot about you, Stuart."

Of course.

We followed Nestle through an entry hall, a large living room and into a large sun porch. We walked over wood floors, oriental rugs, and beside beautiful furniture. "This is my favorite room," she said. "It's a good place to talk."

The house backed up to the forest. "That's where the national park begins," Nestle explained. "Last week, a bear came up to see what we were feeding the birds. The deer eat out of that feeder every day. Along with raccoons, possums, squirrels, and even a bobcat sometimes."

I was glad we were in the sunroom and not sitting out by the feeder.

"Nestle and I have been friends for about fifteen years," Linda said.

We visited for a few minutes and Linda said, "This may be a stretch or overkill. But the closest person to Richard is me. So, I think the way to get to know Richard better might be to get to know me better. And Nestle knows me better than anyone. About now you might be wondering what you've got yourself into. But I hope not. I'm thinking big picture. Richard has great opportunities ahead of him, and I'm praying that you are a part of that plan. So I'm taking maybe an unusual method to . . . " she paused for the word "cultivate his relationship with you for years to come.

"I brought you here so that you can talk to Nestle. She can tell you things about me and maybe Richard that I wouldn't. I will leave you two alone. I'll be back in about an hour."

Nestle gave her a fabulous smile, watched her leave, and turned to me. "There goes one of the best things in my life. When she told me about your interest in Richard, it's the happiest I've ever seen her.

"Linda told me that she wanted you and me to get to know each other. I first met Linda through school. Our kids were the same age, and we've been close friends ever since."

The thought occurred to me of how Nestle and Linda turned a lot of heads when they sat together at Parent-Teacher nights. Some husbands probably got pinched for their frequent stares. And maybe got a lecture on the way home. That made me smile. I didn't share what I was thinking. Maybe Nestle would tell Linda, *He sure does smile a lot!*

"She wants me to help you get to know her better. She also wants my take on you. After all, we're talking about Richard. So, if you don't mind, I'd like to hear more about you." She was sitting on a couch across from me. She was wearing a bright pink sweater and faded blue jeans.

I told Nestle where I lived, what I did, and how long I'd done it.

She asked me about being married and I told her. She asked about the Lodge and I told her. Finally she said, "Tell me about Jillian." So I did.

Nestle was a very good listener. She sat quietly, looking at me. Sometimes she nodded. Occasionally she asked questions. But for the most part, she was silent and still.

Then she asked how Linda, Richard and I met. She liked the part about me as a lawyer.

I had a pretty good idea that Linda had already told her all of this. She asked several questions about how I felt about Richard. She wanted to know what I thought about Linda.

"She is a great mom."

"She certainly is," Nestle responded.

"She is one of the most beautiful women I have ever met," I said.

She smiled. "Agreed. What else?"

"She is very direct,"

"She can be," she said. "Other thoughts?"

"She has a certain characteristic about her that makes others . . . enjoy her presence . . . want to be her friend. It's an energy. Maybe charisma."

She smiled again. "Very perceptive. So, what about you and Linda? Anything going on there?"

That should not have surprised me, but I found myself searching for exactly what *was* going on.

"How about something to drink?" she asked. I needed a drink. I followed her into a large kitchen. She poured us both some fruit tea and motioned for me to sit on a couch in another part of the kitchen next to a fireplace. Another sanctuary from wild animals.

"Do you mind if I talk for a few minutes?" she asked.

I sipped my fruit tea and leaned back.

Chapter Fifty-Seven

We were sitting somewhat close to each other. Personal Space. She turned toward me. I was already leaning against the arm of the couch.

She looked at me for a few seconds. I tried to appear pleasant. Maybe she was sweating me out and wanted me to make a confession. *I admit it. I stole Linda's silverware. I confessed to Cecil May Turnbow.* Maybe she thought I was such a disappointment, she was going to confiscate my fruit tea and make me go wait on the front porch.

"I know the reason Linda wanted us to talk has to do with helping Richard." She smiled and said, "I've watched Richard grow up and feel like a second mother to him in many ways. I'm guessing you are learning about Richard through Linda and some others."

She paused and looked out the window. I was ready to bolt if she yelled, *Bobcat!* "But remember that the key person in Richard's life is Linda. He is like her in many ways. So maybe by me talking about Linda, you'll understand more about Richard." She shrugged. "At least that's what I think."

"I can see why Linda is interested in you. You are handsome, honest, intelligent, and know how to treat a lady. And her son."

Wait. What?

I held up my hand. "Did you say Linda is interested in me?"

She patted me on the shoulder. "Calm down. She is certainly interested in you because of Richard. According to her, you are a *God-send.* And that's the purpose of our conversation. I'm just asking if there's more there. And don't tell me that you haven't thought about it."

I was again blindsided. The only thing Cecil May asked was if I wanted another cookie. I searched for an answer. Linda smiled and decided to continue.

"So, let's talk about Linda. You may or may not know this, but Linda sets a new humility record when it comes to not tooting her own horn.

"For example, did you know that she was valedictorian of her high school class of over two hundred students?"

I didn't know that.

"Did you know that she had full scholarship offers to several universities?"

I didn't know that.

"Some were academic scholarships. Some were cheerleading scholarships, which was unheard of. And some were cheerleading and dance."

"I didn't know she was a cheerleader. I certainly didn't know anything about dance. Or being the valedictorian. Or the scholarships."

Nestle nodded as if to confirm her suspicions. "I didn't know about any of that for years. And even then, Linda didn't bring it up. I'd see an old picture somewhere or hear Richard say something. She was an All-American Cheerleader. And the pompon routines she created were off the scale. They were dance. They were fast and popular and several universities from all over the nation wanted her to create their choreography as well as to be one of the squad."

I shook my head. She never shared any of that.

"As you know, I guess, plans changed when she got married and Richard came along. College went out the window. And she found herself a single mom. She got her bachelor's degree by taking classes at night. During this time, she worked at a men's clothing store and as a secretary in a hospital.

"When they moved to the Smokies, she began working in hotels. She learned the business from the inside. She worked at the front desk. She helped with whatever needed to be done. If they were short-handed, she pitched in to change beds and clean up rooms. She helped in the kitchen. She worked as a server for banquets. Along the way, she saw how hotels attracted groups. She learned how they packaged trips.

"A few years ago, she was offered a job at Trillium. They love her. She loves Trillium. She has contributed in a major way. I'm sure you've heard very little about that."

I nodded and she took a drink, then settled back on the couch.

"She is beyond competent in everything she sets her mind to. Is it any surprise that Richard is already achieving great things?

"No."

"Did you go to *The Harvest?*"

"Yes."

"What was your impression?"

"Positive. I saw a lot of good being done for the community."

"Linda probably left out the part that she was the guiding force in creating the Coffee Shop."

"She did."

Nestle smiled. "Yeah. That's what I thought. Linda and Richard began going to that church just as it was getting started. The sanctuary was built but they ran out of funds to complete the kitchen. Linda saw the potential for community service and raised the money to equip it. Then she, Pastor Jimmy and another one or two formed a master plan for how the Coffee Shop could be used.

"From the first week it was open, people started showing up. Widows, widowers, elderly couples, lonely people, seekers, even some homeless folks. Some of these are people who hadn't set foot inside a church for years. But they came to the Coffee Shop because they could be a part of something. Plus, they are loved and cared for. The Coffee Shop has served a bunch of people. It has saved the lives of a lot of very good people who needed some place to belong.

"Since then, more of the master plan has come into being. Every Monday and Thursday, an exercise class is held. There's a gym that adjoins one side of the Coffee Shop. They exercise and then come over to eat and visit at the Coffee Shop. Linda tells me over one hundred people from the community come to exercise class each time the doors are open. There's also a clothes closet and food pantry for those who need it. Guess who helps keep both of those supplied, organized and manned?"

She paused and I let all of that sink in. "Pretty impressive isn't she?"

"Very."

"I could tell you a lot more stories like that. The way Linda sees a need and develops a plan to meet the need. But you get the idea. So, let me jump horses. As you indicated, you've noticed how drop-dead gorgeous Linda is."

"I have."

"Good. Just checking. I have never met anyone as beautiful as Linda. You don't strike me as a man who has spent a lot of time at the makeup counter, so you don't know how much time and trouble women spend in the interest of beauty. We have to work at it. There are all kinds of stuff we apply at the beginning of the day and take off at the end of it. There's a lot more I could explain, but I don't want to scare you.

“Did you know she uses very little makeup? That probably doesn’t mean anything to you but that’s very unusual. She doesn’t go to the tanning bed. She is quite simply a natural beauty.

“I have been with her when she jumped out of the shower, threw on some sweats and drove to Kroger. Men almost ran their shopping carts into the frozen foods, trying to catch a glimpse of her.”

“Maybe you, too,” I added. Just trying to be helpful.

She smiled widely, “My point is I have to work at it. She was born with it. Here’s something else. Did you know that she’s been asked to model?”

“No.”

“At every hotel she’s worked at, I think, she was asked to be in their ad. Ad agencies have asked her to model for photo shoots in Gatlinburg, Pigeon Forge, Sevierville, Knoxville and surrounding areas. She’s been approached more than once by modeling agencies, trying to sign her up. Every time, she has said no. She doesn’t want that kind of attention. That’s not Linda.”

Finally, she said, “Linda is one of a kind. She has been the best friend I could ever ask for. She is self-sufficient and self-made, in many ways. She does not fear a challenge. She builds up others and helps them feel better about who they are and what they can accomplish.

“At the same time, I think there is something down deep in her that is lonely. I think she would love to share all of who she is with someone else. It would take a very special person not to be overwhelmed by that. It would take a very special person to recognize all that she has to offer. And it would take a very wise person to understand what she needs.”

We heard footsteps and a voice that said, “Linda’s back.”

She came in and joined us.

“Finished?” she asked.

“One more thing,” Nestle said. “You must understand her commitment to God. She and her son are very active Christians. I don’t completely get it. You may not either. But you do have to acknowledge it. “

Chapter Fifty-Eight

Note to self: *The next time I travel to Wears Valley, bring more clothes.*

The noontime air felt good. Linda had the windows down. We were heading toward Townsend, which is at the west end of Wears Valley Road.

We stopped at a restaurant called the *Apple Valley Country Cafe*. It was in the middle of a small cluster of shops at the base of a mountain. At the cafe, you stand in line and place your order. When you place your order, you can sit wherever you want. There were two tour buses in the parking lot, so when we got to the small restaurant, it was full. We stood in line and ordered. Linda got vegetable soup. I got vegetable soup and a ham and cheese sandwich. We found a table outside on the porch.

As we walked out to the porch, I looked to see if Nestle was correct. She was. The geezers from the tour buses gawked at her. They stopped eating mid-bite. I went over the Heimlich maneuver the school nurse had demonstrated yet again during In-Service. I should pay more attention next year.

I looked at Linda. She was not dressed to impress. She still was wearing the shirt over her leggings. The shirt was large for her. But that didn't seem to stop the old goats from watching her every step.

"So, how did it go?" Linda asked.

"For a Marketing Director, you do a terrible job on yourself," I said.

"Assistant Marketing Director. And what are you talking about?"

"I learned a lot of things about you from Nestle, that's all."

"Okay, I'll bite. Like what?"

"You were the valedictorian of your class in high school."

"Yes, that's true."

"And I've never heard anything about that."

"It never came up."

"You had some scholarship offers."

"Yep."

"And you can dance so well that several colleges offered you full scholarships."

"Yes. Is that important?"

"Well, I told you about Jillian dancing with Zachary. Then I told you about Jillian dancing with me. You never shared how well you could dance."

"I didn't want to interrupt."

"It never occurred to you to say anything like, *I can dance, too.*"

"You were talking about Jillian, not me."

Our number was called and I brought our food back to the table. The sun had warmed things up. It was a great day to be eating on the porch. "Anything else you want to share?" she asked.

So, I regaled her with Nestle's accolades. Linda simply listened. She didn't say *Bless her heart* or try to downplay any of the compliments. She let me repeat them. We were about through and ready to leave when I said, "There's one other thing. She said you were a male magnet."

That made Linda laugh.

"She said that you could jump out of the shower with no make-up on and still receive looks from men at Kroger."

That made her smile, too. "I have to say something here. That's not true."

"Really? Let's find out. You go first and I'll video whatever happens with my phone."

She looked at me for several seconds and said, "Are you serious?"

"Just humor me."

"You are going to video those old men to see how they respond as I walk past them?"

"Yep."

She shook her head but stood up. "Roll it Spielberg."

Chapter Fifty-Nine

We were walking along the Chestnut Ridge Trail. Judging from the parking lot at the trailhead, we had it to ourselves. On the way, Linda announced that she needed some exercise and this was one of her favorite hikes. She put her Trillium Inn cap on, tucked her ponytail through the back and that's what I was looking at as we went deeper into the park. It bounced with every step she took.

The trail was full of ferns and rhododendrons. "There are more varieties of flowers in the first three hundred yards of this trail than I've ever seen," Linda said. "But you'll have to come back in April for that."

She turned around and looked at me. "Is that a date?" She lingered on that, smiled, and continued bouncing down the trail. We had traveled about seven miles when she decided to rest. Although it could have been about a mile. We sat on a boulder in a clearing.

The trees were in full color. Linda saw me looking at them. "What's your favorite of all the trees you see?" I looked at the reds, oranges, yellows, and all shades in between.

"It is close to a tie," I said.

"That sounds familiar," she said, still looking at the trees.

"I guess I would have to say, at least for today, that maple over there."

“I hope you’re not always that fickle,” she said.

“I’m not.” Uh-oh.

“Good. I will not give you a hard time here on the trail. Doesn’t it look like a bouquet? I love to see the different colors next to each other. Look at that Dogwood, next to the Sassafras and the Sourwood. And the Sweet Gum next to the Red Maple you were talking about. They look pretty similar, don’t you think? “ She was pointing and looking. “See the yellow tree? That’s my favorite. It’s a Beech. An American Beech to be precise. That other yellow tree is a Yellow Birch. God’s handiwork is amazing.”

She turned toward me and said, “I learned about trees while Richard was getting his Forestry merit badge. He was required to be able to identify and make a field notebook of fifteen species of trees, wild shrubs and vines. So he included one hundred species in his notebook.”

“Were you involved?” I asked.

“Well, enough to know that this tree is a Fraser fir. And that is an Umbrella tree. It blooms during the summer. Okay, break’s over. Let’s head back.”

She was walking fast. She talked during some of it. At one point, she said, “You’re not looking at me the way you said those old men were back at the restaurant, are you?”

“Who me?” I wheezed.

Chapter Sixty

The next stop was back at Linda's home, about twilight. Fortunately, I got to take a shower. I found my Orvis flannel shirt, washed and ironed, along with my boxers from the night before. Also washed and ironed, I should add.

After I finished hosing off, I found Linda in the kitchen. I was not used to a female getting ready faster than me. She had on a white sweater with a lot of buttons in the front. She wore a necklace with several silver strands. She also wore some earrings composed of little blue, black and red bead tapestries, probably made by the Cherokee Indians, just over the mountains in North Carolina. She was wearing some faded jeans and moccasins. Her hair had been washed and was kind of wavy on her shoulders.

She looked at me and smiled. "I like your selection," she said. "I was hoping you'd wear that."

I smiled, too. "You look beautiful," I said.

She paused to acknowledge my compliment with a bright smile.

"Thank you. You need to pack a bag because – oh yeah, you don't have a bag . . . or anything to pack, do you?"

It was a line that seemed to never get old.

"In that case," she said, "follow me."

We were back in the Jeep Cherokee. After a few miles, she turned off Wears Valley Road and we began to ascend rapidly, amid a lot of curves and switchbacks. After a few minutes, she turned on a gravel road and then onto a dirt road, still climbing, until the headlights revealed a cattle gate with a locked chain around it. Linda told me the combination and I opened the lock and then opened the gate. Linda drove through and I relocked the gate. We continued to go up for a few minutes over a farm road. When we got to the tree line, we got out. Linda handed me a picnic basket and a larger case. She strapped on a backpack and took out a flashlight. "Walk this way."

"Yes master."

"What?"

"*Young Frankenstein?*"

"Huh?"

"I think it was before your time."

"Okay. Well, walk this way, just the same.

We walked up a trail for a few minutes until we came to another gate. This was more of a people gate. Too narrow for a vehicle. The gate and the fence on either side were at least eight feet tall and had razor wire at the top. She opened the lock with a combination code and we walked through. She illuminated the area with her flashlight. In the middle of the area was a large flight of steps. She began to climb them.

It turned out there were many flights of steps. "This is top secret. Nobody knows about this," she said.

"Good," I said. "Your secret is safe with me. I have no idea where we are or what we're doing."

She kept climbing.

I think the air was beginning to get thin. Or maybe it was just my lungs giving out. Either way, we came to the top. Linda unlocked another door and we walked up more stairs into a room. She used her light to go to a breaker box. Some small lights came on around the ceiling. We were standing in the middle of a fully furnished room. Linda turned on a lamp and we put our stuff on the floor.

There was a small dining table, couch, a club chair, a coffee table and an end table. In a corner was a refrigerator, stove, oven and a sink. There was a fireplace on another wall. And windows everywhere else.

Linda turned and put her arms around me. "You've received some surprises from others lately. "My turn."

Chapter Sixty-One

"Is this what I think it is?" I asked.

"What do you think it is?"

"A fire tower."

She nodded.

I had no words. I sat on the couch while Linda lit the gas fireplace and stowed our gear. Well, her gear. She sat down beside me. She looked around and smiled.

"This belongs to a very dear friend of mine."

I looked around. "You've been here with him?"

"Of course. It would be a little difficult to borrow if I hadn't been here before."

"I'd like to be his friend, too."

"Maybe you already are. Have you ever heard of Isaiah Gladstone?"

"No, I can't say that I have."

"Oh, I thought you might have gone to school together."

"No, do you know what year he graduated?"

"Not really. I do know he just turned eighty-eight."

I smiled. "He might have been a senior when I was a freshman. Do you share this place with all your freeloading visitors?"

She paused. "I've only shared it with one other."

She didn't elaborate, so I let it go. I spent the next few minutes admiring the place. A telescope and binoculars were positioned next to a bank of windows. There was also a video monitor displaying images from some cameras down below. We looked at some board games and a bookshelf full of old books including my favorite Hardy Boys book, *Cabin Island*. There was an emergency weather radio, a CB radio and some long-range walkie talkies.

Linda announced that she had brought supper and went about getting things ready. She said she needed no help, so I did more exploring. I found a photo album in the bookcase. It contained photos of the fire tower in years gone by, photos of the renovation, and a photo of a very distinguished gentleman and Linda. I assumed I was looking at Isaiah.

The photo was an eight by ten. It was the only large photograph in the book. He had his arm around her and she was smiling brightly. They were sitting on the couch in this room. There was a story here. Linda really did go for older men. I looked at the photo some more. I'm not sure what the connection was with Isaiah, but Linda was high voltage on any level. I hoped paramedics were standing by when the photo was taken.

The little lights in the ceiling went out and I turned around. The lamp had been turned off. The table now had a tablecloth and two candles which were lit. On each side were placemats, dishes, silverware and glasses.

Linda was standing behind the table. Being that far up, it may be what Heaven is like. I hope so. Illuminated by only the flames of the candles, she smiled at me.

"Four months ago, I saw you for the first time," she said. "I was so exasperated during the deposition that I almost took on that half-witted blow hard myself. But then I would have gone to prison. Thank goodness our two attorneys came to save the day. I remember the first time I saw you. I noticed two things. You were handsome and you didn't dress like an attorney. After that, I was so consumed with not committing a felony that I didn't notice you too much. Besides, I've seen handsome before.

"You stole my heart through Richard. You spent time with him. You encouraged him. You validated him in ways that he desperately needed. When we spent the night with you at the Lodge, I saw why Richard liked you so much. I did, too.

"Just so you don't make a break for the steps, which I wouldn't recommend in the dark, I'm talking about a relationship that encompasses Richard, me, and you. I am just glad that you came into our lives. I don't care if your next sentence is to tell me that Jillian is down at a chapel in Gatlinburg with a wedding license and a dance coach.

"From what I can see, Jillian is a good person and loves you. She is my friend and I'm happy for you both. As long as you stay in Richard's life, that's all I need."

Chapter Sixty-Two

Linda provided a gourmet meal. It came compliments of her friends at Trillium Inn.

After the meal, we were sitting on the couch.

"We are here because I mentioned wanting to stay in a fire tower."

"Mark that off your List of Dream Places," she said.

"I am beyond surprised and delighted. Tell me about it," I said. "Who is Isaiah Gladstone?"

Linda folded her arms around her and took a breath. "I met Isaiah many years ago. We had just moved here, from Knoxville. I was a young single mom, trying to start over." She wriggled to get more comfortable. "The only problem was that I had no house, a job that didn't pay much and would never pay much, and no support group. It was really an ambitious move. I'm still not sure whether to call it gutsy or naive.

"I found a place to stay in the guest apartment of a very sweet elderly couple in Gatlinburg. The wife even helped take care of Richard. They knew that I had no money and sometimes told me to forget the rent. They also bought clothes for Richard and food for me.

"Meanwhile, I was trying to find a way to make a living. There were no department stores or clothing stores, so I couldn't do that.

It looked bleak. I had no experience in anything else and was still working on my degree. One day, I applied for a job at a hotel in Gatlinburg. Isaiah happened to be behind the counter. He asked me where I had worked. I told him that I had never worked in a hotel.

"He hired me on the spot. I began as a housekeeper, cleaning the rooms. I became the best housekeeper I could be. Once or twice a week, he'd see me and ask how it was going. He told me I was doing a good job and that I was the hardest worker he'd ever seen. I think he wanted to see if I would stick it out. After a couple of months, he invited me to a sandwich shop. He asked me about Richard. He asked where I lived. He asked me what I wanted in life. Then he asked me about my immediate plans.

"What I didn't realize was that he was not simply some kind old front desk clerk. He owned the hotel. Not just that one, but two others. He also owned other businesses in Gatlinburg and Pigeon Forge. Old Isaiah was probably the richest man in Sevier County.

"On that day in the sandwich shop, he took my hand. He said he decided that he wanted to help me, but it had to be our secret. You are the first person I have ever told. Not Nestle, not even Richard completely. Isaiah handed me an envelope that contained more cash than I had ever seen and said, *I want you to go buy some clothes for you and Richard. And then we're going to find you a place to live.*

"Isaiah owned the house that we now live in. He lived in it at one time. A couple of weeks after our lunch, he drove me to the house and let me look around. Then he handed me the keys and said it was my new home. No rent. No strings attached. After quite a bit of discussion, he convinced me that I should shut up and quit looking a gift horse in the mouth. We lived there very happily. At least once a month, Isaiah would come eat with us.

"Five years after that, he asked me to meet him at his lawyer's office. The lawyer showed me where to sign. Isaiah handed me the deed. The only stipulation was that it had to be our secret.

"Isaiah's wife had died. He had a couple of children, but they moved far away and didn't come see him. He gave them each a large sum of money and told them to take care of it. That's all there was. Well, that wasn't all of Isaiah's money, but it was all of *their* money from Isaiah.

"Isaiah saw to it that I worked in many areas of the hotel, from operations to marketing to sales. I not only learned on the job. I learned from him. I learned why his guests came back year after year. I learned about assembling a good team.

"Isaiah encouraged me to pursue the job at Trillium. He said it was a rare opportunity. He wanted me to see how a World Class organization runs their day-to-day business. I don't know if he had anything to do with me getting the job, but I wouldn't doubt it.

"I have become the daughter that he never had. He is like a father that I always wanted. What we're sitting in is one of Isaiah's projects. He heard that the fire tower was going to be decommissioned. It was not on park land, so he bought it. He let it sit for a few years and decided to turn it into a room with a view.

"Evidently, you and Isaiah have similar tastes."

She paused and smiled.

"I helped him decorate it. I insisted that we have a christening service. The only problem was that he wanted to keep it a secret or the whole county would be crawling with people wanting to see it. Tomorrow you'll see that although he enlarged the structure of this room, it still looks like a fire tower on the outside. It looks old and faded. So, the christening consisted of Richard, Isaiah and me.

"To my knowledge, except for the workers who were from out of state, you make only the fourth person to see the inside of the fire tower."

"Wait, are you forgetting the other person who has been here with you? You said you'd been here with Isaiah and one other person."

"I was wondering if you remembered," she said with a smile. It was Richard."

Chapter Sixty-Three

Isaiah was not just a fond memory. The old boy was still kicking and a regular part of Linda's life. He didn't make it up the stairs much anymore, but he did see Linda at least once a month. In fact, she asked him if she could take me to the fire tower.

He still worked at the same hotel. And most people still knew him as the front desk clerk. "He could do anything or nothing at all, but what he enjoys most is going to work every day," Linda said.

Meanwhile, we were in a five-hundred-foot-high fire tower on top of a mountain. We had a good view. We could see the lights of communities. We could see the blinking lights of planes and satellites. It was a good night to be in a fire tower on a mountain.

I could tell the temperature was dropping. We turned up the fireplace. The room couldn't have been any more comfortable or cozy. Linda walked toward the bathroom with a bag. On the way, she tossed something to me. "Your pajamas," she said.

In a few minutes, she came out, still in her clothes. That was fine, except I had on my pjs. She started laughing. "I'm sorry but those look pretty funny," she said. "Very retro."

I smiled. "May I remind you who gave them to me?" I said. "Who gave them to *you?*"

She began laughing even louder.

Then it hit me. "Isaiah."

She was laughing so hard, she was crying, so she just nodded and pointed to the initials on the pocket – *I.G.*

"Do I want to ask why you have the pajamas of an eighty-eight-year-old man?"

She managed to partially regain her composure and said, "I told him about you some time ago. The next time he saw me, he gave me the pajamas and said they might come in handy. Be grateful that I didn't take the robe and slippers." She motioned toward the bathroom. "Your turn."

I walked into the bathroom. It was small but efficient. It had a toilet, a sink and a small shower. On a little shelf was a small Tupperware container - my toiletries from the house.

I came out of the bathroom to near darkness. The lights were off. I stood there until my eyes adjusted. The fireplace was still on, but it had been turned down to a glow. Linda was sitting in a chair on the other side of the room. As my eyes adjusted, I could see that she had on her own version of Fire Tower pajamas. I could make out a blue shirt and pants, each sporting the Trillium logo.

The floor was now covered with a mattress and some blankets. She crawled onto them and motioned for me to follow. We were lying side by side. "I am so glad we are here," she said.

"Me, too. I can't tell you how much this means to me, Linda."

"Well, this is only half the night's surprise. You told us that one of the things on your Wish List was a fire tower."

"And here we are. It's still hard to believe."

"Do you remember what the other was that you mentioned?"

I thought about that. "I mentioned wanting to see the stars."

"Yes. I adapted this wish a little. You mentioned a campsite in South Dakota. This isn't South Dakota, but you still might like the view. She picked up a remote control and said, "Stuart, I give you, the stars of the Smokies."

She pushed a button. I heard a whir and a buzz. The ceiling of the fire tower disappeared. There above us was a night sky boasting more stars than I had ever seen. And we were watching them from a fire tower.

Chapter Sixty-Four

I was in total shock.

"I'm just spitballing here, but this seems better than leaning back in a camp chair at a campground," Linda commented.

It was. I had never seen nor heard of anything like this.

"The roof just slides away and rolls up," Linda explained. "We're looking through glass. It's a huge sky roof." She gave me time to absorb this. We pointed to various stars and constellations. Even the moon seemed brighter.

"Back at the Lodge, when you mentioned that one of the places you hoped to see was a fire tower, Richard immediately registered that with me. Then, when you said that your next place was a unique spot to see the stars, we knew if things worked out, we'd share our well-kept secret with you.

"And things have worked out," I said.

"They have."

We spent a long time looking at the sky. Then Linda said, "I can't tell you how happy I am to be here. I hope you're having a good time."

"Are you kidding? You have gone so far beyond anything I could have imagined," I said. "I will always remember this night."

Chapter Sixty-Five

I awakened once more to the smell of food.

We had stayed up for as long as we could, watching the stars and talking. I opened my eyes. I had no idea what time it was. The room was full of light. Linda was by the stove, cooking pancakes. She looked very fresh.

While I remained on the pallet during the night, Linda moved to the couch. I could now see blue sky through the ceiling.

I sat up and looked out the windows. There were hues in the sky of purple and blue. The forest canopy was red, gold and orange. The clouds were coming in over the tallest peaks of the mountains. A few hearty winged souls were on a rail by the window. I could hear them. They were happy.

"Good morning!" she said.

I smiled.

"There's coffee on the counter."

"Thanks," I said, trying to sound like a morning person. I walked over in Isaiah's pajamas and poured a cup.

She giggled and flipped a pancake. She was wearing a long sleeve tan shirt with a lot of embroidery on it. One side wrapped around the other. I saw no buttons but it stayed together somehow. She wore jeans and hiking boots.

"How long have you been up?" I asked.

"A couple of hours. Are you ready to eat?"

Breakfast consisted of blueberry pancakes. They were the best I'd ever had. She had some other fruit sliced and ready to eat, as well.

Afterwards, I used the shower. When it was time to go, Linda took out a camera and took several photos of us in the room and on the steps. I didn't want to leave.

Once on the ground, I looked up at the fire tower. I was amazed to see that it indeed did look old and faded, like no one had used it in years.

We spent part of the morning hiking a trail in the surrounding area. Isaiah owned a good bit of land around the fire tower. Some of the trail went through the park. As we were walking toward a stream, Linda caught my belt from the back and pulled it. That's when I saw the bear. It was walking across the trail. It was fifty yards in front of us and didn't see us. Or if it did, it wasn't concerned. Or hungry. We waited until it disappeared and continued our hike.

I love to hike, especially in the mountains. Especially on such a beautiful day. Especially in such a spectacular place. Especially with a spectacular host. I wondered if being eaten by a bear would get me into the photo album.

Chapter Sixty-Six

Back at the Lodge, I was watching three squirrels at my bird feeder. They knocked the feed in every direction and scared each other away. It said on the instructions that the feeder would keep squirrels out. The feeder was pressure sensitive, meaning that the weight of a squirrel would cause the glass door of the feeder to shut. Apparently, the squirrels had figured out that if they didn't touch the pressure sensitive bar, they could get to the food. It's probably humbling to the bird feeder manufacturer people that three squirrels are smarter than all of them.

There were some cardinals and sparrows watching the spectacle from a few feet away. They were not amused. I watched to see how the squirrels were getting up to the feeder. To my amazement, they just scaled up the pole with all four limbs wrapped around it. When I bought the feeder at the local hardware store, the owner suggested I purchase something called Squirrel-Slip "for when the squirrels come to the picnic. And they will." It was non-toxic and wouldn't hurt the birds if it got on their feathers. The soy and coconut oil were supposed to keep the little varmints at bay.

So, I found the container and would shortly apply Squirrel Slip to the pole. Maybe that would help the bird business.

It was Friday. I talked to Jillian for some time the night before. She was not happy that I had spent time with Linda again. But she also trusted us and acknowledged that she was there and Linda was here. "You have to be somewhere, I guess," she said. "I was just hoping it would be just you in the Lodge."

The pretrial work in Los Angeles was taking longer than anticipated. She was asked to be on the actual litigation team. They told her that she received good reviews during the last few weeks. They needed a female on the team for a case on sexual harassment. They thought she would be perfect.

I thought about that. An attractive, intelligent, savvy, charismatic, fast thinking, articulate attorney, representing these three women in a sexual harassment case. It was a good move for Whitsitt's firm. And a chance for Jillian to litigate on a major stage.

That would also mean more time away from home. But, she said she would be back soon for a visit. She didn't know exactly when that would be. Maybe in a week. Maybe longer. So much for Fall Break with Jillian.

My phone beeped. I sometimes get enough reception for a text. Rarely but occasionally. It was a text from Linda, who was back at work. Her note said:

Pumpkin carving contest.

Happy Hollow Road.

This Saturday evening.

Sharp implements and newspaper will be provided.

P.S. Bring your imagination and some extra clothes!

Chapter Sixty-Seven

I drank coffee on Saturday and watched the squirrels take turns sliding down the bird feeder pole. Operation Squirrel Slip had begun. They got about halfway up and slid back down. The bright red male cardinal was eating bird seed from the feeder. He looked smug.

A FedEx truck pulled up outside. A courier hopped out and said, "Stuart Jensen?"

I nodded.

"Good! You weren't easy to find."

It was from Jillian. I opened it.

The first thing I saw were the flowers. A dozen white roses with a vase encased in foam . The next was a clock. The next was a bag of coffee. Then there was the framed photo. And finally an envelope.

I opened the envelope to find a handwritten letter on Ritz Carlton stationary.

Dear Stuart,

Hello from Los Angeles! I did some checking and learned that it is 1,930 air miles from Los Angeles to Spruceviile. It is 2,183 miles by Frank.

As I write to you, it is evening. I'm in my room

on the 21std floor. I can see the illuminated City of Angels and the silhouette of the San Gabriel Mountains. My work here has been the most challenging, borderline intimidating, that I have ever had. But it is exhilarating, and I am grateful for the opportunity to work with some of the nation's top legal minds.

I hope you are doing well, Sweetheart. I am so sorry that I missed Fall Break. We will have to have our own version of it when I return. Speaking of returning, I should be back next Saturday. As I write this, that's nine days away. So that you don't forget, I've included a clock that will tell you exactly how long it will be until touchdown in Knoxville. I hope you can be there to pick me up.

I have included some coffee that I fell in love with out here. You can make it for me at the Lodge. If you can choke down school coffee, you may think you have died and gone to Heaven when you drink this. You can also use it to keep your energy up on Saturday.

Has anyone ever given you flowers before? Well, I wanted to. It occurred to me that you might not have a vase, so I've included one of those, too.

And you'll see a photo of yours truly with The Disney Concert Hall in the background. I want you to be able to pick me out at the airport.

I know that commuting to work across the nation is not a strategic move for our relationship. Especially with you hanging out with other gorgeous women.

I love you Stuart. Can't wait to see you!

Love,

Jillian

I reread the letter. I looked at the flowers. I don't know much about flowers, but these were very pretty. She was right. I had never been given flowers before. And I had no vase at the Lodge. I'm not sure I had one at the house. I took out her vase. It was porcelain. Engraved at the top in script was *Jillian loves Stuart.*

I looked at the digital clock. The thing was actually running backwards. Seven days, eight hours, fifteen minutes and forty-eight seconds. Forty-seven. Forty-six...

The West Coast coffee smelled good.

Which brought me to the photo. There Jillian stood, with the Disney Concert Hall in the background. She had on a white dress with high heels. She was smiling brightly and holding a professional sign, about the size of a real estate sign you see in someone's front lawn. It said, *Jillian loves Stuart.*

Attached was a sticky note: *FYI, to my Match.com traumatized friend. This is a recent photo .*

My first thought, as usual, was Wow!

It was seven days to see Jillian. It was seven hours to see Linda. I looked at the sack of West Coast coffee. I made a fresh pot.

Chapter Sixty-Eight

I turned onto Happy Hollow Road with more clothes this time. I had a feeling I'd be going with Linda and Richard to church in the morning. What did they wear on Sundays at *The Harvest?* I didn't know but brought a coat and tie, just in case.

Before I left, I placed Jillian's photo on my bedside table. I left the flowers on the kitchen counter. And the coffee. And the clock.

When I walked up to Linda's porch, I was met by a scarecrow, sitting in a chair. He was holding a sign,

Welcome Stuart!

If I only had a brain

How's yours working?

I seemed to inspire signs lately. Before I could knock on the door, it opened. Linda came out and gave me a hug. She kissed me on the cheek and said, "Welcome back!"

We walked back to Frank and got my clothes. Richard had taken Scout to a preliminary training session. As we walked back past the scarecrow, I said, "That's not Isaiah, is it?"

She smirked. That's the description I assigned to her expression. I'd seen her make it before. My interpretation of it was, *I know that in your mind that was funny.*

"Besides your clothes and brain, did you bring any creative thoughts with you?" she asked.

"I hope so." I had looked at several websites for jack-o-lantern designs. I had a couple of sketches in my pocket. But I don't think she was talking about pumpkins.

Linda sported a white baseball jersey with green sleeves and some faded jeans. I told her that she looked good. She looked at my t-shirt from the Boulder Lake Lodge and said, "I'm going to miss Mr. Orvis."

"Yes, he couldn't make it this trip. But he sends his regards."

"That's too bad. He was like a member of the family."

"Speaking of clothes," I said. "Are you going to reveal why you happened to have men's boxer shorts on the ready in my time of need?"

She took my clothes and hung them in the hall closet. She sat on a kitchen chair and smiled. "I bought them for the clothes closet at church. They are always in high demand. I held back a package on the chance that they might be needed here."

"When did you decide to hold the package back?" I asked.

She smiled. "A week before *Big Orange Day.*"

I pondered that. "So, back in September, you anticipated that I might be spending the night here sometime?"

She looked at me and said, "Yes."

"And the shaving cream and razor?"

She turned red. "I bought what I thought you'd need if you ever stayed here. I wanted to be ready.

"Good thing." It momentarily entered my mind to tell her about Jillian's shipment. But, unlike the scarecrow outside, my brain kicked in and said that was a bad idea. So, instead, I showed her the video I took at the *Apple Valley Country Café.* It was of the older men's reactions as she went by.

Linda looked at the video with her mouth open. She shook her head. "I can't believe you did that!" she said.

"It was a scientific experiment."

She laughed and shook her head. "You are crazy."

"So, here's the question. Did those men stop what they were doing and stare at you as you walked by? Yes or No?"

She looked at me. The spark in her eyes was there. She smiled. "Yes."

Chapter Sixty-Nine

I had been had.

Linda and Richard were experienced professionals when it came to carving pumpkins. Not one, but both were ringers. I was not going to win.

We were on the floor in the Great Room. The goop that we dug out from the pumpkins was in a big plastic bowl in the middle of us. Scout was having a fine time inspecting it. My preparation was for a face. It was a good face with eyebrows and ears. Linda was working on a jack-o-lantern that looked like a dog's face, complete with the big ears. It was in honor of Scout. And Richard was completing a rendering of Frank. I'm serious.

We put the pumpkins on the hearth. Linda took pictures. She came back with three ribbons. First place went to Richard. Second place went to Linda. The third place ribbon said Nice Try. Each included our names in gold letters at the top. She insisted that each of us hold our pumpkin, with ribbon attached, for a photo.

I pointed out, "You created that ribbon before the contest. Were you that confident I'd finish last?"

She just smiled.

Richard wanted to see the Halloween decorations in Gatlinburg, so we took them in. There were many very large pumpkins on display. When I say large, I'm talking the size of one of those trash cans before the bears squished it. And corn stalks everywhere you looked, with many lighted displays.

Linda wanted to walk down Main Street in Gatlinburg and soak up the full impact of the impressive Halloween scenes. Fortunately, there was no University of Tennessee football game that weekend so the crowd was manageable. We stopped in the Village and I bought some hot chocolate for us at the *Donut Friar*.

Richard saw some friends from school. We agreed to meet back in the Village in an hour. As we sat at a table in the courtyard, Linda said, "Okay, if you'd like, you can tell me about Jillian."

I looked at her.

"I know she couldn't be out in Los Angeles, knowing that you've been with me, and not do something. So, let's hear it."

"With you?"

"Yes. I'm guessing you told her that you're spending a good part of your Fall Break with us."

"Yes. I didn't give too many details, and none about the fire tower."

She drank some hot chocolate and waited for more.

I told her about the letter and each gift. She asked me to describe the photo.

She looked at the fountain in the courtyard and shook her head. ""Are you always this honest?" she asked.

"So far."

Linda drank some more hot chocolate, then asked, "Isn't this where Jillian likes to go?"

I explained it was the cemetery.

"Let's go see it," she said.

"She likes to see it in the daytime so she can think and look out at the view."

"Let's go see it," she repeated.

"You know it's dark and practically Halloween," I reminded her.

"Uh-huh. Is it this way?"

We walked past the art store and past the public restrooms. We followed the road until we came to the *White Oak Flats Cemetery* sign. Due to darkness, we could barely read it. She stood there, taking it in. "Is the bench up there?" she asked, pointing up the hill. You couldn't see it in the darkness. You couldn't see much at all.

"Yep."

"I want to see it."

"Not to be repeating myself, but you do know that its dark and you won't be able to see, and this is a cemetery. It's probably closed."

She took my hand and we began negotiating our way through the monuments as we climbed the hill. Do bears hang out in cemeteries at night?

If Linda was scared or superstitious, she hid it well. The going was slow since we couldn't see. But we didn't hit a single tombstone, and nothing reached out or up to grab us. We arrived at the bench. She looked at it for a few seconds. She walked behind it and put her hands on the back. I think she was trying to imagine Jillian sitting on it.

"Have you ever noticed that cemeteries are often in beautiful spots?" she asked.

I looked down the hill. I could see colorful lights below us on Main Street and lights in cabins from the mountains above. Linda knew the area well enough to know what the daytime view was like.

"I agree with Jillian. It's a good place to get away from it all and think." She was quiet a little longer and said, "I wonder why Jillian chose this place to begin with? I wonder what she thought about. I know she thought about you, but what else?"

That thought had not occurred to me. Had she come up here to think about more than me?

"What would you think about?" I asked.

Linda was still standing behind the bench. She was not sitting. This was Jillian's spot. Not hers. "I'd have to think about these people who are buried here. I would remind myself that because time is rushing past, I must live my life with zest and intention on my way to Heaven,. And then I'd pray."

Chapter Seventy

We went to church the next morning. The service was sincere. The sermon was inspirational. We came home to the enticing smell of a roast and vegetables that Linda had started that morning in her crockpot.

Linda asked Richard and me to help her decorate for Halloween. Then we took a hike up to the Thompson's cabin. Scout went, too, and enjoyed it thoroughly.

Before I left Linda's house, she gave me a present and told me not to open it until I got back to the Lodge

I dutifully waited and unwrapped it when I got back. It was a photo of Linda in a walnut Trillium Inn frame. She was wearing a suede jacket with a lot of fringe. She had on jeans. And leather lace up boots that came up to her knees. She was standing on the bluff. The scene of our first conversation. Behind her was Wears Valley. She was looking directly at the camera. Her brown eyes sparkled. It was a jaw-dropping picture.

Written at the bottom of the photo were these words:

Proverbs 19:21

A letter on Trillium stationary accompanied the photo:

Stuart,

I decided quite impulsively to have Richard take my photo on the spot where we talked. It's for you. It was for Christmas, but since you told me about Jillian's photo . . . well, here's mine, too. I don't know what I was thinking, but I hope you like it.

Hugs, Love, Smiles and Much More,

Linda

I truly didn't know what to think . . . or do with the photo. Jillian's new picture was on my bedside table. I felt awkward about putting the two photos side by side. I also kind of felt that's what Linda wanted me to do. So, that's what I did and fell asleep. It had been a busy Fall Break.

Chapter Seventy-One

I was seated in a large study in a large home in Gatlinburg, across the street from where Battles Grocery Store once was. It was spacious and on one floor. The room's back wall was glass and faced the forest. I liked the room. It had old brown leather chairs, an old brown leather couch, and an old blue tick hound that currently had his head on my leg.

Isaiah Gladstone was fit, agile and looking a hole through me. "Thank you for coming," he said. "I believe Chester likes you."

Chester looked up at me. "I like him, too," I said. It was Monday, a school holiday for a fundraising success. If we were able to raise a certain amount of money, we could have the day off. Funny how that works. So, I slept at the Lodge after my visit with Linda and Richard.

Mr. Gladstone asked me if I minded if he smoked. It was his house, his rules, still polite of him to ask. I smelled the scent as soon as I walked through the front door. He took out a very expensive looking cigar from his humidor and fired it up, taking his time to make sure it was lit properly. He offered me one, but I said no.

He wasn't in a hurry. "As you know, I'm very fond of Linda Eason," he finally said.

I nodded.

"And she is very fond of you."

I smiled but stayed silent.

"That, in itself, got my attention. I have never known her to be truly fond of another man. Well, besides me. She has talked to me about you. She believes that you would be good for Richard."

As he talked, he puffed on his cigar. His eyes never left me. "And so, I wanted to have a look at you and, frankly, see what I think about you. I know this is presumptuous. You are certainly under no obligation to say anything. I assure you that my motives are pure. I want the best for Linda and Richard. I feel protective of her."

I knew he would tell me when to speak.

"And so, if you are so inclined, Stuart, I would like to get to know you."

"It would be an honor to get to know you, Mr. Gladstone. Linda speaks very highly of you. She loves you."

He nodded and checked the business end of his cigar. "Thank you. Call me Isaiah. Tell me about yourself."

I did. I answered his questions. I scratched Chester's ear.

By the time I finished, a cloud of blue smoke had formed above Isaiah's head. "So, are you telling me that your interest is solely in Richard?"

I anticipated this question. That didn't mean I knew how to answer it.

"The short answer is yes."

"What's the longer answer?"

"I cannot have a relationship with Richard without having a relationship with Linda."

Isaiah chose to puff instead of speak. Even after several puffs, he was still silent. He waited me out.

"Did Linda tell you that I have a girlfriend?"

"She did."

"I don't see how I can have a relationship with Linda or anyone else while I am in a relationship with her."

That didn't come out quite the way I intended. It was not on my radar to end things with Jillian. But I didn't really feel the need to clarify it for Isaiah.

He thought about that and said, "So at this point, you are not interested in a romantic relationship with Linda?"

"Correct."

He thought about that, too, and said, "You seem to spend a lot of time with her. Even spend the night sometimes."

"That's true." I thought about mentioning his pajamas but nixed it.

"And it sounds like some of it is when Richard is elsewhere."

I nodded.

"So, if you aren't interested in romance, why are you spending time with her?"

It was a good question.

"I enjoy her company. She has been a good listener. We've had a lot of fun together."

Isaiah smiled. "I can understand that. Of course, I could also say that about Chester, too. "

After another drag, he said, "Linda doesn't know about this little chat. If it's acceptable to you, I'll tell her we talked. I like you, Stuart. I'm a pretty good judge of character. I think you will be a very good friend to Richard. If I can ever help you in that regard, let me know."

We walked to the front door. He shook my hand and said, “I told you that I understand why you are spending so much time with Linda. Do you think she does?”

Chapter Seventy-Two

The first day after Fall Break is not a good one for me. Some teachers enjoy being back in the routine. They enjoy seeing each other and seeing the students. Not me. I need more than a week for that. Even before I got a cup of school coffee, I went to the school library, found a Bible, and looked up Proverbs 19:21, the scripture on Linda's photo.

> *Many are the plans in a person's heart, but it is the Lord's purpose that prevails.*

Chapter Seventy-Three

As close to Halloween as I can get, I schedule *Storytelling* in my class. It's a part of my Speech curriculum. In telling a good story, sometimes there is mystery. Sometimes there is conflict. Sometimes it is a personal narrative. Sometimes it is about someone else. Everyone needs to be able to tell a good story.

On the scheduled day, I borrowed a simulated campfire from the Drama department. It is called BOB, which is an acronym for something. BOB's fan and LED lights simulate a flickering fire against the multicolored silk ribbons that blow in the air.

I ask the students to sit around the fire and tell their stories. They receive a grade, but they also have a lot of fun. It doesn't hurt that they bring some camp food to share. We count donuts and cookies as camp food.

As the day progressed from class to class, I listened to a lot of stories. Some were very good. Some were not. The personal stories were the best. I thought more than once that I had a memorable personal story to tell:

> *Seniors, grab a donut and gather round. Mr. Jensen is going to tell you about the time that he dated a smoking hot woman. This woman was much younger than me and guess what? She thought I was pretty cool. I know! Can you believe it?!*

Now she wasn't only dating me. She wanted to marry me!

I've brought photos from my bedroom. The one in the fringe is Linda. No, she's not my girlfriend. She's another story. The one holding the sign is Jillian. . .

They wouldn't believe it anyway.

Chapter Seventy-Four

It was raining on a Thursday in Wears Valley, where I was waiting in a small restaurant called Stonehouse Pizza. I rarely take a day off work, but I did today. Pastor Jimmy walked over to my booth. I stood up and he hugged me.

He did not look like a preacher. He looked more like a country music entertainer. He was tan and fit.

We were the only ones in the place. Jimmy looked around and commented, “Great pizza here. It will be full after school until about seven tonight.”

We talked about Wears Valley for a minute. “A good place to live,” Jimmy said. The Reverend was easy to talk to and seemed very much at ease. “It was good to see you with Linda and Richard Sunday morning,” he said. “What did you think of the service?”

“I was glad to learn I didn’t have to wear a tie,” I said. “That was a good start.”

He laughed. “Yeah, that’s one of those codes we don’t live by.”

I noticed that he didn’t wear a tie at the service, either. He was dressed casually today, too.

“Just from 30,000 feet, what was your impression?”

I found the service to be very sincere. Pastor Jimmy’s message was encouraging. The singing sounded like angels to me. Of course, the fact that I was sitting next to Linda may have increased the rating. I shared my thoughts with him. Except for the part about Linda. I also didn't tell him that I was responsible for diverting some underwear intended for the homeless.

"Thank you for coming today, Jimmy," I said. "The reason I wanted to meet with you is that I have a situation. And I would like your input."

"I would be honored."

"Well, first, I need you to help me understand something. You are a handsome man. And since there is no ring on your finger, I assume you are single?"

He nodded and smiled. "So what about Linda and me?"

"Yes."

"I appreciate your directness. It has been mentioned to me and to Linda by just about all the members. Especially all the older ladies. More than once. She's single and I'm single. We both love the Lord. Maybe it's God's Will that we marry."

That reminded me of Linda's scripture on her photo, but I chose not to interrupt.

"Understand that I am not a priest. If I want to, nothing prevents me from getting married. And I do think that Linda is – well I know – that Linda is the most beautiful woman I've ever seen. So, I admit the thought has entered my mind. We work on a lot of projects together and I work with the youth, which includes Richard. And more than one good-intentioned soul from our congregation brings it up regularly.

"What I'm about to tell you is going to sound crazy. I know that before I even say it. And I don't expect you to understand fully. But here it is. I feel called by God to be a minister. I want to help the people of Wears Valley in any way I can for as long as I can.

"It's not just about helping them in the sense of providing food, clothes, companionship, inspiration, and shelter. It's about helping them get to Heaven. But it starts with the basics. It's hard for someone to listen about Heaven when he's hungry or lonely.

"I could not do that the way I feel called if I was married. I spend a lot of time with the elderly. I spend a lot of time in assisted living facilities. My ministry often extends into the night. I work with the homeless. I sometimes let them stay with me. I couldn't do nearly as much if I were married.

"I would need to spend time with my wife. I would need to spend quality time with our children. I would not feel comfortable inviting homeless men I know nothing about into our home. I can do that now. I know the risk, but I'm only putting my life at risk. If you read some of the Apostle Paul's writings, you'll find that he was not married and felt that he got more done being single.

"As I said, with Linda sitting in the pews, single and working with me, you may think I'm crazy. It's just the way I feel I'm supposed to live."

I didn't know what to say. He was clearly a man of faith, living his life with purpose and enthusiasm. To bypass a relationship with Linda was inconceivable to me, but not to him. I thanked him for his candor. And, I did think he was crazy on that count.

"I invited you here today to talk about how I can best help Richard. I think you know him and Linda better than most folks. But I also want to fill you in on a few details in my life and get your opinion on how it might affect Richard and any suggestions for the future."

Then I told Jimmy how Linda and I met. And told him about Jillian. I told him about Jillian's perfect storm at Neyland Stadium and her subsequent efforts to reconcile. I told him about my time with Linda and Richard. I left out the fire tower since that was a secret. I left out any mention of Isaiah.

I paused for a second and took a drink of Coke.

He remained silent.

"So what do you think?"

He was a good listener.

He shook his head. "My mind is spinning. I can't imagine what yours is doing. Does Linda know we're talking today?"

"No, I wanted it to be between you and me. Feel free to tell her anything you'd care to."

He nodded. "I've never heard of a situation like this. It is one for the books. I want to help you, but maybe I need to ask you a couple of questions, if you don't mind."

I nodded.

Jimmy said. "In all that you have told me, I have not heard you mention your faith. That is interesting to me, given that Linda's life revolves around hers. I know you have thought about that."

"I have."

"And have you and Linda talked about it?" he asked.

"Not extensively. She asked me to come to the Coffee Shop. She introduced me to you. She invited me to church. She wanted me to experience her world before we talk about it. Ultimately, that may form a boundary for the extent of exposure I have to Richard."

He was silent for a minute. "That sounds like Linda. She wants you to come to your own conclusion about –"he waved his hand – "a tangible Christian lifestyle."

I nodded.

We were both silent. The pizza was gone. We had the place to ourselves.

"I have to ask you the same question you asked me," Jimmy said.

"Okay, shoot."

"What about you and Linda?"

I wondered when that was going to come up. "Well, as I mentioned, I'm sorting things out with Jillian. As you know, Jillian and Linda were friends before I came into the picture. I have shared many of these events with Linda. She has been my primary sounding board. I have tried to keep that boundary between friend and girlfriend."

He smiled. "I think Linda doesn't see that same boundary. And I believe you better buckle up tight, because you are heading for some uncharted waters that include you, Richard and two women who want you."

Chapter Seventy-Five

I just got into my car when I received a call from Linda.

"Richard's old coach is here," she said.

"At your house?"

"Yes, he's still in his car, but he's in the driveway."

"I'm ten minutes away. Don't open the door."

I made it in five minutes. Coach Bodine was just getting out of his car. I could see Linda and Richard watching from the living room window. So far, no police had arrived. I parked closer to the house and stood in the driveway.

He saw me and began to laugh. "So they called you. Are you going to save them from me? Threaten me with a lawsuit?"

He kept walking up.

I didn't say anything. He kept walking.

When he got close enough for me to smell the whisky, I said, "Coach, you need to get back in your car and leave before you get arrested and bad things happen."

He laughed. "Are you going to arrest me?"

"No, not me. I'm just going to keep you from getting to the house."

He snorted. “You think you can stop me?”

“Let’s find out,” I said.

I saw Jimmy’s car wildly turn into the driveway and park right behind mine. He jumped out of his car and walked towards us.

“Two of you? You think you can keep me from doing anything I want to do here?”

By this time, Jimmy was standing next to me. He didn’t say anything. The coach quit walking. He was standing about ten feet away from us.

I said, “You can probably get out of here before the police get here. But if they show up, they’ll get you for trespassing, violating a court order, and maybe something else.”

“Yeah, like manslaughter,” he said.

“I don’t think so,” Jimmy said.

“What are you going to do, pretty boy?” Bodine said.

Jimmy didn’t say anything. He also didn’t seem to be scared.

Bodine started to move toward the house and I pulled something out that I’d put under my belt.

Bodine saw it and stopped again. “What’s that?” he asked.

I looked at it.

“This? It’s a tire iron. You use it for changing tires. Or stopping trespassers.”

“What are you going to do with it?” Coach asked, without as much swagger.

“If you reach me, I’m going to hit you on the side of your head.”

“Now wait a minute, Stuart,” Jimmy said. “You shouldn’t hit him with a tire iron. That could kill him.

Coach looked at my weapon and didn't know what to do.

"I tell you what," Jimmy continued. "Let me reason with him first, and if that doesn't work out, then you can whack him."

Coach came to life. "You going to persuade me to leave?"

"I'd like to see you leave. But I'm also prepared to kick your ample rear-end all over this yard."

Coach and I both looked at him in surprise.

"You are going to kick my butt around the yard?"

Jimmy just nodded.

The coach said, "Well, come on."

"I should tell you that I am a black belt in Shotokan Martial Art and won the Tri-State Golden Gloves tournament. To tell you the truth, and this is a confession, I've heard enough about you that I would love to knock you off your feet with one punch. I think it might help you somehow."

As Jimmy started walking toward the big coach, a truck wheeled into the driveway and pulled up by the house. A very large man got out, followed by Isaiah. Isaiah was holding a double barrel shotgun.

Bodine had waited too long. Two police cars turned into the driveway and quickly had the coach face down on the ground, in handcuffs. Another police car showed up. It was the chief.

He shook hands with Pastor Jimmy who had walked back over to me and suggested I holster my weapon. The chief did everything but bow down to Isaiah. He also spent a moment to pay respect to his vintage 12-guage. Isaiah and Jimmy introduced me to him. Then the chief went to talk to Linda.

Richard came out, shaken but smiling. He shook everyone's hand vigorously. "Thank you for coming," he said very earnestly. Linda soon followed him and hugged each of us. "My favorite men in the whole world," she said.

Isaiah introduced us to his companion, Roscoe. "Roscoe sort of looks after me," he said. From the looks of Roscoe, Bodine picked a bad day to visit Linda and Richard.

Linda invited us in. Our common bond was Linda and her son. After about an hour, I left Linda and Richard in the capable hands of Jimmy, Isaiah and Roscoe.

Chapter Seventy-Six

The plane was late. What would the countdown clock do now? I sat in McGhee Tyson Airport in Knoxville and looked at the new arrival time.

I texted Jillian a brief description of what Bodine did. Since she was out of town, she had another attorney on the case, and had been in contact with Carl Winn, the Ladies Man.

My visit with Jimmy had been helpful. He confirmed what I needed for him to confirm. A relationship with Richard not only involved Richard, and Linda, but also the Man upstairs. And I'm not talking about Isaiah. I didn't mention my conversation with Pastor Jimmy to Linda.

I thought about what Jimmy said about Linda and the boundaries between friend and girlfriend. I wondered if Linda had talked to him about this. He did not say. But he probably wouldn't reveal that they had talked, even if they had, without her permission.

Maybe he was just sharing his observations. If so, he believed that Linda's interest in me was more than just me being a friend to Richard.

Then I thought about my visit with Isaiah. Although he said he approved of my relationship with Richard, he wondered if that's all Linda wanted. I wonder what Roscoe thought.

Since I was waiting on Jillian, I decided to think about her.

She had been gone for a long time. Half of October. She was on business, which was out of her control. She had made an effort to stay in touch with me. I gave her credit for that. Given her schedule and the difference in time zones, she had done a good job. Much better than the previous trip.

The FedEx box was a nice touch. It was thoughtful and took some time. The flowers were on their last legs, but they were still in the vase. The elephant in the room was this - did Jillian strike up another romance while she was in California? She had the kind of beauty that caused men to approach her like heat-seeking missiles. How hard did she try to deflect them? Would it be like this all the time?

I tried to visualize what life with Jillian would be like. It seemed we would be separated a significant amount of the time. She was on her way up. She was making a difference to her law firm. Sooner than later, they would either make her a partner, or some other firm would. Even if she stayed in Spruceville, she would be out of town a good bit. And what if she was offered a job somewhere else, or her firm gave her an opportunity in an office out of town? Would she take it? I did not want to leave. The Lodge had been my dream, and the Smoky Mountains were where I loved to live.

Another issue was money. Jillian and I were in two different income brackets already. And hers was going up. How did she feel about that?

And then there was the matter of how she truly felt about me. She had said many kind and endearing things to me, but I had met only two of her associates. One was her boss. I was introduced to him as a teacher. And then there was Zachary, who needed no introduction.

Why had she not invited me to her office or to a party or some other function?

Weary travelers began walking out of the security zone. They looked like they had been ridden hard and put up wet. Except for Jillian. She walked down the concourse like a model. Her blonde hair was bouncing with every step. She was wearing a charcoal grey business suit. I sometimes marvel at how women's pants seem to come down over their high heels but don't touch the ground. Fellow arriving travelers looked at her covertly. I think they were trying to determine if she was a celebrity from the West Coast.

She scanned the welcoming crowd, saw me, and broke into her million-dollar smile. She waved and picked up her pace. When she got past the ropes, she held out her arms and kissed me for a few seconds. Other passengers may have had to walk around us. Some of the local folks may have enjoyed the spectacle. I'll never know.

She put her arm around mine as we walked to the baggage claim. She held on to it as we waited. "It is sooo good to see you," she said. "I have missed you."

"I have missed you, too," I said. "I didn't get the memo about business attire." I was wearing an old leather jacket, a t-shirt and jeans.

She laughed. "I went straight to the airport from work. It was the only way to catch the flight."

"I like the look," I said. "You cut a very professional image."

"Plus I'm the only one who kissed you" she pointed out.

Chapter Seventy-Seven

The Southern Market in Knoxville doesn't look like much on the outside. Inside, it is full of jewelry, clothes, photographs, paintings, furniture and other home furnishings. It is also full of women. Women who like to talk about what's in each booth.

I was following Jillian around. She was looking for a dresser and maybe some tables. So far, I had not seen anything for the Lodge, but you never know.

I could smell candles and perfume. I excused myself to visit the restroom. There was stuff for sale in there, too. As I walked back, I saw a lady dragging around a little fluffy dog of some kind. I wondered what happened if Fefe heisted a leg on an antique sofa.

When I got back, Jillian had zeroed in on a dresser. It was painted a light blue. I told her I could help her strip off the rest of the paint. She said distressed furniture was in. Go figure.

The dresser barely fit in the Range Rover. We transported her prize out of the parking lot and onto Homberg Drive. "I have a question," I said. "When do I get to see where you work?"

She looked at me. "Are you serious?"

"I would like to see where you spend your time when you go to work. Are people working there today?"

"I don't know. It's Sunday. There could be a few catching up."

"Do you have a key?"

"We don't use keys."

"Okay. Can we swing by there if you don't mind?"

"Yes, I'd love for you to see it."

My first thought was, Then why haven't you asked me?

We parked in the parking garage and rode the elevator up to the twenty-third floor of the Riverview Tower. The elevator opened into a lobby. A guard sat at the desk. Behind him in large brass letters was a sign that said Jordan and Wiser.

The guard said, "Hello Miss Renfro."

"Hello Paul," Jillian said. She motioned for me to follow her down the hall. I waved at Paul. He nodded. At least he didn't shoot me for being in the company of the best-looking attorney in the firm. Jillian was dressed in a red V-neck sweater, blue jeans and some boots with very high heels. Not your typical furniture moving duds. She didn't have on a pinstripe suit, but she still looked striking. I bet Paul agreed.

We walked to a cubicle and Jillian gave me her best Vanna White. "Here it is."

I was expecting an office. It was one of many cubicles. No view. The space was maybe ten by ten feet, with a built-in desk, and bookshelves on the other walls. On the desk was a computer monitor and phone. "This is my domain," she said.

I walked in and looked. Books and notebooks filled most of the bookshelves. Her law degree sat on one of the shelves. There was a football with an inscription,

> *Jillian, thanks for all your help. I appreciate your friendship.*
>
> *Your devoted friend always,*
>
> *Peyton*

I asked, "As in Peyton Manning?"

She nodded. "Number 16 while he was at Tennessee."

"The same number you had on your jersey at the game."

"Yeah."

I think she wanted to zoom past any conversation of that day.

There were a few framed photos scattered among the books. They were group photos of the Jordan and Wiser crew. I recognized Van and Zach. There was no photo of me. But in one of the shelves, I saw Mr. Bear with my watch.

As we walked out, Jillian explained that the partners had the offices with great views. A door to one was opened and I peeked in. It was impressive. You could see the Tennessee River and most of downtown Knoxville. "We have a few offices on the twenty-second floor below us. The senior partners are on the floor above us," she said.

Before we got to Paul, I could see more cubicles. They all had photos of loved ones. I guess a tiny stuffed bear with my watch is better than nothing.

I wondered if I could sneak in sometime and slip a photo of me on Jillian's built-in desk before Paul noticed? Maybe I should just be thankful for the bear.

Chapter Seventy-Eight

In their unsuccessful efforts to climb the slippery pole, the squirrels managed to shake a generous amount of birdseed out of the feeder and on the ground. So, today, the deer stood around the bird feeder, picking corn out of the mix.

I was back at the Lodge on Saturday morning. I had helped Jillian put the dresser in the Great Room. Which meant we had to place another piece of furniture in the Sun Porch. Which meant we had to carry another piece of furniture to the garage. There was paint on the floor. *BELIEVE* in blue. Verification.

Two men had carried the dresser out of the Southern Market and placed it into the Range Rover. It looked heavy. But, after removing the drawers, Jillian and I took it in ourselves. She had no trouble with her end. Her back was strong. And she changed into shoes with no high heels.

I saw her twice more during the week before she went back to Los Angeles. Jury selection started tomorrow. Our time together had been romantic. She was trying hard to be an exemplary girlfriend. She asked me about school. She complimented me regularly. She texted and called more this week than she ever had before. She mailed a humorous greeting card – *To My Boyfriend.* She even sent a couple of selfies of her in the cube.

She took care to do things I might want to do. For example, one of our times together was a picnic. Since it was raining, we had the picnic on her sun porch. We used a picnic basket and a blanket to sit on. She made bacon and tomato sandwiches and brownies because she had asked me what I liked weeks before. She remembered that I'm not a big fan of lettuce on a sandwich and that I enjoy brownies with a lot of icing.

Afterwards, she suggested we go for a walk and produced a very large umbrella. I held the umbrella while she held me. It was a chilly night, and we had our jackets and gloves on.

We laughed and sloshed in the rain and managed to get soaked. "You know what I like about you?" she asked.

"That I don't get sick easily?"

"That, too. You enjoy whatever comes your way. It doesn't take a lot to make you happy. That's coming from someone who enjoys the other end of the spectrum. But I am learning from you."

"I heard it called simple country pleasures once," I said. "But it can be in the city, too."

"I would not have thought so much for me ," she said. "I can tolerate the basics, but I have always preferred the softer side of life. Good restaurants. Fine hotels. Vacations on ships or beaches. Shopping trips to exotic locations. I think it may have to do with the American Dream. Be the best you can be and enjoy the benefits."

"Nothing wrong with that," I said. "Everybody has different tastes."

"Oh, I'm not apologizing," she said with a laugh. "I enjoy walking the streets of Malibu and eating in those ocean side restaurants in Tiburon. I love staying at the Ritz Carlton. And I love shopping in Los Angeles.

"So, you can imagine how surprised I am to be just as happy out in Hooterville with you. You can't even get a cell signal. And let's not even go to the season of the bathroom ladder! But during all of that, I found myself to be happy." As she talked, she kicked up water, in rhythm with her words.

“Sitting outside the Lodge, by the fire. Taking walks on the trails. Sitting on your floor, by the fireplace, just talking about the day. I know a part of it was that I was with you. But another part of it was that you were happy with those simple events. So it was easy for me to enjoy them, too. It’s a skill I’ve learned from you. Be happy where I am. Enjoy what I’m doing. I really like that about you.”

After our walk, she found some sweatpants and a sweatshirt for me to wear while our wet clothes were in dryer. We had hot chocolate by candlelight. The night was simple. It was meaningful. It was fun. It was memorable. And we didn’t have to go anywhere for it to be so. She was learning.

I did not even ask about the clothes she found for me. I was having too much fun to go down that road. I’m just glad they weren’t orange. I’d had enough of that color for the time being.

I took her to the airport Friday evening. She said she was sad to leave. I had seen her upset, but not like this. I asked if there was something else she was upset about. She said no.

She hugged me for a long time. When she looked at me, her eyes were red and the tears were falling. “I love you, Stuart. I have meant every word I said to you. You are the best man I have ever known.” I love being with you. It makes me feel like everything is okay. That’s what makes this so hard. I don’t want to leave. It’s hard to be away. I feel alone. Empty.” She took a deep breath. She kissed me on the cheek and walked to the security area.

Like I said, this was very uncharacteristic for Jillian. And, in my experience, change in behavior is usually not a good thing. But in our situation, who could blame her? She was trying her best with me, but she had no choice. She had to go back out of town and stay out of town. And on top of that, she would encounter a high degree of daily stress in the court case.

By the time I got back to my house, she had sent me a text.

Hello again, I am sorry for that little display. I guess it's just a little too much for me. Thank you for such a great week. I wish with all my heart that circumstances were different. We need more time. More time!

Oh well. Here I go back to the coast, without you. I will miss you. I already do.

Love, love, J

Chapter Seventy-Nine

I attended *The Gathering* with Linda and Richard on Sunday morning. Pastor Jimmy spoke about grace.

He expressed that no one is perfect, and everybody makes mistakes. He said that God is a God of second chances. He encouraged the congregation not to judge someone who made a mistake. He chastised anyone who thought he or she was better than another and said that all have sinned and fallen short of God's expectations.

Brother Jimmy was my kind of preacher. The sermon lasted fifteen minutes. Not that I was watching the clock. I was watching Linda's watch, since I wasn't wearing one these days.

Afterwards, Jimmy put his hand on my shoulder and said, "Stuart, I have been praying for you. I really like you. Let's visit again."

Richard needed to take Scout to a restaurant to get him used to being in places with noise and people. And to teach him not to eat from the table. We were eating at Gepetto's in Wears Valley. Scout was lying down beside Richard's chair. An NFL game was on TV. Marlon Brown caught a touchdown pass for the Denver Broncos. The restaurant patrons erupted in cheers. That unnerved Scout, but Richard reassured him with his hand on Scout's back.

We talked about Jimmy's sermon. I was interested in what Linda and Richard thought. The paraphrase of their comments was that forgiveness was not easy but essential.

I appreciated their comments. It further explained why they lived how they did. I also discovered that the more they talked, the more I could eat. Scout was watching my every bite. I think he had figured out my strategy.

Chapter Eighty

Richard took Scout over for another training session. Linda and I were in the Great Room. "What are your plans for Thanksgiving?" she asked.

I had not thought about Thanksgiving, other than the Speech assignments I usually gave surrounding it.

My parents were deceased. My sister was a crazy woman who lived somewhere in the backwoods of Montana. So there would be no posing for a Thanksgiving family photograph this year.

"Has Jillian invited you to do something with her?" Linda asked.

"No."

"If she doesn't, we would love for you to spend Thanksgiving with us," she said.

"Thank you."

She smiled. "By the way, what did Jimmy mean when he said *Let's visit again?*

I took a breath and told her about my visit with Jimmy at the pizza place.

She listened. I don't think she realized her mouth was open. "You took a day off work to come visit with Jimmy to ask him questions regarding your relationship with Richard?"

"I did."

"And did he give his opinion?"

"He did."

She came over and gave me a hug. "That may be my new favorite thing about you."

Chapter Eighty-One

Trillium Inn became a reality for me today.

I toured the large campus with Linda as my guide. She extended the invitation two weeks prior so I could make preparations. I arranged to leave school at lunch time. It was a test day so it was not difficult for a substitute to proctor as long as Nathan didn't wear his letter jacket. What did Linda say when I asked her about grace? *We have to forgive but not be naïve.*

Linda showed me the meeting rooms, the dining rooms, the barn, the outdoor facilities, the wine cellar, the stables, garden, pastures, the inn and houses, and a lot more. Everywhere we went, her fellow employees gave her hugs and smiles. She introduced me to everyone we met. Several said, "Hello Stuart! I feel like I know you."

She wanted me to meet Pat and Helen Deese, the owners who arranged for us to visit in the library. They seemed genuinely happy to meet me. They treated Linda as a family member. As we were leaving, Helen said, "Better luck next year on the pumpkin carving contest!"

I asked Linda if she would show me her workspace. It was a desk against a wall, with two modular walls on each side. On the walls were photos of many events at Trillium Inn. Linda was in many of the pictures. There were schedules of upcoming events, posters of past and future events, and a photo of Richard, Linda and me holding up our pumpkins. There was also a photo of Richard and the State Representative before they left for Nashville.

She let me look as long as I wanted. "Did you want to go through the drawers, too?" she asked.

"That won't be necessary," I said. "I am very touched that you have a picture of me on your board."

"It helps me remember what you look like when you wander off," she said.

Chapter Eighty-Two

Back in class, we finished our section on Parliamentary Procedure and moved into Debate. I needed Jillian to talk about litigation and how society was affected by both competencies. Even if she was in town and available, I would not have asked her. But if I had, the kids would have never forgotten that day.

The students were expected to form two-person debate teams and hold a debate against another team. As long as the topics were serious, I didn't care what the students debated. I wanted it to be a subject they were interested in. Beyond that, I was more interested in the process than the topic. Some of the topics were controversial. This caused some of the other teachers to become interested in just what was going on in Mr. Jensen's Speech class.

Eventually it would reach my supervisor, the Chairman of the English Department, who knew about as much about Speech as Scout. She would show up for a debate, sit in the back of the room and take notes. Afterwards, she would tell me that she was "concerned." She would also say that certain students and teachers had expressed that they were troubled over such topics. When I asked who, she would say, "It doesn't matter who." We went through this every year. And every year, I would continue to have debates the same way.

Meanwhile I had my own little debate going. Well, maybe not a debate but a discussion. Well, maybe more of a question. Was I really the primary . . . object of two women?

Here's another question. How was I was going to break it to Jillian that I had accepted a Thanksgiving invitation with Linda? And why did I do that? It was the middle of November, so this little talk was coming in for a landing.

Meanwhile, Linda had provided menu options, giving me full veto privileges. I asked her earlier in the week if they would like to have Thanksgiving at the Lodge. She said they would talk it over and let me know.

She called me that night and said that she and Richard discussed it and voted for the Lodge. Then Richard got on the phone and asked if he could bring Scout. "He needs to be in different homes as a part of his training. I will assume full responsibility for any damage he causes."

I was glad to have Scout for Thanksgiving. Since Jillian was a master at short notice and surprise, I wondered if she might surprise all of us, including Scout, with a Thanksgiving appearance.

Chapter Eighty-Three

George Washington used some very long words and sentences in his Thanksgiving address. Years later, Lincoln's sentence structure and words were not simple, either. Both were very different from the way our presidents speak today. The students were not impressed with these Thanksgiving addresses. They were too hard to decipher. Since many of them didn't know the history of this holiday, they were impressed with how both presidents asked the nation to pause and thank God for blessings received. Take, for example, Washington's Thanksgiving Proclamation in 1789. It took the students a while to understand, but it was clear that he was President of a nation under God's guidance.

And also that we may then unite in most humbly offering our prayers and supplications to the great Lord and Ruler of Nations, and beseech Him to pardon our national and other transgressions; to enable us all, whether in public or private stations, to perform our several and relative duties properly and punctually . . .

Although I was not a Bible reading, church going, Scripture quoting, meal praying evangelical, I still felt sadness at how our nation had drifted so far away from its reverence and gratitude to God. It reflected a self-centered, *what's in it for me* attitude. Even I could see that. If there was a God who was actively involved in our day-to-day lives, He had to be sad, too. Maybe mad, as well.

Each student was required to select a President's Thanksgiving address, provide a written analysis of it, and make copies for the other students in the class. Each student was also to bring an empty notebook. With the aid of a three-hole punch, a Thanksgiving notebook was created.

Students were also asked to express what they were thankful for by way of a short speech and paper. Then we had what had become an annual tradition in my class: a Thanksgiving meal. We placed the lecture tables together to form one big table.

In addition to these assignments, the students had to spend a lot more time in preparation for the meal than they would for a class. Each student was responsible for bringing a selected item for the feast. I made it clear to the parents that I didn't want them to make it. I wanted their child to make it, not buy it.

Speaking of Thanksgiving meals, I waited to hear Jillian's final status before I spilled the beans about my Thanksgiving plans. There was no need to tell her that I already made plans with Linda since there was the real chance that she would not be back for Thanksgiving. This kept me from sleeping soundly. But I also think it was why I accepted Linda's invitation. I anticipated that Jillian would not be in town.

She called to tell me the trial would begin on the Monday of Thanksgiving week. Jillian was to deliver the opening remarks. She was being prepped, rehearsed and videoed by legal consultants. On top of that, the judge said he was inclined to keep court in session on Wednesday and resume on Monday. Plus, Jillian needed to work on the case with her team over the weekend. She was very apologetic when she let me know the judge's decision. She said she was sorry and would miss me. I told her that I understood and then breathed a sigh of relief.

I could tell that the trial was on her mind. She had work ahead of her. She said that she and other out-of-town members of the legal team had been invited to Whitsitt's home for Thanksgiving. After the meal, she would go back to a hotel meeting room and put the final touches on her address. She would spend the weekend giving the address to the consultants.

I offered to read Washington's Thanksgiving proclamation

to her, but she said she was tired and was going to bed. Or as Washington would have said, she was performing her duty of rest in her private station to enable her to perform her duty of litigation in a more public theater, properly and punctually.

Sweet dreams, Jillian. See, Washington might have helped after all.

Chapter Eighty-Four

I was delighted that Linda and Richard wanted to celebrate Thanksgiving at the Lodge. I was also delighted that Linda was bringing the food.

The sleeping arrangements had not been difficult. Linda insisted that we repeat the way we did it the last time. I slept in the master. She slept in the other bedroom. Richard and Scout slept downstairs on the couch. All I had to do was clean the house and hide some photos, a cheerleader outfit, and a vase.

When I awoke on Thanksgiving morning, I smelled food. I liked this pattern of smelling food first thing in the morning when I was with Linda.

It was a pleasant feeling to wake up, knowing that Linda and Richard were in the Lodge. I lay there for a minute to absorb it. I saw an envelope that had been slid under the door. It contained a photo of Linda, and me. It was the day we threw the football at the Lodge. I was holding the football. She was behind me, with her arms around me. Her brown eyes were twinkling and she was smiling. I remember the photo. Richard took it. This was before *Big Orange Day*. Interesting.

Written across the bottom of the photo in gold ink was *First Thanksgiving at the Lodge*.

When I walked downstairs, Linda was using my few pots, plus some she brought. I think the turkey was what I smelled. It was in the oven. Richard was watching a Thanksgiving Day parade on TV.

And Scout was sitting on the couch with him but watching Linda and the oven.

Scout saw me first, wagged his tail, jumped off the couch and came over to say hello. Or maybe to see if I had any food. Richard said, "Happy Thanksgiving!" Linda walked over and hugged me and said good morning. She was wearing an apron over a brown cardigan and some blue jeans.

I held up one finger up. Then I told her that I was expecting her to be dressed as a pilgrim or Indian. She smiled, said, "Maybe next year." She looked at me with arched eyebrows, expecting a response.

I switched subjects. "Thank you for your note," I said. "I loved the picture."

"Yeah, I like it, too," she said. "I'm looking forward to seeing all those other photos in your room"

Chapter Eighty-Five

The meal was superb. Linda fixed a baked turkey, cornbread dressing, cranberry sauce, sweet potato casserole, roasted asparagus, green beans and rolls. Dessert was my favorite, lemon icebox pie. That was no coincidence.

Richard led us in prayer, thanking God for our blessings, his mother, and for me. We held hands as he prayed.

During the meal, Linda and Richard talked about what they were thankful for. They said it was a tradition. Then Linda said that they liked to tell each other what they are most grateful for about that person. And so, we took turns expressing our gratitude for each other.

It was the best Thanksgiving I ever had.

After we cleaned up, Richard took Scout out for some exercise. We took turns throwing a toy for him to retrieve. Richard had the foresight to bring a towel for slobber removal.

"I know I am not in your Speech class," Richard said. "But I'd really like to learn the communication skills that you teach. Do you think I could do that as a distance learner?"

No student had ever asked if they could take my class just to learn. Especially from long distance. I told him we'd figure out a way.

Scout was interested in communicating that we needed to

throw his toy more. If we didn't throw it soon enough, he would back up, bark and wag the entire back of his body.

Linda came out, sat in a chair on the porch, and watched. "He seems to like the game," Linda said.

"He has good body language," I said.

Richard asked us if we wanted to go with him while he took Scout on a walk. The walk was not a walk. It was an adventure. And Scout smelled every plant, leaf, rock and tree along the way. At one point, he found an old tin can that had some sort of food in it twenty years ago. He sniffed it for a few seconds, pronounced it worthless and moved on. The highlight of the trip for him was when he came up on a squirrel. The squirrel quickly hightailed it up a tree and Scout stood with his front paws on the base of the tree, barking proudly.

We were back in time to throw a Frisbee around, to Scout's total glee. He chased each throw in hopes he could catch that weird round thing. Occasionally, a throw would go off course and Scout picked it up, prancing for all he was worth. After he slung it around in his mouth sufficiently, he returned it to Richard to start the game over.

While we were out, we filled up the bird feeder and threw some feed on the ground for the deer. Scout took the opportunity to sniff every cubic inch of a five-foot circle around the feeder.

It was almost dark by the time we went inside. Richard built a fire in the fireplace and we sat on the couch. Scout couldn't fit on the couch with us, got aggravated that we wouldn't move, and took up a position in the chair. Two minutes later, he was snoring.

It occurred to me that this was the first time I had not watched football on Thanksgiving afternoon. I didn't miss it. The Lodge offered better memories. I'm pretty sure I was snoring two minutes after that.

Chapter Eighty-Six

It was the end of the second week of December and Christmas was in the air. Christmas decorations were on every street lamp pole in Spruceville. The Christmas parade would be this weekend. The Hallmark Channel was showing its Christmas movies. Our local radio station was playing all Christmas music.

Jillian was still in Los Angeles. Her opening statement went well. She said the defense counsel was excellent. It would not be a slam dunk for Whitsitt and associates.

She hoped that the judge would give them more time for Christmas than he had for Thanksgiving. But if he didn't, there was no need for me to even think about me coming to Los Angeles to celebrate Christmas with her. She would be working. As a matter of fact, I hadn't thought of that. I didn't mind not going to Los Angeles for Christmas.

Linda and Richard had decorated their house for Christmas and wanted me to see it. They also wanted me to come to the Christmas party at church. When I arrived at their house on Saturday morning, I saw a wreath on the front door. It was decorated with pinecones, cranberries and a red velvet bow.

I found Linda, a couple of her friends, Richard and a couple of his friends in the Great Room. It had been transformed into Santa's Workshop. Two eight-foot tables were full of gift-wrapping paper, bows, ribbons, tape and scissors. And a lot of toys.

Linda gave me a hug, a kiss on the cheek, and some tape. "We are wrapping presents for the foster children who will be there tonight." She introduced me to everyone and showed me my spot. Two hours later, we were finished.

Linda's Christmas tree was a Douglas Fir and about ten feet tall. It was decorated with ornaments, lights and a lighted bear at the very top. Three stockings with embroidered names hung on the mantle: *Linda, Richard, and Scout.*

Everyone packed the presents into their vehicles and traveled to the *The Harvest.* The meeting room was decorated with a Christmas tree, Christmas lights and all kinds of Christmas goodies on tables covered in green and red tablecloths. We placed the presents under the tree. I was put in charge of making the coffee.

As more people began to arrive, Linda gave them jobs and introduced them to me. Pastor Jimmy showed up and pitched in. The foster children and their families began to arrive. Before long, the room was filled with conversation and laughter. After we ate, everyone sat down and listened to Jimmy talk about the birth of Jesus. He was very animated, especially when he imitated some of the animals in the stable. The kids loved it.

Then it was time to hand out the presents. After that, someone turned off all the lights except for the lights on the tree. We sang a few Christmas songs. Jimmy thanked everyone for coming and reminded the faithful that there was some cleaning up to do. This was my first religious Christmas party. I enjoyed seeing the smiles and hearing the story of Christmas.

Chapter Eighty-Seven

I pulled into the driveway at my house after school on Wednesday, December seventeenth. It was the first day of our three-day semester exam schedule. The Range Rover pulled up next to me.

Jillian jumped out. She held onto me and danced around the driveway. "We're off until after Christmas and I beat a trail to your house as quickly as I could."

"Long trail," I managed to say between kisses.

She was wearing a black leather jacket over a blue t-shirt with black pants.

"You timed it just right," I said.

She laughed and said, "Well, I've been circling. I made two stops at a Starbucks close by that you probably don't even know exists. I'm hoping you didn't convert your bathroom into a ladder."

After the bathroom break, she wanted to hear about the incident with Bodine at Linda's house. I gave her the details and answered her questions. She was both fascinated and angry.

I did not tell her about my visit with Isaiah. I did tell her about my visit to see Linda and Richard and the Christmas party. She chose not to comment. Instead, she caught me up on the trial. She was trying the case just as much as the other attorneys. She felt good about it. The case was a strong one and they were confident.

"Of course, it ain't over till' it's over," she said.

I wonder if she left out some details, too.

She said she was hungry and wanted to go out to eat. So, we went to a local steak place. Neither of us ordered steak, but the other food was good there, too. She looked at me and smiled the million watt smile. "Now, what do you want to do about us?" she asked.

Chapter Eighty-Eight

She continued to smile and softly said, "I really want to talk about it. It doesn't have to be over supper, but soon."

When we got back to my house, she said, "I know you have exams to grade, so I will leave. Do you think we could spend the weekend together?"

I agreed. She kissed me and left.

It is hard to grade exams after a surprise visit from Jillian. I needed to put in a direct line to Pastor Jimmy. Instead, I made another call. Which is how I found myself in Knoxville the next afternoon, sitting across from Van Wiser. We were in his office on the twenty-fourth floor of the Riverview Tower.

It was a large office. A beautiful antique mahogany desk was in the back of the room. An equally old table and four chairs were positioned to the side. On the other side of the room were two overstuffed leather chairs, in front of a glass wall. That's where we were sitting. I watched a barge making its way down the Tennessee River while cars crossed the bridge over it.

"I never get tired of the view," Van said.

It was 4:00. The afternoon traffic was beginning to pick up. I was through with school for the day. Because of exams, we got out at noon. I had also confirmed that Jillian wasn't working. I was drinking a Coke. He drank bottled water.

I thanked Van for seeing me. “I wanted to talk to you about Jillian,” I said. “You probably know about Jillian’s relationship with Zachary?”

“I do,” he said.

I nodded. “Do you also know of her relationship with me?”

“I know some. Zachary gave me an idea.”

“So you had an idea of what this was about.”

He nodded and smiled. “Unless you need a really good law firm.”

We both smiled at that because we both knew I couldn’t afford it.

“I do know of your association with Richard Eason. I have followed his case through Jillian. What a day that must have been when Bodine showed up at their residence. I understand you were the first on the scene to delay his progress to the house.”

I nodded.

“I’d love to hear the story.”

So I told him.

He shook his head. “Not only did you show up, but an elderly man with his bodyguard, the pastor, and the police. Bodine had no chance.”

“The elderly man and his twelve gauge didn’t need the rest of us. His bodyguard made the coach look like a midget. And the pastor is a martial arts and boxing champion. What we all shared in common is our concern for Richard and for Linda Eason.”

“And, in your case, Jillian.”

“So, that’s why you agreed to see me? You knew this was somehow about Jillian?”

He smiled some more. "Call it intuition."

"I am about to make a large decision that will impact her."

He nodded.

"I am trying to decide about my future with Jillian. And her future with me."

He nodded again.

"Would you mind telling me whatever you choose about Jillian as a lawyer?"

Van put the tips of his fingers below his chin. "I am making an exception, just so you know. Ordinarily, I never talk about a lawyer in our firm, without the lawyer being here. But I sense what this is about.

"Jillian is one of the most gifted trial attorneys I have ever worked with. She has learned quickly. She has the kind of mind that retains facts, cases, motions, verdicts, appeals, names, judges, even birthdays. Her presence in the courtroom is . . . impressive. She is a natural. I know she's something to look at, but that's not what I'm talking about. She is formidable as an opponent. You should watch her in action."

"If I may ask, what does her future look like?"

Van paused again. He looked at me and said. "I don't think you're asking this because you want to know how much money she'll be making."

"Correct."

"As I said, I think I know what you're doing, so I'm going to try to help. Jillian is on a fast track to be a partner here. Everybody knows that. She will be a partner before she is thirty-five. For our firm, that's unheard of. We aren't doing this out of the goodness of our hearts. We're doing it to try our best to keep her. Frankly, I don't think we can."

I thanked him for his candor. "And how is she doing in the Los Angeles trial?"

He shook his head. "If the truth were known, William requested her help because he needed a female lawyer just to be visible in this particular case. She has become lead counsel. William said she has taken the defense by surprise. She is playing in the big leagues against the best. And she is winning. On top of that, there is a large payout for both William's firm and our firm. William says that Jillian has made it look easy."

I thought about that. "Does Jillian enjoy her job?"

"Oh my, yes. She loves the courtroom. She loves helping others. She loves being a lawyer. And to be so good and so young . . . she has a lot of options.

"Jillian lights up the room, any room. And she is good at it. Her clients and associates enjoy her company. I'm not a marriage counselor, but I realize it would be hard on any man to know that his beautiful and talented wife was being admired, wined and dined both near and far away from home."

He let that hang there and when I didn't bite, he crossed his legs and said, "At the same time, she's young and very ambitious and good. Would being married to you affect her career progress? Probably. I guess it comes down to what she really wants. That, I don't know. In total candor, I wonder if she does.

"You are beginning to understand how talented Jillian is. I will share another thought. The kind of talent Jillian has is a double-edged sword. While she is vivacious and spontaneous and articulate and dynamic, she needs to realize that she is not bulletproof. Nor is she the first talented, attractive attorney that has walked into a courtroom. She must not allow her looks, charm and talent to create arrogance. That has caused the downfall of many talented lawyers. Success sometimes causes egotism and overconfidence.

"She must realize what's most important to her and what she

can live without. That should be the compass that guides her. It seems to me you are trying to understand where her compass is pointing. Perhaps along the way, it will help Jillian understand, too.

As I walked out the door, he said, "Whether she fully understands this or not, Jillian is very fortunate to have you in her life."

I looked at him. "Thank you. You are a smart man, Van."

Chapter Eighty-Nine

I looked across the table at Jillian. We were at the Grand Bohemian Hotel in Asheville, North Carolina. It was a two-hour drive. Jillian had made the arrangements. The Red Stag Grill in the hotel was lit with candles. I could still make out the head of what I think was an elk, staring down at us.

It was Saturday night and had snowed all day. We spent most of that time visiting the shops of Biltmore Village which were within walking distance of the hotel. They were decorated for Christmas, with Christmas trees and garland and red bows and lights.

Tonight, Jillian was wearing a red cardigan and some gray slacks, both of which she bought in one of the shops. I was wearing a sports jacket. Her suggestion.

We sat at a corner table. The weather was cold like Christmas should be, and it felt good to be close to a fireplace. "Can you see us being married?" Jillian asked.

Right to the heart of the matter.

"I can," I said. "Can you?"

She smiled and took my hand. "Yes. Can you see us being married soon?"

I looked at Jilllian. "Maybe you can help me with where we are."

She smiled. "I can definitely help."

"Do you have a life plan?"

She paused and smiled. "A what?"

"You know, where do you want to be in five, ten, twenty years?"

She thought about that. "I've given it some thought. Five years – a partner at Jordan and Wiser or some other firm. Ten years – managing partner or maybe start my own firm. Twenty years – that's pretty far off. I'd be about your age. Maybe I'd want to retire," she said and smiled. "Why do you ask?"

"I don't know. We've never talked about it. I don't know what your future goals are. You don't know what mine are. If they conflict, how do we make a decision?"

"I guess the way you make any decision. We talk about it, hear what the other person wants, and then make the best choice we can."

"Okay. One of the ways we differ in our life plans is that your's focus on your job. Mine don't focus around my job. It's more about what I want out of life. What I want to experience. My bucket list doesn't include my job experiences. Yours does."

She looked at me, thinking. I let her think for a few moments. "We've never talked about children," I said.

She smiled. "Do you want children?"

"Only if you really wanted them. I am pushing fifty."

"I don't want children. But I think you would look cute sitting in those little desks, listening to the preschool teacher tell us about our three-year old."

"Do you think I would interfere with your life plan?" I asked.

"What do you mean?"

"I heard someone describe it like this. *You must realize what's most important to you, what's most important to Jillian, and what she can live without. That should be your compass.*

"Can you help me understand where your compass is pointing?"

She leaned back in her chair and widened her eyes. "Wow. My compass. I haven't thought of it like that." She was quiet, thinking about her compass.

"I know. But where your compass is pointed determines your decisions. Where to live, job decisions, finances, religion, marriage. Things like that. For example, what if you got a great job offer in LA and what if I didn't want to move to LA?"

She took a drink and said, "Good question. As for moving, it would have to be a combined decision. No matter how good the offer was, if you weren't in, I wouldn't go."

"Are you sure you'd be happy if you wanted to go and I didn't?"

She thought about that. "I would try to convince you. I would try to figure out a way to make it work. Yes, I think I would be disappointed if my heart was set."

I tapped my fork on the table. "*That's* what I mean. How would that get resolved?"

She took my fork and put it on the table. "You've had a chance to think about this and I am just considering it now. I think the question is, which is more important – a career opportunity or," she picked up the fork and pointed it at me, "you?"

I put the fork back beside my plate.

"Correct."

Chapter Ninety

I looked at her for several seconds. She was beautiful. And she was smiling at me.

What else do we need to talk about?" she asked.

"Are you okay with the fact that you make twice as much money as I do?" I asked.

She paused and said, "What you do is honorable. It's a shame that teachers don't make more." She paused and continued. "And I make way more than twice as much. It should make it that much clearer that my motives are pure."

"Good to know. Why in the world do you want to marry me?"

She picked up the fork. "You don't know by now? We've talked about this back at the Lodge on *Believe Day*."

"I'm asking. Humor me."

"I love you Stuart. I was probably in love with you back in high school or had a schoolgirl crush on you. Or just associated you with lunch which put you on the plus side. As I've said, I've never felt this way for any other man. I want a life filled with adventure and laughs and romance. I want it to be like that until they put you in the White Oak Flats Cemetery. And I want to be buried right beside you thirty years later."

"Wouldn't your new husband mind?"

"Perhaps. But he won't realize that I put it in writing in the prenups."

"What if you get an offer to join William Whitsitt's firm?" I asked. "Maybe become a partner. And let's say that I didn't want to move to California. What then?"

She put the fork down and spun it. "Yeah, that's a tough one."

"If you know now that I would refuse to move with you, is that a deal breaker?"

She spun the fork again. "Are we talking hypothetically you wouldn't move. Or are we talking, there's no way you would move?"

"I know. I think that's an area where our life plans conflict. Ultimately you are going to move. And one of my life goals is to live in the Smoky Mountains. How can you fix that? Is that a deal breaker?"

She looked at the fork. She looked at the elk. Then she looked at me. "There's no way you would move? There are many incentives on the table."

I shook my head. "My home is in the mountains. With the squirrels and the ticks. It's waking up to see the Smokies. Hiking and camping. Looking up to see the stars. Hearing coyotes. That's been my life plan for a long time."

She was quiet again and said, "But if you love me, shouldn't you at least be willing to consider the option? Isn't that what love is about?"

"I think it is. And it bothers me that neither one of us would find it easy to give in on this one. But that's where we are. Aren't we?"

She grabbed my hand. "Maybe. I would like to think that you are more important than any job I might ever be offered, even if it raises my salary by another zero. I have never thought about us having conflicting life plans. I guess I assumed that if I made enough money, you'd be willing to go. And you hoped that I would choose you over the opportunity, every time one came up."

"And at your age, that's going to be a lot of opportunities."

She sighed, put the fork down, and said, "You sure know how to sabotage a good wedding conversation."

Chapter Ninety-One

"Can we take a walk?" I asked.

"It's cold out there. Wouldn't you rather stay in the bar and drink?" she asked.

"I need some air. Come on, if you can go to Los Angeles, you can go on a walk with me."

She got up and said she needed to change. I decided I did, too. On the way up, I think I heard her mutter, "Stupid analogy."

We walked back through Biltmore Village. She had on a pair of jeans and a down jacket. I had on jeans and my leather jacket. She held on to my arm and was quiet. Some of the stores had already closed. Others were still opened.

"Now what?" she asked.

"We'll keep walking unless you're too cold."

"Not what I meant, and you know it. Is this the deal breaker? Is this where you go your way and I go mine?" She started to cry.

"I hope not," I said.

"But we have different life plans," she sobbed. "You don't want to move away from the Lodge and I almost have to if I want the best version of my life plan." She was holding on to my arm and suddenly hit it very hard. "I've never even said life plan before. Where did you come up with that term?"

I hesitated, then confessed, "Van Wiser."

She stopped. "Van Wiser?"

"Yeah. I visited with him this week and he talked about your life plan."

She was still standing still. "You talked to Van?"

"Yes."

"About me?"

"Yes."

She thought about it and then said, "I don't know whether to be flattered or furious."

She started walking again and said, "So what did he say?"

"He said if you loved me, you would move into the Lodge and support me for the rest of my short life."

We continued to walk and she said, "How short?"

Chapter Ninety-Two

I told her what Van said. It made her cry some more.

"So Van thinks I'm an emerging great lawyer?"

"No. He thinks you're a great lawyer now who can pick her professional destiny. That's when he brought up the life plan."

"I think I hate that word," she said.

"Did he tell you that I was the best thing that could ever happen to you?" she asked.

"Well, not exactly. He did say that you were fortunate to have someone like me in your life."

"He was right. But he should have mentioned my virtues, too."

"He did plenty of that. He is a huge advocate."

"So how can you think twice about marrying me?" she asked, crying again. "I'm cute, I'm smart, I'm vivacious. What else did he call me?"

"Formidable."

"Yeah, skip that one. What else?"

"Beautiful, smart, able to retain names, dates and facts, and very impressive in the courtroom."

She stopped again. "See! Van gets it. Why don't you? What else did he say?"

“He said you need to make sure you don’t get too cocky and self-assured. He thinks I could help you in that regard.”

She nodded. “Did he say I was the most wonderful female you would ever go out with, not to mention the youngest? Did he say how charismatic I am? Did he say that I have a heart of gold? Did he say you’d be an absolute moron if you did not say yes to this human being who is walking out in the freezing cold and desperately in love with you?”

We kept walking. “Well, did he?”

“Not exactly.”

We kept walking.

“He should have.”

Chapter Ninety-Three

It was Tuesday, the twenty-third day of December. Classes were only a memory. The exam, quarter and semester grades were posted and approved. I had shopped for Linda, Richard, Scout and Jillian.

I looked at my Christmas tree in the Lodge. The Wears Valley elves had paid a visit while I was in Asheville. It was a tall Douglas Fir, decorated with a variety of creative ornaments - photos in stick frames (as in tree sticks), photos in hollowed out pine cones, photos hanging from ribbons, including one of Cecil May Turnbow, a fire tower made out of wooden matches, and a rusted tin can from Scout. It took a lot of work and I enjoyed looking at each ornament.

Speaking of Asheville, Jillian was in a funk the rest of the trip. Oh, she was pleasant. But she was frustrated about our conflicting life plans. If she said it once, she said it many more times that my analogy and the actual word *life plan* were both "stupid."

The day after my return, I told Linda about the Asheville trip. I told her about our unresolved issues. I told her about my conversation with Van Wiser and his responses to me.

Linda was silent.

"Thoughts?" I asked.

She shook her head. She was still silent. What was going on inside her brain? It seemed to me that she was deciding what to say. Finally, she said, "You are an amazing man. I love your question about life plans and what that looked like in the future. And talking to Van . . . very direct and filled with integrity."

It turns out that Isaiah had paid Linda a visit. He spilled the beans about my visit to his house.

"He likes you," Linda said. "He said that Chester is a good judge of character."

Chapter Ninety-Four

That night, I went to Jillian's house. She had two trees. Both had themes. The one in the front room was artificial, elegant and may have been decorated by a professional. The one in the den was a Spruce and had more casual ornaments from her childhood days.

On her mantel were two stockings. One for her. One for me.

Jillian greeted me at the door. She was wearing a green Christmas sweater and leggings that made me think of an elf. Also because of the elf hat she was wearing. As I walked in, I smelled the scents of Christmas. I heard Christmas music.

I noticed that there were many presents under the tree in the den. If those were for me, she might be disappointed with the four presents I had for her.

We cooked hotdogs on her outside kitchen grill and ate them in the den by the fireplace.

"I've been thinking about this life plan business," she said as she chewed. "I even talked to Van about it.

"I have now decided to come out in favor of life plans. And after we eat, I'll show you my work on the matter."

So, after some homemade Christmas cookies, she pulled out her laptop and showed me a chart. "I wanted to show you some of my life's plan," she said.

"First and foremost, I want you to know that you, Stuart, trump any career plan. That means if I get the job of the century in Big Sur, but you don't want to move to Big Sur, bye-bye job. Although let me just say, if that opportunity should happen, I think you'd really like it. It's where the mountains meet the ocean. Plenty of room to feed birds and squirrels and sea otters.

"To review, in the next five years, I want to be a partner at Jordan and Wiser. It's a good job. Van has assured me that I would get it and that I would not be sorry. I like Van. I like the firm. Yes, it would mean some traveling, but not more than any other law firm. And that would keep me right here.

"That's the professional goal. The personal goal is to make our marriage everything it should be. Period. I want to be a great wife. I want us to grow in our love for each other. And I want us to make memories on a regular basis.

"I love the Lodge. Some of my best memories have already happened there. I'm game for spending as much time as you want there. And I would like to find a way to communicate with the outside world from there."

She moved to the next power point. "In *ten* years? You will be about 60 and I will be in my 40s. Career wise, as I said before, maybe work to be a managing partner. Maybe start my own firm.

"Personal goals might be to stay in shape – both of us. Perhaps travel a little bit. I'm hoping that just as I will stretch to live and do what you want to do, you'll agree to travel some. In the states. To other countries.

"I want our marriage to stay fresh. That's a goal. I want to hear you like it's the first time I've heard you. And I want you to light up when you see me walking through the door. I don't ever want your heart to quit skipping a beat when I'm around. Unless it's a medical emergency."

Chapter Ninety-Five

The squirrels were at it again at the Lodge. They were trying their best to scale the pole to get to the birdseed. I found that I had to apply Squirrel-Slip to the pole every other day. That's about how long it took them to wipe it off with their white furry bellies. One squirrel thought if he could jump high enough up the pole, he would bypass the lubricant. This resulted in something closely akin to a fireman sliding down the fire pole. He always landed on his feet, though.

It was the night before Christmas. Jillian had something to go to which was fine because I did, too. It was Linda's annual Christmas Eve party.

It occurred to me that maybe I was supposed to bring something, like food. But then again, what would I bring? North Pole Vienna sausage? Holly Jolly hot dogs? That's probably why I was not asked to bring food.

Not too long ago, we had quite an episode with Coach Stupid at Linda's house. Maybe things would not be as dramatic tonight.

Then again, you never know. As it turned out, I didn't.

Chapter Ninety-Six

Christmas Eve was a festive occasion at Linda's home. When I arrived, cars filled the driveway and lined the street. Linda told me earlier that she hosted an annual Christmas party and insisted that I be there.

I found her laughing with guests in the kitchen. When she saw me, she greeted me with a hug and a kiss and introduced me to some of her neighbors. I smelled the Douglas Fir and the freshly baked party food assembled on the kitchen island.

Nestle came up and gave me a hug and kiss. I also saw Cecil May Turnbow and several other church members. Richard came up and introduced me to some of his friends. I also said hello to Pat and Helen Deese, Linda's bosses.

Linda held onto my arm. The mood was fun, celebratory, and happy. The ladies wore Christmas attire. There were a lot of Christmas sweaters. Some of the men were wearing Christmas ties. Linda wore a red knit shirt, tucked into jeans, which were tucked into leather boots. She was wearing a large leather belt and Santa earrings. Scout was sitting off to the side, sporting a Christmas bandana.

Me? I chose the ever-popular red Orvis quilted sweatshirt, a gift from Jillian that she insisted I wear, and khaki pants.

The house was filled with laughter and people. I walked over to Pastor Jimmy at the fireplace. He gave me a hug and said, "Merry Christmas, Stuart."

I wished him a Merry Christmas and traded some Christmas memories. I visited with a few other people, all connected to Linda. Then I saw Isaiah, sitting in a chair by the wall. I walked over and sat beside him. He nodded. I said, "I understand you and Linda have talked."

"That's correct," he said.

"Where's Roscoe?"

"He's around. I told him to dispose of any fruitcake he might discover."

Pastor Jimmy clinked a glass and asked for our attention. "Linda has asked me to thank you for coming to this year's Christmas Eve get-together. I think we would all agree that it is Linda we need to thank." He led the applause, and everyone cheered.

"Linda, you do this for us every year. It is a tradition that means so very much to me and to each person in this room.

"Linda has asked me to share a few words with you again this year. But first, I want to tell you about something I'm very excited about. It's our mission trip this summer. Linda and Richard are joining our team to work at the Village of Hope in Ghana. But I'll save that for another gathering. Except to say, please keep them in your thoughts and prayers. And, as I say each year, do not panic. I will be brief and there will be no collection."

This got a laugh and allowed people to find a seat. I looked at Linda. She was looking down.

Jimmy smiled and said, "The ancient physician Luke tells us about one of the most dramatic episodes in the Bible, a time when shepherds met angels. Even Charlie Brown talks about it in his Christmas special.

"The shepherds were some of the toughest, bravest men around. They slept with the sheep and protected them from wolves using only staffs and slingshots. You could tell who a shepherd was by his leathery skin and the look in his eye. You didn't mess with a shepherd.

"These men had no fear. Until they met the angel. Then they were scared. We don't know what angels look like, but every time angels met a human, the Bible says they had to tell the human not to be afraid, including these shepherds that night. The angel said he was there to share some good news. News about a Savior who was born in Bethlehem. And when he said that the sky became *full* of angels! What a night that must have been!

"As you know, the shepherds found Jesus in a manger. He was actually in a feeding trough. It was filled with hay. That's how our Savior came into this world. We celebrate tomorrow and each Sunday not just for the story of baby Jesus, but for what would happen to Him a little over thirty years later. He would be killed for you and me. And three days later, He would come out of that tomb, again for you and for me. I think the celebration that night was not just about Jesus' birth. It was also about God's love for us.

"You see, God knew what was going to happen to Jesus when He allowed him to be born in that stable. Isn't it great to know that we have a God who loves us that much? As a matter of fact, He wants you and me to live with Him and celebrate Christmas for eternity. That is the reason we can have joy on earth, despite life's circumstances. And with that, I wish you a Merry Christmas and invite you to join me in singing Joy to the World"

Joy to the world, the Lord is come!

Let earth receive her King

Let every heart prepare Him room

And Heaven and nature sing

And Heaven and nature sing

And Heaven, and Heaven, and nature sing.

Chapter Ninety-Seven

Roscoe and I folded up some tables that Jimmy was taking back to church. When Jimmy left, Linda touched my arm.

"Stuart, I did not know Jimmy was going to make that announcement. It was to be a secret until the first of the year. I was going to tell you soon. It all happened so fast."

She needed to tell me this, and I listened.

"As you know, one of Richard's goals is to visit the Village of Hope and to assist the medical team. Earlier this week, we learned of an opening for him. To make a long story short, with the blessing of Pat and Helen and the assistance of Isaiah, I'm going, too. I'm sorry you had to learn about it this way."

I assured her that I was happy for her, and I would miss them.

"We'll talk more about it later," she said.

I helped clean up. Linda had plenty of help from the guests and the work was accomplished quickly with much laughter. I think they might have stayed much later if I hadn't reminded them that Santa wouldn't visit them if they weren't asleep in their beds. Plus, Scout's earlier holiday meatball consumption was having some gastric consequences.

Linda invited me to spend the night. I thanked her and explained that I would be with Jillian early Christmas morning and would see them around lunch.

I went home and then went to Jillian's house the next morning. It turns out all of those presents around Jillian's tree were for me. Shirts, sweaters, socks, pants, belts, and more. I detected a theme. We had a great time. I told her about Linda's party and the surprise announcement. My presents to her included framed photos which she immediately put on the table behind the couch. I also wrote her a letter.

Dear Jillian

I love you. I want to spend the rest of my life with you.

Being in your company makes everything better and brighter.

Thank you for your gift of you.

I don't need anything else.

Merry Christmas.

Stuart.

When she read the letter, which I saved for last, she began to cry in really big sobs. She could not speak or even see. Finally, when she was able to breathe, she told me that was the sweetest letter she had ever received and if she wasn't so vain, she might have it tattooed somewhere. Then she said, "Maybe on you as a reminder."

After many photos, hugs and kisses, I said goodbye to Jillian and made my way to eat lunch with Linda and Richard. Although that may sound unusual, it was sanctioned by Jillian. She understood, better than I did, the importance of these next few days. That took a lot of faith in me and our future.

Our Christmas day was full of laughter and sentimental presents. Richard made a birdhouse for me. Linda gave me a printed book of our year in review, a book to identify trees, plus a wristwatch.

I gave Richard a camera for his telescope. I gave Linda my very orange UT jersey. Just kidding. I gave Linda a large framed photo of the three of us. It was taken at the Village in Gatlinburg. We were standing in front of the fountain. There were pumpkins, hay bales and corn stalks all around. I made the frame out of some left-over lumber from the Lodge, with Richard's help. She loved it. I gave Scout a larger bed with his name embroidered on the front. I also received a wrapped present from Jimmy. It was a Bible.

I spent a good part of the afternoon with them and, again after some hugs and photos, left to go back to Jillian's house. She called and asked to meet at the Lodge.

She was inside, looking at my Christmas tree. She thought it was cute and I told her the story behind some of the ornaments.

She said, "I would like to start a tradition with you. I would like to go to Gatlinburg tonight, drink some hot chocolate and ride the chair lift."

That sounded like a good tradition. Hopefully it wouldn't include a trip to the cemetery. That seemed to be a popular stop these days.

The night was cold when we got out of Jillian's car on River Road. Jillian pulled out a blanket. "We'll need this," she said. We walked up the street to the *Gatlinburg SkyLift* and prepared to board. Once we caught the chair lift, Jillian spread the blanket over us. It helped. There weren't many people on the lift. "I have always loved this chair lift," she said. "For some reason, it was important for me to ride it with you tonight."

When we got to the top, it was colder. We walked inside the store and warmed up. Jillian purchased the photo that was automatically taken of us on the way up. We stood out on the deck and looked down at the lights of the city and up at the stars. She positioned herself between me and the view, put her arms around me and looked into my eyes. "My hope is that we will do this for so many years, we will fill up a photo album with *SkyLift* pictures."

She put her head on my chest and breathed. She said, "I want two things. I want to make you and me a forever thing. And I want some hot chocolate."

Chapter Ninety-Eight

I was back at Linda's house. Richard was gone.

We were drinking some spiced tea and trying out some of the leftover Christmas cookies, as we looked out the kitchen window. We talked about Christmas and Richard and Jillian and even a little about Nestle.

"I wanted to talk to you some more about Jimmy's announcement," she said.

I said. "It's a great opportunity. I think it's the right thing to do."

She was quiet. Maybe a little too long. Then she said, "There's more to it. I'm doing this for Richard. But I'm also" she paused as if she did not want to say what was coming next "doing it for Jimmy . . . and for me."

I was silent. That seemed understandable.

"The night that Coach Bodine made his visit, Jimmy stayed a longer than anyone else. That's been the beginning of a new type of relationship for us. I wouldn't call it romantic, but it could get that way. I know it's a mission trip, but it will also be a chance for the two of us to see how things go.

"He said he has reevaluated things and is interested in us seeing each other. His only stipulation is that we have your blessing."

By this time, she was crying profusely.

Chapter Ninety-Nine

I didn't know what to say. I didn't see that coming. I thought Jimmy had taken some kind of personal vow and sworn off women forever. But if someone could make you rescind that vow, it would be Linda.

She continued to cry and fell into my arms. I held her as she shook. I cried a little bit, too.

After gaining some composure she looked at me through the tears. "I will say this once. It is only for your ears. If I had my way, I would marry you tomorrow. There are many reasons. One of the biggest ones is Richard. But there are many others, too. I would love to spend the rest of my life with you. I've prayed about it. I've thought about it. I've even dreamed about it.

"However, we have a big reason not to get married. We do not share the same . . . values. You have more integrity than any man I've ever known. But serving God is the center of my life and you're just not there right now. You respect my beliefs, and I think you would participate in a good bit of what I might ask. And maybe one day, you would share my faith. I don't know.

"I can't make that assumption. And it's not fair to you for me to do that. There's also something, well somebody else. I think you know that I love you. Everybody else does, so why shouldn't you? But the very fact that you know me and are still in a relationship with Jillian tells me what I need to know. I like her, Stuart. Despite any shortcomings, I think she will be good for you.

“So, if I’m honest, it has hurt me a good bit to watch you choose Jillian and not me. I’m not bitter. I understand. She knew you before I did. I just see you as such a good man, I would love for you to be my husband.”

She took a second to breathe. She looked at the ceiling for a minute and continued. “Jimmy is a good man. He shares my faith. He will be good for me and good for Richard.

She started to cry again. In the midst of the sobs she said, “But you are the best thing that’s ever happened to Richard. I will not do anything that jeopardizes his relationship with you.”

Chapter One Hundred

I was back at Jillian's house on December 27th. We were sitting in her Great Room. More photos had been added. All photos of us.

I recounted my conversation with Linda. I did not tell her the part that Linda said were for my ears only. But I didn't have to. Jillian listened as tears flowed down her cheeks.

"Why are you crying?" I asked.

It took her a while to be able to talk. "I am so sad for her. She loves you. She loves the way you and Richard get along. And she would like for that to be forever. You are the man she always dreamed about marrying. I feel the same way. And I know how devastated I would be if you chose Linda and not me."

She blew her nose and wiped her eyes. "I am also sad because I love Linda and Richard. And I am the cause of her sadness."

She broke down and cried some more.

I waited until she was somewhat composed. "First of all, none of this is your fault. You need to understand that very clearly. Secondly, Linda is in a good place. Even if you were not in the picture, she made it clear that we did not have the same life plan."

"I hate that word again," Jillian choked out. "I cannot imagine her saying you are not good enough. In my book, you are close to sainthood."

“I think you only become a saint after you pass on,” I said.

“Good to know,” she said. “Maybe it will fit on our monument.”

“And I think you know what she’s saying. Jimmy is a good man and will be good for her and for Richard.”

“And he has the same you-know-what,” she added.

“True,” I said.

“But she doesn’t love him,” she said.

I didn’t tell her that part. But she knew.

“Not yet, but I think she’s moving in that direction.”

She was silent. Her tears were drying up.

“If I might go where angels fear to tread, no pun intended,” I said, “aren’t you supposed to be somewhat happy or relieved that Linda is no longer your competition?”

She sighed. “Is that what you think?”

“That’s what you told me.”

“Okay, yes, was I concerned that you were spending so much time with a beautiful, incredible, wonderful woman? Yes. Was I concerned that you had both our photos on your nightstand? Yes. That was weird, by the way.”

“Wait a minute,” I said. “How did you know that?”

“I’ve been at the Lodge waiting on you before.”

I looked at her. “And you snooped around?”

“Absolutely.”

I decided to leave that alone. “So aren’t you glad the . . . situation is resolved?”

She stood up and walked to the window. “Of course I am. I

love you and want to spend my life with the remaining days of your life. You know that. I can't wait. But Linda is my friend. And so is Richard. I have to know they will be okay."

I shook my head. I didn't know what that meant. But I was pretty sure she was planning it.

Chapter One Hundred and One

It was December 30. Richard, Jillian and I were at the Lodge. Richard had made a fire in the fireplace and we were sitting around it. I called this Phase Three.

Jillian did indeed create and execute a plan. Phase One was for her to visit with Linda. That took place without me. Jillian said it went well. After some tears, Linda told her that she knew I had made my decision and it was Jillian. She also knew that the only other person that she had ever considered as husband material was Jimmy.

Furthermore, at least on paper, Jimmy scored higher than I did, since he was on the same spiritual page as Linda. Jillian seemed to spend more time than was necessary to tell me that part. Linda said that she would always love me and told Jillian how important it was that I continue an active relationship with Richard.

Phase Two was for me to meet with Jimmy. She wanted to be in on that, too. I wavered but said okay. We met at the Lodge.

"I know I said I would never marry," Jimmy said. "But something happened that day the coach showed up. I realized that I had very deep feelings Linda and Richard. There was no way he was getting to them."

I nodded. "The part about martial arts and boxing was news to me."

"I trust in God to protect me but believe he has equipped

me to learn how to protect myself and others. That's why I keep the trophies in my closet. I don't broadcast it. Might be bad for business."

Jillian jumped in. "Jimmy, you don't know me. But I'm sure you've heard my name. I'm the other woman in Stuart's life. I'm also Linda's friend. Linda speaks so highly of you. She can't wait to get away to be in Ghana. She thinks it will be good in many ways. She's very anxious to see what the future holds for you two."

"Thank you. It's three and not two, though. I want to see what God has in store for *us.* I also know that Linda's heart does not really favor me. She wants it to. Maybe she will in time. It is no secret that she loves you, Stuart. She also realizes that you can't marry two women."

How did everyone know so much about who Linda loved? I seemed to remember from somewhere that Abraham and Solomon and some others in the Bible had more than one wife. But I couldn't see how that would play well with either Jimmy or Jillian, so I sat on it.

"My prayer is that as time goes on, she will love me as much, even more than she loves you," Jimmy continued.

We were quiet for a few moments, except for Jillian who started to sniff. Finally, I asked, "What about Richard?"

He smiled and said, "I really like Richard. I think he likes me, too. Through the years, we've had many wonderful conversations. We've also worked side-by-side at the Coffee Shop, on mission trips, at the homeless shelter, and even in Boy Scouts. I'm an old Eagle Scout, and I participate in just about all the camping trips.

"It would be my honor to spend the rest of my life with Linda and Richard. And I would solicit you to be a part, as well, Stuart. Richard needs you."

Back to Phase Three. Jillian went over to Richard, who was sitting on the couch by himself. She put her arm around him and said, "Busy holiday season, huh?"

He smiled and said, "And how."

"So what do you think about what's going on?" she asked.

Chapter One Hundred and Two

Richard was quiet. When he spoke, he asked a question.

"What do you think, Stuart?"

I wasn't expecting the question. But Richard is very sensitive and very perceptive. I stretched and stood up. "This is awkward for me. I love your mom. She is smart, impressive, compassionate, beautiful, and a wonderful mom.

"I love Jillian. My life has never been the same since. She loves me and despite a few bumps in the road, we've weathered the storm. I look forward to living with her for many years."

That got Jillian going. She whipped out a Kleenex.

"And I love you, Richard. I want you in my life, period. In many ways, you are my best friend."

"We both want you in our lives," Jillian said.

Richard was quiet again. "Thank you. I love both of you. You have been such good friends. Stuart, I can't begin to express how grateful I am for all you've done. You too, Jillian. And I look forward to more great memories.

"I want you both to know that I really like Jimmy. He's a great man. I have no idea what will happen between him and mom. I do believe that God has a plan for each of us. If that's part of the plan, I'm in. If it doesn't work out, we're okay with that, too.

"But whatever happens, I hope to keep our friendship alive and active. Mom will always love both of you, and I will, too."

Well, that did it for Jillian. She grabbed Richard, hugged him, and cried all over him. He looked at me and gave me a thumbs-up.

Chapter One Hundred and Three

It was Spring Break for Richard and me. Linda and Jimmy were at some type of spiritual retreat for ministers. Richard was staying with me at the Lodge. Jillian had come out for the weekend. We had just finished a vigorous hike for everyone but Scout.

As we sat on the porch, I looked at Jillian and Richard. It was less than a year ago that our adventure began. That's a lot of memories in a short period of time. I hope I never forget them.

Jillian had made subtle changes to the Lodge. Some rugs. A few mirrors. Some Kleenex boxes. Flowers for her flower vase with the *Jillian loves Stuart* engraving. A very comfortable dog bed with Scout's name on it for the Lodge. And of course, more photos. Oh, yes and plans for a new bed after our wedding in a few months.

Speaking of romance, Linda and Jimmy were still seeing each other. The trip to Village of Hope seemed to cement their relationship. Richard predicted a wedding in less than a year.

And speaking of Jimmy, I continued our friendship. Under the radar, we had many spiritual discussions and Biblical studies. While it's a bit too far to attend each Sunday, Jillian and I have attended the Harvest many times. That has caused some very interesting conversations between us. Conversations neither one of us ever foresaw happening.

We discussed that scripture that Linda referred to in Proverbs 19:21 of how the Lord's plans prevail over ours.

"So," I asked Jimmy, "was it always God's plan for me to marry Jillian and you to marry Linda?" We were back at Stonehouse Pizza.

He smiled and was silent for several seconds. "It's a question I've asked God myself. The best answer I've come up with is that God hears us when we pray and I've prayed a lot for many years about how I should live. He knows what's going on in our lives and He doesn't leave us alone." He gazed over the pizza shop and thought.

"Is all of this God's will? I believe some of it is. Maybe all. He says He is with us in every adventure of our lives. Even in terrible times. And He tells us that if we believe in a God we can't see that He not only will be with us now, but forever in a place far better than even this." He pointed to the mountains that surrounded us.

"My faith is pretty simple, Stuart. I believe the words written long before us that all things work together for good for those of us who love God. So, I believe that God leads His followers."

There was that word again, Believe.

"So, just to be clear, you think it was God's will for us to have the wives that we will soon have?"

He smiled at me for a long time. Then he started laughing. And then he nodded.

The last time I saw him nod was when the coach asked him if he was going to kick his rear. So I decided to quit while I was ahead and went back to the pizza. My faith was not as long or as strong as Jimmy's but I was convinced of a few things.

We both agree that we think God is real, that Jesus lived on the earth and went from being dead to alive. We think Heaven is real and have every intention of being there. Jillian's only concern is that I might hook up with some "good looking angel" before she gets there.

Chapter One Hundred and Four

If the Lodge could speak, it would have plenty to say about its first year. A lot of photos. Some drama. Much laughter. A few tears.

But, of course, it can't talk because it's just a building. Just some boards and stones with a roof on top. As buildings go, it's nothing special. Nothing to write home about. It will never be in a magazine. And I can't take it with me when I kick the bucket.

However, it does serve as a symbol on which to hang those memories.. I can still see Jillian drive up for the first time. I can see *BELIEVE* on the porch. I can see the Christmas tree with the tin can ornament. I can see Scout watching the turkey bake. I can see Jillian covered in primer, trying to blow hair out of her eyes. I can see Linda holding the blanket around my shoulder while Richard pointed to the stars. I can see Richard cooking over the campfire.

The Lodge helps me remember. I associate the memories with the Lodge. It keeps the memories real. It also reminds me of how important it is to make new memories.

Jillian and Richard joined me on the porch. Scout was already there. He was basically asleep, but had one eye open for squirrels, lizards, wasps or fast-moving leaves.

"We've got a proposition," Jillian began.

Oh boy.

www.ingramcontent.com/pod-product-compliance
Lightning Source LLC
Chambersburg PA
CBHW030351310726
48979CB00001B/263

9780998268675